I0667637

THE SAGEBRUSHER

A STORY OF THE WEST

EMERSON HOUGH

1st WORLD
LIBRARY
Literary Society

The Sagebrusher

Emerson Hough

© 1st World Library, 2007
PO Box 2211
Fairfield, IA 52556
www.1stworldlibrary.com
First Edition

LCCN: 2007927772

Softcover ISBN: 978-1-4218-4533-3
Hardcover ISBN: 978-1-4218-4449-7
eBook ISBN: 978-1-4218-4617-0

Purchase *"The Sagebrusher"*
as a traditional bound book at:
www.1stWorldLibrary.com/purchase.asp?ISBN=978-1-4218-4533-3

1st World Library is a literary, educational organization
dedicated to:

- Creating a free internet library of downloadable ebooks

- Hosting writing competitions and offering book
publishing scholarships.

Interested in more 1st World Library books?
contact: literacy@1stworldlibrary.com
Check us out at: www.1stworldlibrary.com

1ˢᵗ World Library Literary Society

Giving Back to the World

"If you want to work on the core problem, it's early school literacy."

- James Barksdale, former CEO of Netscape

"No skill is more crucial to the future of a child, or to a democratic and prosperous society, than literacy."

- Los Angeles Times

"Literacy... means far more than learning how to read and write... The aim is to transmit... knowledge and promote social participation."

- UNESCO

"Literacy is not a luxury, it is a right and a responsibility. If our world is to meet the challenges of the twenty-first century we must harness the energy and creativity of all our citizens."

- President Bill Clinton

"Parents should be encouraged to read to their children, and teachers should be equipped with all available techniques for teaching literacy, so the varying needs and capacities of individual kids can be taken into account."

- Hugh Mackay

CONTENTS

I. SIM GAGE AT HOME 9

II. WANTED: A WIFE 18

III. FIFTY-FIFTY 26

IV. HEARTS AFLAME...35

V. BEGGAR MAN—THIEF...39

VI. RICH MAN--POOR MAN 42

VII. CHIVALROUS; AND OF ABUNDANT
      MEANS..47

VIII. RIVAL CONSCIENCES 53

IX. THE HALT AND THE BLIND..............................65

X. NEIGHBORS 83

XI. THE COMPANY DOCTOR 89

XII. LEFT ALONE 99

XIII. THE SABCAT CAMP 110

XIV. THE MAN TRAIL..118

XV. THE SPECIES..132

XVI. THE REBIRTH OF SIM GAGE..........................139

XVII. SAGEBRUSHERS 156

XVIII. DONNA QUIXOTE...164

XIX. THE PLEDGE..172

XX. MAJOR ALLEN BARNES, M.D.,
     PH.D.—AND SIM GAGE 182

XXI. WITH THIS RING...................................191

XXII. MRS. GAGE.......................................195

XXIII. THE OUTLOOK................................207

XXIV. ANNIE MOVES IN 213

XXV. ANOTHER MAN'S WIFE................222

XXVI. THE WAYS OF MR. GARDNER....229

XXVII. DORENWALD, CHIEF 236

XXVIII. A CHANGE OF BASE 244

XXIX. MARTIAL LAW...............................250

XXX. BEFORE DAWN 258

XXXI. THE BLIND SEE.............................269

XXXII. THE ENEMY 278

XXXIII. THE DAM.....................................289

XXXIV. AFTER THE DELUGE................298

XXXV. ANNIE ANSWERS.........................301

XXXVI. MRS. DAVIDSON'S CONSCIENCE...........304

CHAPTER I

SIM GAGE AT HOME

"Sim," said Wid Gardner, as he cast a frowning glance around him, "take it one way with another, and I expect this is a leetle the dirtiest place in the Two-Forks Valley."

The man accosted did no more than turn a mild blue eye toward the speaker and resume his whittling. He smiled faintly, with a sort of apology, as the other went on.

"I'll say more'n that, Sim. It's the blamedest, dirtiest hole in the whole state of Montany—yes, or in the whole wide world. Lookit!"

He swept a hand around, indicating the interior of the single-room log cabin in which they sat.

"Well," commented Sim Gage after a time, taking a meditative but wholly unagitated tobacco shot at the cook stove, "I ain't saying she is and I ain't saying she ain't. But I never did say I was a perfessional housekeeper, did I now?"

"Well, some folks has more sense of what's right, anyways," grumbled Wid Gardner, shifting his position on one of the two insecure cracker boxes which made the only chairs, and resting an elbow on the oil cloth table cover, where stood a few broken dishes, showing no signs of any ablution in all their hopeless lives. "My own self, I'm a bachelor man, too—been batching for twenty years, one place and another—but by God! Sim, this here is the human limit. Look at that bed."

He kicked a foot toward a heap of dirty fabrics which lay upon the floor, a bed which might once have been devised for a man, but long since had fallen below that rank. It had a breadth of dirty canvas thrown across it, from under which the occupant had crawled out. Beneath might be seen the edges of two or three worn and dirty cotton quilts and a pair of blankets of like dinginess. Below this lay a worn elk hide, and under all a lower-breadth of the over-lapping canvas. It was such a bed as primarily a cow-puncher might have had, but fallen into such condition that no cow camp would have tolerated it.

Sim Gage looked at the heap of bedding for a time gravely and carefully, as though trying to find some reason for his friend's dissatisfaction. His mouth began to work as it always did when he was engaged in some severe mental problem, but he frowned apologetically once more as he spoke.

"Well, Wid, I know, I know. It ain't maybe just the thing to sleep on the floor all the time, noways. You see, I got a bunk frame made for her over there, and it's all tight and strong—it was there when I took this cabin over from the Swede. But I ain't never just got around to moving my bed offen the floor onto the bedstead. I may do it some day. Fact is, I was just a-going to do it anyways."

"Just a-going to—like hell you was! You been a-going to move that bed for four years, to my certain knowledge, and I know that in that time you ain't shuk it out or aired it onct, or made it up."

"How do you know I ain't made her up?" demanded Sim Gage, his knife arrested in its labors.

"Well, I know you ain't. It's just the way you've throwed it ever' morning since I've knowed you here. Move it up on the bedstead?—First thing you know you can't."

"Well," said Sim, sighing, "some folks is always making other folks feel bad. I ain't never found fault with the way you keep house when I come over to your place, have I?"

"You ain't got the same reason for to," replied Wid Gardner. "I ain't no angel, but I sure try to make some sort of bluff like I was human. This place ain't human."

"Now you said something!" remarked Sim suddenly, after a time spent in solemn thought. "She ain't human! That's right."

He made no explanation for some time, and both men sat looking vaguely out of the open door across the wide and pleasant valley above which a blue and white-flecked sky bent amiably. A wide ridge of good grass lands lay held in the river's bent arm. The wind blew steadily, throwing up into a sheet of silver the leaves of the willows which followed the water courses. A few quaking asps standing near the cabin door likewise gave motion and brightness to the scene. The air was brilliantly cool and keen. It was a pleasant spot, and at that season of the year not an uncomfortable one. Sim Gage had lived here for some years now, and his homestead, originally selected with the unconscious sense for beauty so often exercised by rude men in rude lands, was considered one of the best in the Two-Forks Valley.

"Feller, he loses hope after a while," began the owner of the place after a considerable silence. "Look at me, for instance. I come out here from Ioway more'n twenty-five years ago, when I was only a boy. When my pa died my ma, she moved back to Ioway. I stuck around here, like you and lots of other fellers, and done like you all, just the best I could. Some way the country sort of took a holt on me. It does, ain't it the truth?"

His friend nodded silently.

"Well, so I stuck around and done about what I could, same as you, ain't that so, Wid? I prospected some, but you know how hard it is to get any money into a mine, no matter what you've found fer a prospect. I got along somehow—seems like folks didn't use to pester so much, the way they do to-day. And you know onct I was just on the point of starting out fer Arizony with that old miner, Pop Haynes—do you suppose I'd struck anything if I'd of went down there?"

"Nobody can say if you would or you wouldn't," replied Wid. "Fact is, you never got more'n half started."

"Well, you see, this old feller, Pop Haynes, he'd been down in Arizony twenty years before, and he said there was lots of gold out there in the desert. Well, we got a team hooked up, and a little flour and bacon, and we did start—now, I'll leave it to you, Wid, if we didn't. We got as far as Big Springs, on the railroad. What did we hear then? Why, news comes up from down in Arizony that a railroad has went out into the desert, and that them mines has been discovered. What's the use then fer us to start fer Arizony with a wagon and team? Like enough all the good stakes would be took up before we could get there. Old Pop and me, we just turned back, allowing it was the sensiblest thing to do."

"And you been in around here ever since."

"Yes, sir; yes, sir, that's what I been. Been around here ever since. I told you the country kind of takes a holt on a feller. Ain't it the truth? Well, I trapped a little since then in the winters, and killed elk for the market some, like you know, and fished through the ice over on the lakes, like you know. Some days I'd make three or four dollars a day fishing. So at last when that Swede, Big Aleck, got run out of the county, I fell into his ranch. There ain't a better in the whole valley. Look at that hay land, Wid. You got to admit that this here is one of the best places in Montany."

"Well, maybe it is," said his friend and neighbor. "Least-ways, it's good enough to run like you mean to run it."

"I'm a-going to run her all right. She's all under wire—the Swede done that before I bought his quit claim. Can't no sheep get in on me here. I'll bet you all my clothes that I'll cut six hundred ton of hay this season—leastways I would if my horse hadn't hurt hisself in the wire the other day. Now, you figure up what six hundred ton of hay comes to in the stack, at prices hay is bringing now."

"Trouble is, your hay ain't in the stack, Sim. You'll just about cut hay enough to buy yourself flour and bacon for next winter, and that'll be about all. If you worked the place right you'd make plenty fer to—"

"Fer to be human?"

"Well, yes, that's about it, Sim."

"That's right hard—doing all your own work outside and doing all your own cooking and everything all the time in your own house. Just living along twenty years one day after another, all by your own self, and never—never—"

His voice trailed off faintly, and he left the sentence unfinished. Wid Gardner completed it for him.

"And never having a woman around?" said he.

"Ain't it the truth?" said Sim Gage suddenly. His eyes ran furtively around the room in which they sat, taking in, without noting or feeling, the unutterable squalor of the place.

"Well," said his friend after a time, rising, "it'd be a fine place to fetch a woman to, wouldn't it? But now I got to be going—I got my chores to do."

"What's your hurry, Wid?" complained the occupant of the cabin. "Cow'll wait."

"Yours might," said the other sententiously. As he spoke he was making his way to the door.

The sun was sinking now behind the range, and as he stood for a moment looking toward the west, he might himself have been seen to be a man of some stature, rugged and bronzed, with scores of wrinkles on his leathery cheeks. His garb was the rude one of the West, or rather of that remnant of the Old West which has been consigned to the dry farmers and hay ranchers in these modern polyglot days.

Sim Gage, the man who followed him out and stood for a time in the unsparing brilliance of the evening sunlight, did not compare too well with his friend. He was a man of absolutely no presence, utterly lacking attractiveness. Not so much pudgy as shapeless; he had been shapeless originally. His squat figure showed, to be sure, a certain hardiness and vigor gained in his outdoor life, but he had not even the rude grace of a stalwart manhood about him. He sank apologetically into a lax posture, even as he stood. His pale blue eyes lacked fire. His hair, uneven, ragged and hay-colored, seemed dry, as though hopeless, discouraged, done with life, fringing out as it did in gray locks under the edge of the battered hat he wore. He had been unshaven for days, perhaps weeks, and his beard, unreaped, showed divers colors, as of a field partially ripening here and there. In general he was undecided, unfinished—yes, surely nature must have been undecided as he himself was about himself.

His clothing was such as might have been predicted for the owner of the nondescript bed resting on the cabin floor. His neck, grimed, red and wrinkled as that of an ancient turtle, rose above his bare brown shoulders and his upper chest, likewise exposed. His only body covering was an undershirt, or two undershirts. Their flannel over-covering had left them apparently some time since, and as for the remnant, it had known such wear that his arms, brown as those of an Indian, were bare to the elbows. He was always thus, so far as any neighbor could have remembered him, save that in the winter time he cast a sheepskin coat over all. His short legs were clad in blue overalls, so far as their outside cover was concerned, or at least the overalls once had been blue, though now much faded. Under these, as might be seen by a glance at their bottoms, were two, three, or possibly even more, pairs of trousers, all borne up and suspended at the top by an intricate series of ropes and strings which crossed his half-bare shoulders. One might have searched all of Sim Gage's cabin and have found on the wall not one article of clothing—he wore all he had, summer and winter. And as he was now, so he had been ever since his nearest neighbor could remember. A picture of indifference, apathy and hopelessness, he stood, every rag and wrinkle of him sharply outlined in the clear air.

He stood uncertainly now, his foot turned over, as he always stood, there seeming never at any time any determination or even animation about him. And yet he longed, apparently, for some sort of human companionship, but still he argued with his friend and asked him not to hurry away.

None the less after a few moments Wid Gardner did turn away. He passed out at the rail bars which fenced off the front yard from the willow-covered banks of a creek which ran nearby. A half-dozen head of mixed cattle followed him up to the gate, seeking a wider world. A mule thrust out his long head from a window of the log stable where it was imprisoned, and brayed at him anxiously, also seeking outlet.

But Sim Gage, apathetic, one foot lopped over, showed no agitation and no ambition. The wisp of grass which hung now from the corner of his mouth seemed to suit him for the time. He stood chewing and looking at his departing visitor.

"Some folks is *too* damn dirty," said Wid Gardner to himself as he passed now along the edge of the willow bank toward the front gate of his own ranch, a half-mile up the stream. "And him talking about a woman!" He flung out his hand in disgust at the mere thought.

That is to say, he did at first. Then he began to walk more slowly. A touch of reflectiveness came upon his own face.

"Still," said he to himself after a time—speaking aloud as men of the wilderness sometimes learn to do—"I don't know!"

He turned into his own gate, approached his own cabin, its exterior much like that of the one which but now he had left. He paused for a moment at the door as he looked in, regarding its somewhat neater appearance.

"Well, and even so," said he. "I don't know. Still and after all, now, a woman—"

CHAPTER II

WANTED: A WIFE

"I couldn't have ate at Sim's place if he would of asked me to," grumbled Wid Gardner aloud to himself as he busied himself about his own household duties in his bachelor cabin. "He's too damn dirty, like I said, and that's a fact."

Wid's cabin itself was in general appearance no better, if no worse, than the average in the Two Forks Valley. There was a bed on a rude pole frame—little more than a heap of blankets as they had been thrown aside that morning. The table still held the dishes which had been used, but at least these had been washed, and there was thrown across them what had served as a dish-towel, a washed and dried, fairly clean flour sack which had been ripped out and turned into a towel. There was a box nailed up behind the stove which served as a sort of store room for the scant supplies, and this had a flap at the top, so that it was partly curtained off. Another box nailed against the wall behind the table served as book case and paper rack, holding, among a scant array of ancient standard volumes, a few dog-eared paper-backed books of cheap and dreadful sort, some illustrated journals showing pictures of actresses and film celebrities—precisely the sort of literature which may be found in most wilderness bachelor homes.

　　　　Emerson Hough

At one end of the up-turned box which served as a sort of reading table lay a pile of similar magazines, not of abundant folios, but apparently valued, for they showed more care than any other of the owner's treasures. It was, curiously enough, to this little heap of literature that Wid Gardner presently turned.

Forgetful of the hour and of his waiting cows, he sat down, a copy in his hands, his face taking on a new sort of light as he read. At times, as lone men will, he broke out into audible soliloquy. Now and again his hand slapped his knee, his eye kindled, he grinned. The pages were ill-printed, showing many paragraphs, apparently of advertising nature, in fine type, sometimes marked with display lines.

Wid turned page after page, grunting as he did so, until at last he tossed the magazine upon the top of the box and so went about his evening chores. Thus the title of the publication was left showing to any observer. The headline was done in large black letters, advising all who might have read that this was a copy of the magazine known as *Hearts Aflame*.

Curiously enough, on the front page the headline of a certain advertisement showed plainly. It read, "Wanted: A Wife."

From this it may be divined that here was one of those periodicals printed no one knows where, circulated no one knows how, which none the less after some fashion of their own do find their way out in all the womanless regions of the world—Alaska, South Africa, the dry plains of Canada and our Western States, mining camps far out in the outlying districts beyond the edge of the homekeeping lands—it is in regions such as these that periodicals such as the foregoing may be found. Their circulation is among those who seek "acquaintance with a view to matrimony." They are the official organs of Cupid himself—*or* Cupid commercialized, or Cupid much misnamed and sailing his craft upon a wide and uncharted sea. In lands of the first pick or the first plow, these half-illicit pages find their way for their own reasons; and men and women both sometimes have read them.

Wid Gardner finished his own brief work about the corral, came in, washed his hands, and began to cook for himself his simple supper. Then he washed his dishes, threw the towel above them as before, and went to bed, since he had little else to do.

Early the next morning Wid had finished his breakfast, and was at the edge of the main valley road, which passed near to his own front gate. He lighted a pipe and sat down to smoke, now and again glancing down the road at a slowly approaching figure.

It was the schoolma'am, Mrs. Davidson, who daily presided at the little log schoolhouse a mile further on up the road, where some twenty children found their way over varying distances from the surrounding ranches. This lady was of much dignity and of much avoirdupois as well. Her ruddy face was wrinkled up somewhat like an apple in the late fall. She walked slowly and ponderously, and her gait being somewhat restricted, it was needful that she make an early start each day to her place of labor, since the only possible boarding place lay almost a mile below Sim Gage's ranch. She had been the only applicant for this school, and perhaps was the only living being who could have contented herself in that capacity in this valley. Wid Gardner pulled at the edge of his broken hat as he stepped down the narrow road to meet her.

"'Morning, Mis' Davidson," said he.

"Good morning, Mr. Gar-r-r-dner," boomed out the great voice of Mrs. Davidson. "It is apparently promising us fair weather, sir-r-r."

Mrs. Davidson spoke with a certain singular rotund exactness, and hence was held much in awe in all these parts.

"Yes, ma'am," said Wid, "it looks like it would rain, but it won't."

"Your hay in that case would not flourish so well, Mr. Gar-r-r-dner?" said she.

"Without rain, not worth a damn, ma'am, so to speak. But I'll get by if any one can. This is one of the best locations in the valley. Me and Sim Gage; and Sim, he says—"

"Sim Gage!" The lady snorted her contempt of the very name. "That man! Altogether impossible!"

"He shore is. He certainly is," assented Wid Gardner. "He seems to be getting impossible-er almost every year, now, don't he?"

"I do not care to discuss Mr. Gage," replied the apostle of learning. "I was in his abode once. I should never care to go there again."

Already she was leaning partially forward, ponderously, as about to resume her journey toward the school house.

"Well, now, Sim Gage," began Wid, raising a restraining hand, "he ain't so bad as you might think, ma'am. He's just kind of fell into this way of living."

"Mr. Gar-r-r-dner," said the lady positively, "I doubt if he has made a bed or washed a dish in twenty years. His place is worse than an Indian camp. I have taught schools among the savages myself, in Government service, and therefore I may speak with authority."

"Well, now, ma'am, I reckon that's all true. But you see, if more women come out in here, now, things'd be different. I been thinking of Sim Gage, ma'am. I wanted you to do something fer me, or him, ma'am."

"Indeed?" demanded she. "And what may that be?"

"I don't mean nothing in the world that ain't perfectly all right," began Wid, hesitatingly. "I only wanted you to write something fer me. I'm this kind of a man, that when he wants anything to be fixed up, he wants it to be fixed up right. I kind of got out of practice writing. I want you to write a ad fer me."

"A what?" she demanded. "Oh, I see—you have something to sell?"

"No, ma'am, I ain't got nothing to sell—not unlessen—well, I'll tell you. I want to advertise fer a woman—fer a wife—that is to say, really fer him, Sim Gage—a feller's got to have something to sort of occupy his mind, hain't he?"

Mrs. Davidson was too much astonished to speak, and he blundered on.

"Folks has done such things," said he.

"You offer me a somewhat difficult problem," rejoined the other, "since I do not in the least understand what you desire to do."

"Well, it's this away, ma'am. There's papers that prints these ads—sometimes big dailies does, they tell me—where folks advertises for acquaintances just fer to get acquainted, you know—'acquaintance with a view to matrimony' is the way they usually say it—and that may be a tip fer you—I mean about this here ad I want you to write. Why, folks has got married that way, plenty of 'em—I'll bet there ain't more'n half the homesteaders in this state out here, leastways in the sagebrush country, that didn't get married just that way—it's the onliest way they *can* get married, ma'am, half the time.

"Once, up in Helleny, years ago, right after the old Alder Gulch placer mining days, there was eleven millionaires, each of 'em married to a Injun woman, and not one of them women could set on a chair without falling off. Now, there wasn't no papers then like this one here, or them millionaires might of done better."

She gasped, unable to speak, her lips rotund and pursed, and he went on with more assertiveness.

"They turn out just as good as any marriages there is," said he. "I've knowed plenty of 'em. There's three in this valley—although they don't say much about it now. *I* know how they got acquainted, all right."

"And you desire me to aid you in your endeavor to entr-r-r-ap some foolish woman?"

"They don't have to answer. They don't have to get married if they don't want to. You can't tell how things'll turn out."

"Indeed! *Indeed!*"

"Well, now, I was just hoping you would write the ad,

that's all. Just you write me a ad like you was a sagebrusher out here in this country, and you was awful lonesome, and had a good ranch, and was kind-hearted—and not too good-looking—and that you'd be kind to a woman. Well, that's about as far as I can go. I was going to leave the rest to you."

Mrs. Davidson's lips still remained round, her forehead puckered. She leaned ponderously, fell forward into her weighty walk.

"I make no promise, sir-r-r!" said she, as she veered in passing.

But still, human psychology being what it is, and woman's curiosity what it also is, and Mrs. Davidson being after all woman, that evening when Wid Gardner passed out to his gate, he found pinned to the fastening stick an envelope which he opened curiously. He spelled out the words:

"Wanted: A Wife. A well-to-do and chivalrous rancher of abundant means and large holdings in a Western State wishes to correspond with a respectable young woman who will be willing to appreciate a good home and loving care. Object—matrimony."

Wid Gardner read this once, and he read it twice. "Good God A'mighty!" said he to himself. "Sim Gage!"

He turned back to his cabin, and managed to find a corroded pen and the part of a bottle of thickened ink. With much labor he signed to the text of his enclosure two initials, and added his own post office route box for forwarding of any possible replies. Then he addressed a dirty envelope to the street number of the eastern city which appeared on the page of his matrimonial journal. Even he managed to fish out a curled stamp from somewhere in the wall pocket. Then he sat down and looked out the door over the willow bushes shivering in the evening air.

"'Chiv*al*erous!'" said he. "'Well-to-do! A good home—and loving care!' If that can be put acrosst with any woman in the whole wide world, I'll have faith again in prospectin'!"

CHAPTER III

FIFTY-FIFTY

It was late fall or early winter in the city of Cleveland. An icy wind, steel-tipped, came in from the frozen shores of Lake Erie, piercing the streets, dark with soot and fog commingled. It was evening, and the walks were covered with crowded and hurrying human beings seeking their own homes—men done with their office labors, young women from factories and shops. These bent against the bitter wind, some apathetically, some stoutly, some with the vigor of youth, yet others with the slow gait of approaching age.

Mary Warren and her room-mate, Annie Squires, met at a certain street corner, as was their daily wont; the former coming from her place in one of the great department stores, the other from her work in a factory six blocks up the street.

"'Lo, Mollie," said Annie; and her friend smiled, as she always did at their chill corner rendezvous. They found some sort of standing room together in a crowded car, swinging on the straps as it screeched its way around the curves, through the crowded portions of the city. It was long before they got seats, three-quarters of an hour, for they lived far out. Ten dollars a week does not give much

Emerson Hough

in the way of quarters. It might have been guessed that these two were partners, room-mates.

"Gee! These cars is fierce," said Annie Squires, with a smile and a wide glance into the eyes of a young man against whom she had been flung, although she spoke to her companion.

Mary Warren made no complaint. Her face, calm and gentle, carried neither repining nor resignation, but a high and resolute courage. She shrank far as she might, like a gentlewoman, from personal contact with other human beings; the little droop beginning at the corners of her mouth gave proof of her weariness, but there was a thoroughbred vigor, a silken-strong fairness about her, which, with the self-respecting erectness in her carriage, rather belied the common garb she wore. Her frock was that of the sales-woman, her gloves were badly worn, her boots began to show signs of breaking, her hat was of nondescript sort, of small pretensions—yet Mary Warren's attitude, less of weariness than of resistance, had something of the ivory-fine gentlewoman about it, even here at the end of a rasping winter day.

Annie Squires was dressed with a trifle more of the pretension which ten dollars a week allows. She carried a sort of rude and frank vitality about her, a healthful color in her face, not wholly uncomely. She was a trifle younger than Mary Warren—the latter might have been perhaps five and twenty; perhaps a little older, perhaps not quite so old—but none the less seemed if not the more strong, at least the more self-confident of the two. A great-heart, Annie Squires; out of nothing, bound for nowhere. Two great-hearts, indeed, these two tired girls, going home.

"Well, the Dutch seems to be having their own troubles

now," said Annie after a time, when at length the two were able to find seats, a trifle to themselves in a corner of the car. "Looks like they might learn how the war thing goes the other way 'round. Gee! I wish't I was a man! I'd show 'em peace!"

She went on, passing from one headline to the next of the evening paper which they took daily turns in buying. Mary Warren began to grow more grave of face as she heard the news from the lands where not long ago had swung and raged in their red grapple the great armies of the world.

Then a sudden remorse came to Annie. She put out a hand to Mary Warren's arm. "Don't mind, Sis," said she. "Plenty more besides your brother is gone. Lookit here."

"He was all I had," said Mary simply, her lips trembling.

"Yes, I know. But what's up to-night, Mollie? You're still. Anything gone wrong at the store?" She was looking at her room-mate keenly. This was their regular time for mutual review and for the restoring gossip of the day.

"Well, you see, Annie, they told me that times were hard now after the war, and more girls ready to work." Mary Warren only answered after a long time. A passenger, sitting near, was just rising to leave the car.

Annie also said nothing for a time. "It looks bad, Mollie," said she, sagely.

Mary Warren made no answer beyond nodding bravely, high-headed. Ten dollars a week may be an enormous sum, even when countries but now have been juggling billions carelessly.

They were now near the end of their daily journey. Presently they descended from the car and, bent against the icy wind, made their way certain blocks toward the door which meant home for them. They clumped up the stairs of the wooden building to the third floor, and opened the door to their room.

It was cold. There was no fire burning in the stove—they never left one burning, for they furnished their own fuel; and in the morning, even in the winter time, they rose and dressed in the cold.

"Never mind, dear," said Annie again, and pushed Mary down into the rocking chair as she would have busied herself with the kindling. "Let me, now. I wish't coal wasn't so high. There's times I almost lose my nerve."

A blue and yellow flame at last began back of the mica-doored stove which furnished heat for the room. The girls, too tired and cold to take off their wraps, sat for a time, their hands against the slowly heating door. Now and again they peered in to see how the fire was doing.

Mary Warren rose and laid aside her street garb. When she turned back again she still had in her hands the long knitting needles, the ball of yellowish yarn, the partially knitted garment, which of late had been so common in America.

"Aw, Sis, cut it out!" grumbled Annie, and reached to take the knitting away from her friend. "The war's over, thank God! Give yourself a chanct. Get warm first, anyways. You'll ruin your eyes—didn't the doctor tell you so? You got one bum lamp right now."

"Worse things than having trouble with your eyes, Annie."

"Huh! It'll help you a lot to have your eyes go worse, won't it?"

"But I can't forget. I—I can't seem to forget Dan, my brother." Mary's voice trailed off vaguely. "He's the last kin I had. Well, I was all he had, his next of kin, so they sent me his decoration. And I'm the last of our family—and a woman—and—and not seeing very well. Annie, he was my reliance—and I was his, poor boy, because of his trouble, that made him a half-cripple, though he got into the flying corps at last. I'm alone. And, Annie—that was what was the trouble at the store. I'm—it's my *eyes*."

They both sat for a long time in silence. Her room-mate fidgeted about, walked away, fiddled with her hair before the dull little mirror at the dresser. At length she turned.

"Sis," said she, "it ain't no news. I know, and I've knew it. I got to talk some sense to you."

The dark glasses turned her way, unwaveringly, bravely.

"You're going to lose your job, Sis, as soon as the Christmas rush is over," Annie finished. She saw the sudden shudder which passed through the straight figure beside the stove.

"Oh, I know it's hard, but it's the truth. Now, listen. Your folks are all dead. Your last one, Dan, your brother, is dead, and you got no one else. It's just as well to face things. What I've got is yours, of course, but how much have we got, together? What chanct has a girl got? And a blind woman's a beggar, Sis. It's tough. But what are you going to *do*? Girls is flocking back out of Washington. The war factories is closing. There's thousands on the streets."

"Annie, what do you *mean*?"

"Oh, now, hush, Sis! Don't look at me that way, even through your glasses. It hurts. We've just got to face things. You've got to live. How?"

"Well, then," said Mary Warren, suddenly rising, her hands to her hot cheeks, "well, then—and what then? I can't be a burden on you—you've done more than your half ever since I first had to go to the doctor about my eyes."

"Cut all that out, now," said Annie, her eyes ominous. "I done what you'd a-done. But one girl can't earn enough for two, at ten per, and be decent. Go out on the streets and see the boys still in their uniforms. Every one's got a girl on his arm, and the best lookers, too. What then? As for the love and marriage stuff—well—"

"As though you didn't know better yourself than to talk the way you do!" said Mary Warren.

"I'm different from you, Mollie. I—I ain't so fine. You know why I liked you? Because you was different; and I didn't come from much or have much schooling. I've been to school to you—and you never knew it. I owe you plenty, and you won't understand even that."

Mary only kissed her, but Annie broke free and went on.

"When they come to talk about the world going on, and folks marrying, and raising children, after this war is over—you've got to hand it to them that this duty stuff has got a strong punch behind it. Besides, the kid idea makes a hit with me. But even if I did marry, I don't know what a man would say, these times, about my bringing some one else into his house. Men is funny."

"Annie—Annie!" exclaimed Mary Warren once more. "Don't—oh, don't! I'd die before I'd go into your own real home! Of course, I'll not be a burden on you. I'm too proud for that, I hope."

"Well, dope it out your own way, Sis," said her roommate, sighing. "It ain't true that I want to shake you. I don't. But I'm not talking about Mary Warren when she had money her aunt left her—before she lost it in Oil. I'm not talking about Mary Warren when she was eighteen, and pretty as a picture. I ain't even talking about Mary a year ago, wearing dark glasses, but still having a good chanct in the store. What I'm talking about now is Mary Warren down and out, with not even eyes to see with, and no money back of her, and no place to *go*. What are you going to *do*, Sis? that's all. In my case—believe me, if I lose my chanct at this man, Charlie Dorenwald, I'm going to find another some time.

"It's fifty-fifty if either of us, or any girl, would get along all right with a husband if we *could* get one—it's no cinch. And now, women getting plentier and plentier, and men still scarcer and scarcer, it's sure tough times for a girl that hasn't eyes nor anything to get work with, or get married with."

"Annie!" said her companion. "I wish you wouldn't!"

"Well, I wasn't thinking how I talked, Sis," said Annie, reaching out a hand to pat the white one on the chair arm. "But fifty-fifty, my dear—that's all the bet ever was or will be for a woman, and now her odds is a lot worse, they say, even for the well and strong ones. Maybe part of the trouble with us women was we never looked on this business of getting married with any kind of halfway business sense. Along comes a man, and we get foolish. Lord! Oughtn't both of us to know about bargain counters and basement sales?"

"Well, let's eat, Mary," she concluded, seeing she had no answer. And Mary Warren, broken-hearted, high-headed, silent, turned to the remaining routine of the day.

Annie busied herself at the little box behind the stove—a box with a flap of white cloth, which served as cupboard. Here she found a coffee pot, a half loaf of bread, some tinned goods, a pair of apples. She put the coffee pot to boil upon the little stove, pushing back the ornamental acorn which covered the lid at its top. Meantime Mary drew out the little table which served them, spread upon it its white cloth, and laid the knives and forks, scanty enough in their number.

They ate as was their custom every evening. Not two girls in all Cleveland led more frugal lives than these, nor cleaner, in every way.

"Let me wash the dishes, Sis," said Annie Squires. "You needn't wipe them—no, that's all right to-night. Let me, now."

"You're fine, Annie, you're fine, that's what you are!" said Mary Warren. "You're the best girl in the world. But we'll make it fifty-fifty while we can. I'm going to do my share."

"I suppose we'd better do the laundry, too, don't you think?" she added. "We don't want the fire to get too low."

They had used their single wash basin for their dish pan as well, and now it was impressed to yet another use. Each girl found in her pocket a cheap handkerchief or so. Annie now plunged these in the wash basin's scanty suds, washed them, and, going to the mirror, pasted them against the glass, flattening them out so that in the morning they might be "ironed," as she called it. This done, each girl deliberately sat down and removed her shoes and stockings. The stockings themselves now came in for washing—an alternate daily practice with them both since Mary had come hither. They hung the stockings over the back of the solitary spare chair, just close enough to the stove to get some warmth, and not close enough to burn—long experience had taught them the exact distance.

They huddled bare-footed closer to the stove, until Annie rose and tiptoed across to get a pair each of cheap straw slippers which rested below the bed.

"Here's yours, Sis," said she. "You just sit still and get warm as you can before we turn in—it's an awful night, and the fire's beginning to peter out already. I wish't Mr. McAdoo, or whoever it is, 'd see about this coal business. Gee, I hope these things'll get dry before morning—there ain't anything in the world any colder than a pair of wet stockings in the morning! Let's turn in—it'll be warmer, I believe."

The wind, steel-pointed, bored at the window casings all that night. Degree after degree of frost would have registered in that room had means of registration been present. The two young women huddled closer under the scanty covering that they might find warmth. Ten dollars a week. Two great-hearts, neither of them more than a helpless girl.

CHAPTER IV

HEARTS AFLAME

They rose the next morning and dressed in the room without fire, shivering now as they drew on their stockings, frozen stiff. They had their morning coffee in a chilly room downstairs, where sometimes their slatternly landlady appeared, lugubriously voluble. This morning they ate alone, in silence, and none too happily. Even Annie's buoyant spirits seemed inadequate. A trace of bitterness was in her tone when she spoke.

"I'm sick of it."

"Yes, Annie," said Mary Warren. "And it's cold this morning, awfully."

"Cotton vests, marked down—to what wool used to be. Huh! Call this America?"

"What's wrong, Annie?" suddenly asked Mary Warren, drawing her wrap closer as she sat.

"I'd go to the lake before I'd go to the streets, though you mightn't think it. But how about it with only the discards in Derby hats and false teeth left? If we two are going to get married, Mollie, we got to look around among the remnants and bargains—we can't be too particular when we're hunting bargains. Whether it's all off for you at the store or not ain't for me to say, but you might do worse than listen to me."

Mary Warren looked at her in a sort of horror. "Annie, what do you mean?" she demanded.

The real reply came in the hard little laugh with which Annie Squires drew from the pocket of her coat—in which she also was muffled at the breakfast table—a meager little newspaper, close-folded. She spread it out before she passed it to her companion.

"*Hearts Aflame!*" said she. "While you have to dry your own socks, while you break the ice in your coffee! Can't you feel your heart flame? Anyway, here you are— bargains in husbands and wives! Take 'em for the asking. Here's a lot of them advertised. Slightly damaged, but serviceable—and marked down within the reach of all.

"Why, us girls over at the shop, we read these things regular," she rattled on in explanation, her mouth full. "Some of the girls answer these ads—it's lots of fun. You ought to see what some of the men write back. Look at this one, Sis!" said she, chuckling. "Some class to it, eh?" She pointed to an advertisement a trifle larger than its fellows, a trifle more boldly displayed in its black type.

"Wanted: A Wife. A well-to-do and chivalrous rancher of abundant means and large holdings in a Western State wishes to correspond with a respectable young woman who will appreciate a good home and loving care. Object—Matrimony."

"How ridiculous," said Mary Warren simply.

"Uh huh! Is it, though? I don't know. I put this thing to my ear, and it sort of sounded as if there was something behind it. That fellow wants a woman of his own to keep house for him. Out there women are scarce. It's supply and demand, Sis, same as in your store. Well, here's a man looking for goods. So'm I. I've been looking him over for myself, because I ain't as strong for Charlie Dorenwald as I might be, even if he's foreman. He talks so damn much Bolshevik, somehow. Of course, the country's rotten, but it's ours! Still and all, I'll tell you what I'll do, Sis, with you!"

She pulled her chair up to the side of her companion, fumbling in her little purse as she did so; drew out a copper coin and held it balanced between her fingers.

"'The one shall be taken and the other left,' Sis," said she. "Two women, grinding at the mill, the same little old mill, as the Bible said; and 'The one shall be taken and the other left.' Which one? One throw, Mary. Heads or tails. It's got to hit the ceiling before it falls."

"Why, nonsense, Annie— No, no!"

"Heads or tails!" insisted Annie Squires; and as she spoke she flipped the coin against the ceiling. It rolled toward the street window, where neither of them at first could see it.

"Tails!" called Mary Warren faintly, suddenly. It seemed to her she heard some other voice, speaking for her, without her real volition.

"You're on!" said Annie. They both rose and walked toward the darker side of the room.

"I can't see," said Mary. "Strike a match."

Annie did so, and they both bent over the coin.

"Tails—you win!" said Annie Squires. "Well, what do you know about that?"

She was half in earnest about her chagrin—half in earnest as she spoke. "I'd saved him for myself. Sometimes, I say, I don't know about this Charlie Dorenwald, even if he is crazy over me—I'm mostly being beware of foremen, me. And here's a chivalrous and well-to-do ranchman—out West! Gee! Congratulations, Sis!"

CHAPTER V

BEGGAR MAN—THIEF

They laughed like girls, each with slightly heightened color in spite of all the make-believe. Then Annie ran to a vase of artificial flowers which stood upon the mantel, and pulled out a draggled daisy.

"What's he going to be, Kid—your man? Is he rich or poor? Listen! 'Lawyer—doctor—merchant—chief—rich man—poor man—beggar man—thief—'" She stopped in a certain consternation, the last petal in her hand—"A thief?—"

"Why, Annie, you surely don't believe in such things," said Mary Warren reprovingly. "And of course we oughtn't to have done anything foolish as this. It's—it's awful."

Annie, her mood suddenly changing, drew apart and sat down moodily.

"You couldn't blame a fellow for trying to forget things, Sis," said she. "Look at me. I'm on the street, you might say—they canned me yesterday! Yes! that's the truth. I wasn't going to tell you—you looked so cold last night, and you with your eyes what they are. It—it looks like

Charlie had a chance, eh?"

Mary Warren looked at her for a time in silence. "You'll never have to toss a copper for a husband, I'm sure of that. If I were handsome as you—"

"Oh, am I?" said her companion. "Men hang around—what does it get me? Time passes. Where are we pretty soon? Men ain't all husbands that make love."

"How much money you got saved up, Mary?" she asked suddenly.

"Just one hundred thirty-five dollars and eighty cents," said Mary, not needing to consult her pass book. "I can pay for my bond now."

"Got me beat. Best I can do for my life savings is fifty-eight dollars and seventy-five cents. How long will that last you and me?"

"You're despondent, Annie—you mustn't feel blue—why, to-morrow we'll both go out and see what we can do."

"About me? I like that! It's *you* we got to bother about. My Lord! It ain't so far off, this ad in *Hearts Aflame*! What you really *do* need is a man who'll be kind and chivalrous with you."

"I haven't got to that yet," said Mary Warren, stoutly. Her color rose.

"No? Funnier things have happened. You might do worse."

"I'm not *bred* that way, Annie," said Mary Warren slowly; but her color rising yet more as she realized that perhaps she had been cruel.

"You needn't explain anything to me," replied Annie. "I'm not sore. You came of a better family, and so it'll be harder for you to get through life than it is for me."

As she spoke she had risen, and was buttoning her street wraps. Mary Warren sat silent, the dark lenses of her glasses turned toward her companion.

"Beggar man—thief!" she said at last. "I'd be robbing him, even then!" She smiled bitterly. "Who'd take *me*?"

CHAPTER VI

RICH MAN—POOR MAN

When spring came above the icy shores of the inland seas, Mary Warren had been out of work for more than three months. She was ill; ill of body, ill of mind, ill of heart. Her splendid, resilient courage had at last begun to break. She was facing the thought that she could not carry her own weight in the world.

She sat alone once more one evening in the little room which after all thus far she and Annie had been able to retain. Her oculist had taken much from her scanty store of money. She held in her hand his last bill—unpaid; and though she had paid a score of his bills, yet her eyesight now was nearly gone. Her doctor called it "retinal failure"; and it had steadily advanced, whatever it was. Now she knew that there was no hope.

She greeted the homecoming of her room-mate each nightfall with eagerness. Annie by this time had found harder and worse paid work in another factory. She came in with her hands scarred and torn, her nails broken and stained. She had grown more reticent of late.

"Well, how are things coming along, Sis?" said she this evening on her return, after she had thrown her wrap across a chair back. "How much money have you got left? You look to me like you was counting it."

"Not very much, Annie—not very much. The doctor—you see, I can't take his time and not pay him."

"You're too thin-skinned. What are doctors for?"

"But, Annie, I don't know what to do. I'm scared. That's the truth about it—I'm scared!"

Her companion smiled, with her new slow and cynical smile. "Some of us go to the lake—or to a man—or to men," said she, succinctly. "Look over the stock of goods that's within your means. Bargains. Odds and Ends."

"What could I *do*?"

"Suppose you got married to your gentle and chivalrous rancher out West. Maybe you'd be able to stand it after a while, even if he dyed his hair, or had his neck shaved round. Mostly they have false teeth—before they'll advertise. Probably he's a widower. Object: matrimony; that mostly is a widower's main object in life; and you can't show 'em nothing except when you bury 'em."

"I'd die before I'd answer that sort of a thing!" said Mary Warren hotly.

"You would," replied Annie. "I know that. I knew it all along. That's why I had to take it into my own hands." Again the cynical smile of Annie Squires, twenty-two.

"Your own hands—what do you mean by that?"

"I might as well tell you. I've been writing to him in your name! I've sent him a *picture* of you—I got it in the bureau drawer. And he's crazy over you!"

Mary Warren looked at her with wrath, humiliation and offended dignity showing in her reddened cheeks.

"You had the audacity to do that, Annie! How *dared* you? How *could* you?"

"Well, I was afraid of the lake for you, and I knew that something had to be done, and you wouldn't do it. I've got quite a batch of letters from him. He's got three hundred and twenty acres of land, eight cows, a horse and a mule. He has a house which is all right except it lacks the loving care of a woman! Well, stack that up against this room. And we can't even keep this for very long.

"Listen, Mary," she said, coming over and putting both her broken hands on her friend's shoulders. "God knows, if I could keep us both going I would, but I don't make money enough for myself, hardly, let alone you. You don't belong where you've been—you wouldn't, even if you was well and fit, which you ain't. Mollie, Mollie, my dear, what is there ahead for you? We *got* to do some thinking. It's up to us right now. You're too good for the lake or the poor farm—or—why, you *belong* in a home. Keep house? I wish't I knew as much as you do about that."

"I'll tell you," she resumed suddenly. "I'll tell you what let's do! A stenographer down at our office does all these letters for me—she's a bear, come to correspondence like that. Now, I'll have her get out a letter from you to him that will sort of bring this thing to a head one way or the other. We'll say that you can't think of going out there to marry a man sight-unseen—"

"No," said Mary Warren. "The lake, first." She was

wringing her hands, her cheeks hot.

"But now, as a housekeeper—" After a long and perturbed silence Annie spoke again. "That's the real live idea, Sis! That's the dope! You might *think* of going out there as a housekeeper, just to see how things *looked*—just so that you could look things *over*, couldn't you? You wouldn't marry any man in a hurry. You could say you'd only do your best as a sincere, honest woman—why, I have to tell that stenographer what to write, all the time. She's sloppy."

"But *look* at me, Annie—I wouldn't be worth anything as a housekeeper." Mary Warren was arguing! "As to marrying that way—"

—"Letter'll say you're not asking any pay at all. You don't promise anything. You don't ask *him* to promise anything. You don't want any wages. You don't let him pay your railroad fare out—not at all! You ain't taking any chances nor asking him to take any chances,—unless she falls in love with you for fair. Which I wouldn't wonder if he did. You're a sweet girl, Mollie. Put fifteen pounds on you, and you'd be a honey. You are anyway. Men always look at you—it's your figure, part, maybe. And you're so good—and you're a *lady*, Sis. And if I—"

"Tell him," said Mary Warren suddenly, pulling herself together with the extremest effort of will and in the suddenest and sharpest decision she had ever known in all her life, "tell him I'm square! Tell him I'll be honest all the time—all the time!"

"As though you could be anything else, you poor dear!" said Annie Squires, coming over and throwing a strong arm about Mary Warren's neck, as though they both had done nothing but agree about this after a dozen conversations. And then she wept, for she knew what Mary Warren's surrender had cost. "And game! Game and square both, you sweet thing," sobbed Annie Squires.

"Give me fifteen pounds on you," she wept, dabbing at her own eyes, "and I wouldn't risk Charlie near you,—not a minute!"

CHAPTER VII

CHIVALROUS; AND OF ABUNDANT MEANS

Around the Two Forks Valley the snow still lay white and clean upon the peaks, but the feet of the mountains were bathed in a rising flood of green. On the bottom lands the grasses began to start, the willows renewed their leafery. On the pools of the limpid stream the trout left wrinkles and circles at midday now, as they rose to feed upon the insects swarming in the warmth of the oncoming sun.

On this particular morning Wid Gardner turned down the practically untrod lane along Sim's wire fence. Now and again he glanced at something which he held in his hand.

When he entered Sim Gage's gate, the ancient mule, his head out of the stable window, welcomed him, braying his discontent. Here lay the ragged wood pile, showing the ax work of a winter. At the edge of a gnawed hay stack stood the remnant of Sim's scant cattle herd, not half of which had "wintered through."

No smoke was rising from Sim Gage's chimney. "Feller's hopeless, that's what," complained Wid Gardner to himself. "It gravels me plenty."

A muffled voice answered his knock, and he pushed open

the door. Sim Gage was still in bed, and his bed was still on the floor.

"Come in," said he, thrusting a frowsy head out from under his blankets. He used practically the same amount of covering about him in winter and summer; and now, as usual, he had retired practically without removing his daily clothing. His face, stubbled and unshaven, swollen with sleep and surmounted by a tangled fringe of hair, might not by any flight of imagination have been called admirable or inviting, as he now looked out to greet his caller.

"Oh, dang it! Git up, Sim," said Wid, irritated beyond expression. "It's after ten o'clock."

His words cut through the somewhat pachydermatous sensibilities of Sim Gage, who frowned a trifle as, after a due pause, he crawled out and sat down and reached for his broken boots.

"Well, I dunno as it's anybody's damn business whether I git up a-tall or not, except my own," said he. "I'll git up when I please, and not afore."

"Well, you might git up this morning, anyhow," said Wid.

"Why?"

"I got a letter for you."

"Look-a-here," said Sim Gage, with sudden preciseness. "What you been doing? Letter? What letter? And how come you by my letters?"

"Well, I been talking with Mis' Davidson—she run the whole correspondence, Sim. We—now—we allowed we'd ought to take care of it fer you. And we done so, that's all."

"Huh!" said Sim Gage. "Fine business, ain't it?"

"Well, she's a-coming on out," said Wid Gardner, suddenly and comprehensively.

"*What's that*? Who's a-coming on out?"

The face of Sim Gage went pale even under the cold water to which at the moment he was treating his leathery skin in the basin on top the stove.

"Sim," said Wid Gardner, "it was understood that this thing was to run in your name. Now, Mis' Davidson—when it comes to fixing up a love correspondence, she's the ace! It all ain't my fault a-tall, Sim. We advertised—and we got a answer, and we follered it up. And this here letter is the *re*-sult. I allowed we'd ought to tell you too, by now."

"What you been doing—fooling with me, you two?" demanded Sim. "That whole thing was a joke."

"It's one hell of a fine joke now," rejoined Wid Gardner. "She's a-coming on out. Sim, it's up to you. *I* ain't been advertising fer no wife. This here letter is *yours*."

"That's a fine thing you done, ain't it?" said Sim Gage, turning on to his neighbor. "When you find the ford's too deep to git acrost, you begin to holler fer help."

"That's neither here nor there. That ain't the worst—I've got her picture here, and her letters too. She's been plumb honest all along. She says she's pretty much broke, and not too well. She says when she sees you she hopes you won't think she's deceived you. She says she knows you're everything you said you was—a gentle and chiva*l*erous ranchman of the West, sure to be kind to a woman. She's scared—she's that honest. But she's a-coming. She's going to try housekeeping though—no more'n that. Rest's all up to you, not her. She balked from the jump on all marrying talk."

"Mis' Davidson ought to take care of this thing," said Sim Gage, his features now working, as usual, in his perplexity.

"Mis' Davidson is due to pull her freight. She's going down on her own homestead. I'm some scared too, Sim. You don't really *know* how you been making love to this woman. I didn't know Mis' Davidson had it in her. You got to come through now, Sim."

"Who says I got to come through?"

"You got to go to town to-morrow."

"So you're a-going to make me go in to town tomorrow and marry a woman I never seen, whether I want to or not?"

"No, it ain't right up to that—you needn't think she's coming out here to hunt up a preacher and git married to you right away. Not a-tall, Mr. Gage, not none a-tall! She never onct said she'd do any more'n come out here and keep house fer you one season—that's all. Said she wouldn't deceive you. God knows how you can keep from deceiving *her*. Look at this place. And you got to bring her here—to-morrow. She'll be at Two Forks station to-morrow morning at eight-thirty, on the Park train. This here thing is up to you right now. You made such a holler about needing a woman to make things human fer you.

Emerson Hough

Well, here you are. There's the cards—play 'em the way they lay. You be human now if you can. You got the chance."

"I ain't got no wagon, Wid," said Sim, weakly. "You know I ain't got none."

"You'll have to take my buckboard."

"And you know I ain't got no team—my horse, he ain't right strong—didn't winter none too well—and I couldn't go there with just one mule, now could I?"

"You'll have to take my team of broncs," said Wid. "You can start out from my place."

"But one thing, Sim Gage," he continued, "when you've started, I'm a-coming down here with a pitch-fork and I'm a-going to clean out this place! It ain't human. We'll do the best we can. Since there ain't a-going to be no marrying right off, you'll have to sleep in your wall tent outside. You'll have to git some wood cut up. You'll have to git a clean bed here in the house,—this bed of yours is going to be burned out in the yard. You'll have to git new blankets when you go to town."

"As fer your clothes"—he turned a contemptuous glance upon Sim as he stood—"they ain't *hardly* fit fer a bridegroom! Go to the Golden Eagle, and git yourself a full outfit, top to bottom—new shirts, new underclothes, new pants, new hat, new socks, new gloves, new everything. This girl can't come out here and see you the way you are, and this place the way it's been. She'd start something."

"Well, if you leave it to me," said Sim Gage mildly, "all this here seems kind of sudden. You come in afore I'm up, and tell me to burn my bed, and sleep in a tent, and borry a wagon and team and go to town fer to marry a girl I never seen. That don't look reason'ble to me, especial since I ain't had no hand in it."

"It's up to you now."

"How do I know whether I want that girl or not? I ain't read no letters—nor wrote none. I ain't seen no picture of her—"

"Well," said Wid, and reached a hand into his breast pocket, "here she is."

In a feeling more akin to awe than anything else, Sim Gage bent over, looking down at the clear oval face, the piled dark hair, the tender contour of cheek and chin of Mary Warren, as beautiful a young lady as any man is apt ever to see; so beautiful that this man's inexperienced heart stopped in his bosom. This picture once had been buttoned in the tunic of an aviator who flew for the three flags; her brother; and before his death and its return more than one of Dan Warren's army friends had looked at it reverently as Sim Gage did now.

"Wears glasses, don't she," said he, to conceal his confusion. "Reckon she's a school ma'am?"

"Ask me, and I'll say she's a lady. She says she's a working girl. Says she's had trouble. Says she's up against it now. Says she ain't well, and ain't happy, and—well, here she is."

"My good God A'mighty!" said Sim Gage, his voice awed as he looked at the high-bred, clear-featured face of Mary Warren.

CHAPTER VIII

RIVAL CONSCIENCES

The transcontinental train from the East rarely made its great climb up the Two Forks divide on time, and to-day it was more than usually late. A solitary figure long since had begun to pace the station platform, looking anxiously up and down the track.

It was Sim Gage; and this was the first time he ever had come to meet a train at Two Forks.

Sim Gage, but not the same. He now was in stiff, ill-fitting and exclaimingly new clothing. A new dark hat oppressed his perspiring brow, new and pointed shoes agonized his feet, a new white collar and a tie tortured his neck. He had been owner of these things no longer than overnight. He did not feel acquainted with himself.

He was to meet a woman! Her picture was in his pocket, in his brain, in his blood. A vast shyness, coming to consternation, seized him. He felt a sense of personal guilt; and yet a feeling of indignity and injustice claimed him. But all this and all his sullen anger was wiped out in this great shyness of a man not used to facing women. Sim Gage was product of a womanless land. This was the closest his orbit ever had come to that of the great mystery. And he had been alone so long. A sudden surging longing came to his heart. Sim Gage was shy always, and he was frightened now; but now he felt a longing—a longing to be human.

Sim Gage never in all his life had seen a young woman looking back at him over his shoulder. And now there came accession of all his ancient dread, joined with this growing sense of guilt. A few passengers from the resort hotel back in the town began to appear, lolling at the ticket window or engaged at the baggage room. Sim Gage found a certain comfort in the presence of other human beings. All the time he gazed furtively down the railway tracks.

A long-drawn scream of the laboring engines told of the approaching train at last. Horses and men pricked up their ears. The blood of Sim Gage's heart seemed to go to his brain. He was seized with a panic, but, fascinated by some agency he could not resist, he stood uncertainly until the train came in. He began to tremble in the unadulterated agony of a shy man about to meet the woman to whom he has made love only in his heart.

Sim Gage's team of young and wild horses across the street began to plunge now, and to entangle themselves dangerously, but he did not cross the street to care for them. *She* was coming! The woman from the States was on this very train. In two minutes—

But the crowd thinned and dissipated at length, and Sim Gage had not found her after all. He felt sudden relief that she had not come, mingled with resentment that he had been made foolish. She was not there—she had not come!

But his gaze, passing from one to another of the early tourists, rested at last upon a solitary figure which stood close to the burly train conductor near the station door. The conductor held the young woman's arm reassuringly, as they both looked questioningly from side to side. She was in dark clothing. A dark veil was across her face. As she pushed it back he saw her eyes protected by heavy black lenses.

Sim Gage hesitated. The conductor spoke to him so loudly that he jumped.

"Say, are you Mr. Gage?"

"That's me," said Sim. "I'm Mr. Gage." He could not recall that ever in his life he had been so accosted before; he had never thought of himself as being Mr. Gage, only Sim Gage.

One redeeming quality he had—a pleasant speaking voice. A sudden turn of the head of the young woman seemed to recognize this. She reached out, groping for the arm of the conductor. Consternation urged her also to seek protection. This was the man!

"Lady for you, Mr. Gage," said the conductor. "This young woman caught a cinder down the road. Better see a doctor soon as you can—bad eye. She said she was to meet you here."

"It's all right," said Sim Gage suddenly to him. "It's all right. You can go if you want to."

He saw that the young woman was looking at him, but she seemed to make no sign of recognition.

"I'm Mr. Gage, ma'am," said he, stepping up. "I'm sorry you got a cinder in your eye. We'll go up and see the doctor. Why, I had a cinder onct in my eye, time I was going down to Arizony, and it like to of ruined me. I couldn't see nothing for nearly four days."

He was lying now, rather fluently and beautifully. He had never been in Arizona, and so little did he know of railway travel that he had not noted that this young woman came not from a sleeping car, but from one of the day coaches. The dust upon her garments seemed to him there naturally enough.

She did not answer, stood so much aloof from him that a sudden sense of inferiority possessed him. He could not see that her throat was fluttering, did not know that tears were coming from back of the heavy glasses. He could not tell that Mary Warren had appraised him even now, blind though she was; that she herself suffered by reason of that wrong appraisal.

The throng thinned, the tumult and shouting of the hotel men died away. Sim Gage did not know what to do. A woman seemed to mean a sudden and strangely over-whelming accession of problems. What should he do? Where would he put her? What ought he to say?

"If you'll excuse me," he ventured at last, "I'll go acrosst and git my team. They're all tangled up, like you see."

She spoke, her voice agitated; reached out a hand. "I—I can't see at *all*, sir!"

"That's too bad, ma'am," said Sim Gage, "but don't you worry none at all. You set right down here on the aidge of the side walk, till I git the horses fixed. They're scared of the cars. Is this your satchel, ma'am?"

"Yes—that's mine."

"You got any trunk for me to git?" he asked, turning back, suddenly and by miracle, recalling that people who traveled usually had trunks.

He could not see the flush of her cheek as she replied, "No, I didn't bring one. I thought—what I had would do." He could not know that nearly all her worldly store was here in this battered cheap valise.

"You ain't a-going to leave us so soon like that, are you?"

She turned to him wistfully, a swift light upon her face. He had said, "leave us"—not "leave me." And his voice was gentle. Surely he was the kind-hearted and chivalrous rancher of his own simple letters. She began to feel a woman's sense of superiority. On the defensive, she replied: "I don't know yet. Suppose we—suppose—"

"Suppose that we wait awhile, eh?" said Sim Gage, himself wistful.

"Why—yes."

"All right, ma'am. We'll do anything you like. You don't need no trunk full of things out here—I hope you'll git along somehow."

Knowing that he ought to assist her, he put out a hand to touch her arm, withdrew it as though he had been stung, and then hastily stood as he felt her hand rest upon his arm. He led her slowly to the edge of the platform. Then she heard his footsteps passing, heard the voices of two men—for now a bystander had gone across to do something for the plunging horses, one of which had thrown itself under the buckboard tongue. She heard the two men as they worked on. "Git up!" said one voice. "Git around there!" Then came certain oaths on the part of both men, and conversation whose import she did not know.

Their voices were as though heard in a dream. There suddenly came an overwhelming sense of guilt to Mary Warren. She had been unfair to this man! He was a trifle crude, yes; but kind, gentle, unpresuming. She felt safer and safer—guilty and more guilty. How could she ever explain it all to him?

"I reckon they're all right now," said Sim Gage, after a considerable battle with his team. "Nothing busted much. Git up on the seat, won't you, Bill, and drive acrosst—I got to help that lady git in."

"Who is she?" demanded the other, who had not failed to note the waiting figure.

"It's none of your damn business," said Sim Gage. "That is, it's my housekeeper—she's going to cook for the hay hands."

"With a two months' start?" grinned the other.

"Drive on acrosst now," said Sim Gage, in grim reply, which closed the other's mouth at once.

Mary Warren heard the crunch of wheels, heard the thump of her valise as Sim Gage caught it up and threw it into the back of the buckboard. Then he spoke again. She felt him standing close at hand. Once more, trembling as in an ague, she placed a hand upon his arm.

"Now, when I tell you," he said gently, "why, you put your foot up on the hub of the wheel here, and grab the iron on the side, and climb in quick—these horses is sort of uneasy."

"I can't see the wheel," said Mary Warren, groping.

She felt his hand steadying her—felt the rim of the wheel under her hand, felt him gently if clumsily try to help her up. Her foot missed the hub of the wheel, the horses started, and she almost fell—would have done so had not he caught her in his arms. It was almost the first time in his life, perhaps the only time, that he had felt the full weight of a woman in his arms. She disengaged herself, apologized for her clumsiness.

"You didn't hurt yourself, any?" said he anxiously.

"No," she said. "But I'm blind—*I'm blind*! Oh, don't you know?"

He said nothing. How could she know that her words brought to Sim Gage not regret, but—relief!

He steadied her foot so that it might find the hub of the wheel, steadied her arm, cared for her as she clambered into the seat.

"All right," she heard him say, not to her; and then he replaced the other man on the high seat. The horses plunged forward. She felt herself helpless, alone, swept away. And she was blind.

All the way across the Middle West, across the great plains, Mary Warren had been able to see somewhat. Perhaps it was the knitting—hour after hour of it, in spite of all, done in sheer self-defense. But at the western edge of the great Plains, it had come—what she had dreaded. Both eyes were gone! Since then she had not seen at all, and having in mind her long warning, accepted her blindness as a permanent thing.

She passed now through a world of blackness. She could not see the man who had written those letters to her. She could catch only the wine of a high, clean air, the breath of pine trees, the feeling of space, appreciable even by the blind.

Suddenly she began to sob. Sim Gage by now had somewhat quieted his wild team, and he looked at her, his face puckered into a perturbed frown.

"Now, now," he said, "don't you take on, little woman." He was abashed at his daring, but himself felt almost like tears, as things now were. "It'll all come right. Don't you worry none. Don't be scared of these horses a-tall, ma'am; I can handle 'em all right. We got to see that doctor."

But when presently they had driven the half mile to the village, he learned that the doctor was not in town.

"We can't do anything," said she. "Drive on—we'll go. I don't think the doctor could help me very much."

All the time she knew she had in part been lying to him. It was not merely a cinder in her eye—this was a helpless blindness, a permanent thing. The retina of each eye now was ruined, gone. So she had been warned. Again she reached out her hand in spite of all to touch his arm. He remained silent. She cruelly misunderstood him.

At last she turned fully towards him, and spoke suddenly. "Listen!" said she. "I believe you're a good man. I'll not deceive you."

"God knows I ain't no good man," said Sim Gage suddenly, "and God knows I'm sorry I deceived you like I have. But I'll take care of you until you can do something better, and until you want to go back home."

　　　　　　　Emerson Hough

"Home?" she said. "I haven't any home. I tell you I've deceived you. I'm sorry—oh, it's all so terrible."

"It shore is," said Sim Gage. "I didn't really write them letters—but it's my fault you're here. You can blame me fer everything. Why, almost I was a notion never to come near this here place this morning. I felt guilty, like I'd shot somebody—I didn't know. I feel that way now."

"You're all your letters said you were," said Mary Warren, weeping now. "Any woman who would deceive such a man—"

"You ain't deceived me none," said Sim Gage. "But it's wrong of me to fool a woman such as you, and I'm sorry. Only, just don't you git scared too much. I'm a-going to take care of you the best I know how."

"But it wasn't true!" she broke out—"what the conductor said! It isn't just a cinder in my eye—it's worse. My eyes have been getting bad right along. I couldn't see *anything* to-day. You didn't know. I lost my place. I have no relatives—there wasn't any place in the world for me. I was afraid I was going blind—and yesterday I *did* go blind. I'll never see again. And you're kind to me. I wish—I wish—why, what shall I *do*?"

"Ma'am," said Sim Gage, "I didn't know, and you didn't know. Can you ever forgive me fer what I've done to you?"

"Forgive you—what do you mean?" she said. "Oh, my God, what shall I do!"

Sim Gage's face was frowning more than ever.

"Now, you mustn't take on, ma'am," said he. "I'm sorry as

I can be fer you, but I got to drive these broncs. But fer as I'm concerned—it ain't just what I want to say, neither—I *can't* make it right plain to you, ma'am. It ain't right fer me to say I'm almost *glad* you can't see—but somehow, that's right the way I do feel! It's mercifuler to *you* that way, ma'am."

"What do you mean?" said Mary Warren. She caught emotion in this man's voice. "Whatever can you *mean*?"

"Well," said Sim Gage, "take me like I am, setting right here, I ain't fitten to be setting here. But I don't *want* you to see. I got that advantage of you, ma'am. I can *see* you, ma'am"; and he undertook a laugh which made a wretched failure.

"How far is it to your—our—the place where we're going?" she asked after a time.

"About twenty-three mile, ma'am," he answered cheerfully. "Road's pretty fair now. I wish't you could see how pretty the hills is—they're gitting green now some."

"And the sky is blue?" Her eyes turned up, sensible of no more than a feeling that light was somewhere.

"Right blue, ma'am, with leetle white clouds, not very big. I wish't you could see our sky."

"And trees?"

"Dark green, ma'am—pine trees always is."

She heard the rumble of the wheels on planks, caught the sound of rushing waters.

"This is the bridge over the West Fork, ma'am," said her

companion. "It's right pretty here—the water runs over the rocks like."

"And what is the country like on ahead, where—where we're going?"

"It's in a valley like, ma'am," said Sim Gage.

"There's mountains on each side—they come closest down to the other fork, near in where I live. That fork's just as clean as glass, ma'am—you can see right down into it, twenty feet—" Then suddenly he caught himself. "That is, I wish't you could. Plenty of fish in it—trout and grayling—I'll catch you all you want, ma'am. They're fine to eat."

"And are there things about the place—chickens or something?"

"There's calves, ma'am," said Sim Gage. "Not many. I ain't got no hens, but I'll git some if you want 'em. We'd ought to have some eggs, oughtn't we? And I got several cattle—not many as I'd like, but some. This ain't my wagon. These ain't my horses; I got one horse and a mule."

"What sort is it—the house?"

Sim Gage spoke now like a man and a gentleman.

"I ain't got no house fitten to call one, ma'am," said he, "and that's the truth. I've got a log cabin with one room. I've slept there alone fer a good many years, holding down my land."

"But," he added quickly, "that's a-going to be your place. Me—I'm out a leetle ways off, in the flat, beyond the first row of willers between the house and the creek—I always sleep in a tent in the summer time. I allow you'd feel safer in a house."

"I've always read about western life," said she slowly, in her gentle voice. "If only—I wish—"

"So do I, ma'am," said Sim Gage.

But neither really knew what was the wish in the other's heart.

CHAPTER IX

THE HALT AND THE BLIND

The sweet valley, surrounded by its mountains, was now a sight to quicken the pulse of any heart alive to beauty, as it lay in its long vistas before them; but neither of these two saw the mountains or the trees, or the green levels that lay between. Long silences fell, broken only by the crackling clatter of the horses' hoofs on the hard roadway.

It was Mary Warren who at last spoke, after a deep breath, as though summoning her resolution. "You're an honest man," said she. "I ought to be honest with you."

"I reckon that's so enough, ma'am," said Sim Gage. "But I just told you I ain't been honest with you. I never wrote one of them letters that you got—it was some one else."

"But you came to meet me—you're here—"

"Yes, but I didn't write them letters. That was all done by friends of mine."

"That's very strange. That's just the reason I wanted to tell *you* that I hadn't been honest—I never wrote the letters that *you* got! It was my room-mate, Annie Squires."

"So? That's funny, ain't it? Some folks has funny idees of jokes. I reckon they thought this was a joke. It ain't."

"Your letters seemed like you seem now," she broke in. "It seems to me you must have written every word."

"Ma'am—" said Sim Gage; and broke down.

"Yes, sir?"

"Them is the finest words I ever heard in my life! I ain't been much. If I could only live up to them words, now—

"Besides," he went on, a rising happiness in his tones, "seems like you and me was one just as honest as the other, and both meaning fair. That makes me feel a heap easier. If it does you, you're welcome."

Blind as she was, Mary Warren knew now the gulf between this man's life and hers. But his words were so kind. And she so much needed a friend.

"You're a forgiving man, Mr. Gage," said she.

"No, I ain't. I'm a awful man. When you learn more about me you'll think I'm the worst man you ever seen."

"We'll have to wait," was all that Mary Warren could think to say. But after a time she turned her face toward him once more.

"Do you know," said she, "I think you're a gentleman!"

"Oh, my Lord!" said Sim Gage, his eyes going every which way. "Oh, my good Lord!"

"Well, it's true. Look—you haven't said a word or done a

thing—you haven't touched me—or laughed—or—or hinted—not once. That's being a gentleman, in a time like this. This—this is a very hard place for a woman."

"It ain't so easy fer a man! But I couldn't have done no other way, could I?"

She made no answer. "Are there many other women in this valley, Mr. Gage?" she asked after a time. "Who are they? What are they like?"

"Five, in twenty-two miles between my place and town, ma'am," he answered, "when they're home. The nearedest one to us is about couple miles, unless you cut through the fields."

"Who is she? What is she like?"

"That is Mis' Davidson, our school ma'am— She's the only woman I seen a'most all last summer, unlessen onct in a while a woman would come out with some fishing party in a automobile. Most of them crosses up above on the bridge and comes down the other side of the creek from us. Seems to me sometimes women has always been just acrosst the creek from me, ma'am. I don't know much about them. Now, Wid—Wid Gardner—he's the next rancher to me, this side—he sometimes has folks come there in the fishing season."

"Your log house is all painted and nice, isn't it?"

"*Painted*, ma'am? Lord, no! You don't paint a log house none."

"I never saw one in my life," said she contritely; then, sighing. "I never will, now."

"Do men come to your place very much, then?" she asked at length.

"Why, Wid, he sometimes comes over."

"And who is Wid?"

"Like I said, he's got the next ranch to mine. He's maybe a forwarder sort of man than me."

"Did he have anything to do with—that advertisement?"

"How can you guess things like that?"

"He thought you were all alone?"

"We did have some talk. But I want to tell you one thing, ma'am—if I had ever thought onct that we'd a-brung a woman like *you* here, I'd never of been part nor party to it. I guess not!"

"And yet you can't see why you're a gentleman!" said she again slowly.

"You said you'd be going back home again before long?" It was the first thing Sim Gage could say.

"I haven't any home."

"Nor no folks neither?"

"There's not a soul in the world that I could go back to, Mr. Gage. So now, I've told you the truth."

"But there was oncet, maybe?" he said shrewdly. "How old are you?" He flushed suddenly at this question, which he asked before he thought.

"I'm twenty-five."

"You don't look that old. Me, I'm thirty-seven. I'm too old to marry. Now I never will."

"How do you know?" she said. "What do you mean?" As she spoke she felt the tears come again on her cheeks, felt her hands trembling.

"Well, ma'am, I know mighty well I'll never marry now. Of course, if one sort of woman had came out here—big and strong enough to be a housekeeper and nothing else, and all that, and one thing with another—I won't say what might have happened. Strange things has happened that way—right out of them damn *Hearts Aflame* ads—right around along in here, in this here valley, too, I know. Well, of course, a man can't get along so well, ranching, unless he has a wife—"

"Or a housekeeper?"

"Why, yes. That's what we advertised fer. I didn't know it."

Mary Warren pondered for a long time.

"Look at me," she said at last. "There's no place for me back home, and none here. What sort of housekeeper would I make—and what sort of—of—wife? I'm disappointing you; and you're disappointing me. What shall we both do?"

"Why, how do you mean?" said Sim Gage, wonderingly. "Disappoint you? Of course I couldn't marry a woman like you! You don't want me to do *that*? That wouldn't be right."

"Oh, I don't mean that! I don't know what I did mean!"

Some sense of her perturbation must have come to him. "Now don't you worry, ma'am. Don't you git troubled none a-tall. I'm a-goin' to take care of you myself until everything gits all right."

"I'm a thief! I'm a beggar!" was all she could say.

"The same here, ma'am! You've got nothing on me," said Sim Gage. "What I said is, we're in the same boat, and we got to go the best way we can till things shapes out. It ain't very much I got to offer you. Us sagebrushers has to take the leavings."

"You've said the truth for me—the very truth. I'm of the discard—I can't earn my living. Leavings! And I wanted to earn my living."

"You've earned it now, ma'am," said Sim Gage; and perhaps made the largest speech of all his life.

"Well, anyways, we're going to come to my land right now," he added after a time. "We've passed the school house, only couple mile from my place. On ahead here is Wid Gardner's ranch, on the left hand side. I don't reckon he's at home. I told you the school ma'am had maybe went off to her homestead, didn't I? Maybe Nels Jensen, he's maybe driving her to the Big Springs station down below. This here is Wid Gardner's team and buckboard, ma'am. I ain't got around to fixing mine up this spring. I've got to drive back after a while and take these things back to Wid."

Her situation grew more tense. They were coming now to the end of the journey—to her home—to his home. She did not speak. To her ears the sound of the horses' feet seemed less, as though they were passing on a road not so much used.

"This is a sort of alley, like, down along between the willers and the rail fence," explained Sim Gage. "It's about half a mile of this. Then we come to my gate."

And presently they did come to his gate, where the silver-edged willows came close on the one side and the wide hay meadows reached out on the other toward the curving pathway of the river. He pulled up.

"Could you hold these horses, ma'am, fer a minute? I got to open the gate."

He handed her the reins, it never occurring to him that there was any one in the world who had never driven horses. She was frightened, but resolved to appear brave and useful.

Sim Gage began to untwist the short club which bound the wire gate shut. He pulled it back, and clucked to the horses, seeing that she did not start them.

Mary Warren knew nothing of horses. It seemed to her that the correct thing to do was to drop the reins loosely, shaking them a little. The half wild horses, with their uncanny brute sense, knew the absence of a master, and took instant advantage of the knowledge. With one will they sprang, lunged, and started forward, plunging. Mary Warren dropped the lines.

"*Sit still there*!" she heard a voice call out imperatively. Then, "Whoa! damn you, whoa now!"

She could see nothing, but sensed combat. Sim Gage had sprung forward and caught the cheek strap of the nearest horse. It reared and struck out wildly. She heard an exclamation, as though of pain, but could not see him as he swung across to the other horse and caught his fingers in its nostrils, still calling out to them, imperiously, in the voice of a commander.

At length they halted, quieted. She heard his voice speaking brokenly. "Set still where you are, ma'am. I'll tie 'em."

"You're hurt!" she called out. "It was my fault."

"I'm all right. Just you set still."

Apparently he finished fastening the horses to something. She heard him come to the end of the seat, knew that he was reaching up his arms to help her down. But when she swung her weight from the seat she felt him wince.

"One of 'em caught me on the knee," he admitted. "It was my new pants, too."

She could not see his face, gray with pain now under the dust.

"It's all my fault—I didn't dare tell you—I don't know anything about horses. I don't know anything about anything out here!"

"Take hold of my left hand coat sleeve," he answered to her confession. "We'll walk on into the yard. Keep hold of me, and I'll keep hold of them horses. I'll look out if they jump."

For some reason of their own the team became less fractious. He limped along the road, his hand at the bit of the more vicious. She could feel him limp.

"You're hurt—they did jump on you!" she reiterated.

"Knee's busted some, but we'll git along. Don't you mind. Anyhow, we're here. Now, you go off, a little ways—it's all level here—and I'll unhitch these critters."

"That's the barn over there," he added, pointing in a direction which she could not see. "Plain trail between the house and the corral gate. On beyond is my hay lands and the willers along the creek. There's a sort of spring that-away"—again he pointed, invisibly to her—"and along it runs a band of willers—say a hundred yards from the house. It all ain't much. I never ought to of brought you here a-tall, but like I said, we'll do the best we can. Please don't be afraid, or nothing."

Stripped of their harness, the wild team turned and made off at a run down the road, through the gate and back to their own home.

"Good riddance," said Sim Gage, stooping, his hands at his cut knee-cap. "Wid can come over here fer his own buckboard, fer all of me."

"Take right a-holt of my arm tight, and go easy now," he added, turning to Mary Warren. She felt his hand on her arm.

They passed around the corner of the cabin. She reached out a hand to touch the side post as she heard the door open.

"It's a right small little place inside," said Sim Gage, "only one bunk in it. I've got some new blankets and I'll fix it all up. Maybe you'll want to lay down and rest a while before long.

"Over at the left is the stove—when I git the fire going you can tell where it is, all right. Between the stove and the bunk is the table, where we eat—I mean where I used to eat. It all ain't so big. Pretty soon you'll learn where the things all is. It's like learning where things is in the dark, ma'am, I suppose?"

"Yes. What time is it?" she asked suddenly. "You see, I can't tell."

"Coming on evening, ma'am. I reckon it's around three or four o'clock. You see, I ain't got a clock. I ain't got round to gitting one yet. Mine's just got busted recent.

"This here's a chair, ma'am," he said. "Jest set down and take it right easy. Lay off your wraps, and I'll put 'em on the bunk. You mustn't worry about nothing. We're here now."

By and by she felt his hand touch her sleeve.

"Here's a couple of poker sticks," said he. "I reckon maybe you'll need to use one onct in a while to kind of feel around with. Well, it's the same with me—I'm going to need something, kind of, my own self. That knee's going to leave me lame a while, *I* believe."

A sudden feeling that they two were little better than lost children came to her as she turned toward him. A strange, swift feeling of companionship rose in her heart. Her vague fears began to vanish.

"You're hurt," said she. "What can I do? Can't you put some witch hazel on your knee?"

"I ain't got none, ma'am."

"Isn't there some alcohol, or anything, in the place?"

"No, ma'am—why, yes, there is too! I got some whiskey left. Whiskey is good fer most anything. I'll tell you what I'll do. I'll just go round the house, and I'll rub some of that whiskey on my knee."

She heard him pass out of the door. She was alone. Absolutely she welcomed the sound of his foot again. He might have seen her face almost light up.

"When you git kicked on a bone," he said, "it hurts worse. She's swelled up some, but I reckon she'll get well in a few days or weeks. I don't think she's busted much, though at first I thought he'd knocked the knee cap plump off. There's a cut in above there. Cork of the shoe must of hit me there."

The gravity of her face was her answer. She could see nothing.

"I reckon you can smell that whiskey," said he, "but I ain't drunk none—it's just on my leg, that's all."

"You're not a drinking man?" she asked.

"Why, yes, of course I am. All of us people out here drinks more or less when they can git it—this is a dry state. But I allow I'll cut it out fer a while, now, ma'am."

"Ain't you hungry now, ma'am?" he added. "We didn't have a bite to eat all day."

"Yes," said she. "But how can I help cook supper—what can I do?"

"There ain't much you need to do, ma'am. If I've lived

here alone all this time, and lived alone everywhere else fer thirty-seven years, I reckon I can cook one more meal."

"For your housekeeper!" she said, smiling bitterly.

"Well, yes," he replied. "You don't know where things is yet. I got some bacon here, and aigs too. I brought out some oranges from town—fer you." She did not see him color shyly. Oranges were something Sim Gage never had brought to his ranch before. He had bought them of the Park commissary at the station.

"Then I got some canned tomatoes—they're always good with bacon. Out under my straw pile I got some potatoes that ain't froze so very bad anyways, and you know spuds is always good. I didn't bring no more flour, because I had plenty. I can make all sorts of bread, ma'am—flapjacks, or biscuits, or even sour dough—even dough-gods. I ain't so strong when it comes to making the kind of bread you put in the oven."

"Why, I can make that—I know I can do that!" she said, pleased at the thought.

"We'll start in on that to-morrow," said he. "I'll just cook you one meal—as bad as I can, ma'am—so as to show you how bad I needed a housekeeper out here."

The chuckle in his tones was contagious, so that she almost laughed herself. "All right," said she.

She heard him bustling around here and there, rattling pans, stumbling over sticks of wood on the floor.

"Haven't you any chickens?" she asked.

"No, ma'am, I ain't got around to it. I was a-going to have some."

"I'd like awfully well to have some chickens. Those little yellow things, in my hands—"

"We can get plenty, ma'am. I can drive out just a leetle ways, about forty miles, to where the Mormons is at, and I can get plenty of 'em, even them yeller ones."

"Where is the dog? Haven't you got a dog?"

"No, ma'am, I ain't. The wolves got mine last winter, and I ain't got round to getting another one yet. What kind would you like?"

"Why, a collie—aren't they nice?"

"Yes, ma'am, I reckon. Only thing is, they might take me fer a sheep man. I'd hate that."

"Well—even a little dog?"

"I'll get you one, any kind you want. I allow myself, a dog is a heap of comfort. I'm about the only homesteader in this valley that ain't got one right now. Some has sever'l."

"I can make the coffee, I'm sure," she said, still endeavoring to be of use. But she was skimpy in her measurement, and he reproached her.

"That won't make it strong enough. Don't you like it right strong?"

"Well, Annie and I," said she honestly, "couldn't afford to make it very strong. Annie was my roommate, you see."

"We can afford anything we want out here, ma'am. I got a credit at the store. We're going to make six hundred tons of hay right out there in them medders this summer. We're going to have plenty of money. Hay is mighty high. I can get eight dollars a ton standing out there, and not put a machine into it myself. Wheat is two dollars and twenty cents a bushel, the lowest."

"Why, that's fine, that's fine!" said she. "I'm so glad." She knew nothing in the world about hay or wheat.

The odors from the stove appealed pleasantly enough to the tired woman who sat on the box chair, in the same place she originally had taken. "Draw up," said Sim Gage. But it was clumsy work for her to eat, newly blind. She was so sensitive that she made no pretence of concealing her tears.

"I wouldn't worry none, ma'am," said Sim Gage, "if I could help it. I wouldn't worry any more'n I could help, anyways. I'll put things where you can find 'em, and pretty soon you'll get used to it."

"But at least I can wash the dishes."

"That's so," said he. "That's so. I reckon you could do that. It ain't hard." And indeed in due course he made arrangements for that on the table in front of her, so that she might feel easier in being useful.

"Why, that isn't the dish pan," said she.

Sim Gage flushed with great guiltiness.

"No, ma'am, it ain't. It's only the wash pan. Fact is, some one has been in this place since I been away, and they stole my dish pan, the low-down pups. I didn't know as you'd notice the wash pan."

"Well, it will do for once," she said dubiously, and so she went on, making good shift, wiping the dishes carefully and placing them before her on the table. Then she laughed. "It was the same with Annie and me—we only had the one pan. Yours is much larger than ours was. I always helped with the dishes."

"That's fine," said he. "Do you know, that's the part of keeping house I always hated more'n anything else, just washing dishes."

"I almost always did that for Annie and me," said Mary Warren, feeling out with her hands gently and trying to arrange the battered earthenware upon the table.

"Now," said Sim Gage, "I reckon I'd better get them new blankets in and make up that bed. Come along, ma'am, and I'll show you." And in spite of all he took her arm and led her to the side of the rude bunk.

"I'm so tired," she said. "Do you know, I'm awfully scared out here." Her lips were quivering.

"Ain't a woman a funny thing, though?" said Sim Gage. "No use to be scared, none a-tall. I'll show you how us folks makes a bed. There's willer branches and pine underneath, and hay on top. Over that is the tarp, and now I'm spreading down the blankets. You can feel 'em—soft ones—*good* blankets, I can tell you! Whole bed's kind of soft and springy, ma'am. You reckon you can sleep?"

Responsively she stretched out a hand and felt across the surface of the soft new blankets.

"Why, where are the sheets?" said she.

"Sheets!" said Sim Gage in sudden consternation. "Now, look at that! That ornery low-down pup that come and stole my dish pan must of took all my sheets too! Fact is, I just made it up with blankets, like you see. But you needn't mind—they're plumb new and clean. Besides, it gets cold here along toward morning, even in the summer time. Blankets is best, along toward morning."

She stood hesitant as she heard his feet turning away.

"I'm going away fer a hour or so," said he. "I got to take care of my horse and things. Now, you feel around with your stick, sort of. I reckon I better go over before long and make up my own bed—my tent is beyond the willers yonder."

She could not know that Sim Gage's bed that night would be composed of nothing better than a pile of willow boughs. He had given her the last of the new blankets— and his own old bed was missing now. Wid had fulfilled his threat and burned it.

She stood alone, her throat throbbing, hesitant, at the side of the rude bunk.

"He's a kind man," said she to herself, half aloud, after a time. "Oh, if only I could see!"

She began to feel her way about, stood at the door for a time, looking out. Something told her that the darkness of night was coming on. She turned, felt her way back to the edge of the bunk, and knelt down, her head in her hands. Mary Warren prayed.

She paused after a long time—half-standing, a hand upon the soft-piled blankets, her eyes every way. Yes, she was sure it was dark. And above all things she was sure that she was weary, unutterably, unspeakably weary. The soft warmth of the blankets about her was comforting.

Sim Gage in his own place of rest was uneasy. Darkness came on late by the clock in that latitude. Something was on Sim's mind. He had forgotten to tell his new house-keeper how to make safe the door! He wondered whether she had gone to bed or whether she was sitting there in the dark—an added darkness all around her. He was sure that if he told her how to fasten the door she would sleep better.

Timidly, he got up out of his own comfortless couch, and groped for the electric flash-light which sometimes may be seen in places such as his to-day. He tiptoed along the path through the willows, across the yard, and knocked timidly at the door. He heard no answer. A sudden fear came to him. Had she in terror fled the place—was she wandering hopelessly lost, somewhere out there in the night? He knocked more loudly, pushed open the door, turned the flash light here and there in the room.

He saw her lying, the blankets piled up above her, a white arm thrown out, her eyes closed, her face turned upon her other arm, deep in the stupor of exhaustion. She was a woman, and very beautiful.

Suddenly frightened, he cut off the light. But the glare had wakened her. She started up, called out, "Who's there?" Her voice was vibrant with terror. "Who's *there*?" she repeated.

"It's only me, ma'am," said Sim Gage, his voice trembling.

"You said you wouldn't come!—Go away!"

"I wanted to tell you—"

"Go away!"

He went outside, but continued stubbornly, gently.

"—I wanted to say to you, ma'am," said he, "you can lock this here door on the inside. You come around, and you'll find a slat that drops into the latch. Now, there's a nail on a string, fastened to that latch. You can find that nail, and if you'll just drop that bar and push the nail in the hole up above it—why, you'll be safe as can be, and there can't *no* one get in."

He stood waiting, fumbling at the button of the flash light. By accident it was turned on again.

He saw her then sitting half upright in the bed, both her white arms holding the clothing about her, the piled mass of her dark hair framing a face which showed white against the background. Her eyes, unseeing, were wide open, dark, beautiful. Sim Gage's heart stopped in his bosom. She was a woman. She had come, of her own volition. They were utterly alone.

Emerson Hough

CHAPTER X

NEIGHBORS

Sim Gage, hesitant at the door of his bare-floored tent in the cool dawn, saw smoke arising from the chimney of Wid Gardner's house. From a sense of need he determined to pay Wid a visit. His leg was doing badly. He needed help, and knew it. He hobbled over to the cabin door, where all was silent; knocked, and knocked again, more loudly. She still slept—slept as she had not dreamed she could.

"Who's there?" she demanded at length. "Oh yes; wait a minute."

He waited several minutes, but at length heard her at the door. His eyes fell upon her hungrily. She was fresher, her air was more eager, less pitiful.

"Good morning, ma'am," said he. "I've come to get the breakfast." All she could do was to stand about, wistful, perplexed, dumb.

"Now, ma'am," said he, after he had cooked the breakfast—like in all ways to the supper of the night before—"I'm a-going to ask you to stay here alone a little while to-day. You ain't afraid, are you?"

"You'll not be gone long? It's lonesome to me all the time, of course." In reality she was terrified beyond words at the thought of being left alone.

"I know that. But we got to get a dog and some hens for you. I just thought I'd go over and see Wid Gardner, little while, and talk over things."

"How is your knee now?" she asked. "It seemed to me you sounded rather limpy, Mr. Gage."

"Is that what you want to call me, ma'am?" said he at last—"Mr. Gage? It sounds sort of strange to me, but it makes me feel taller. Folks always called me Sim."

She heard him turn, hesitant. "You'll not be gone long?" said she.

"I reckon not."

"Then bring me the pan of potatoes in here, so that I can peel them."

"You're mighty helpful, ma'am. I don't see how I kept house here at all without you.

"Ma'am," he went on, presently, hesitating, after his bashful fashion. "This here is a right strange place, way you and me is throwed in here together. I only wish't you wouldn't git scared about anything, and you'd sort of— *believe* in me, till we can shape things out somehow, fairer to you. Don't be scared, please. I'll take care of you the best I can. The only trouble is I'm afraid about folks, that's all."

"What do you mean—about folks?"

84 Emerson Hough

"If there was a woman within fifty miles of you knowed you wasn't married to me, she'd raise hell sure. All women is that way, and some men is, too. There ain't been no room for talk—yet."

"Yet?" she said. "What do you mean?"

But this was carrying Sim Gage into water too deep for him. He only stepped closer to the door. "Don't you be scared to be alone a little while. So long," he added, and so he left her.

She heard his hobbling footfalls across the boards at the end of the house, heard them pass into silence on the turf. What had he meant? How long could she maintain her supremacy over him, here alone in the wilderness, help-less, blind? And those other women? What, indeed, was her status to be here? When would he tire of this? When would he change?

Questions came to Sim Gage's mind also. Now and again he paused and leaned against the fence. He was in much pain alike of body and of mind.

He saw Wid himself turn out at his gate and approach him; dreaded the grin on Wid's face even before he saw it.

"Well, there, neighbor," said the oncomer. "You're out at last. How's everything?"

Sim looked down at his bandaged leg with a gesture.

"How come that?"

"One of them damn broncs cut me with his forefoot when I was unhitching. Did you git track of them anywhere? They run off."

"They're hanging around here," said Wid indifferently. He bent over the wounded member. "So struck you with his front hoof? That's a bad leg, Sim. It's getting black; and here's some red streaks."

"I'm some scared about it," said Sim. "Seems to me I'd better get to a doctor. I got to get me a dog first, and some hens."

Wid Gardner took a hasty but careful inventory of his friend's appearance, his shaven face, his clean hands, his new clothing.

"How's your wife, Sim?" he said, grinning.

"That lady, she's all right. Left her paring spuds. And I want to say to you, Wid, while I'm away from there, everybody else stays away too."

"What, not get to see the bride? That ain't very friendly, seems to me."

"Well, what I said goes."

"You're a jealous sort of bridegroom?" said Wid, laughing openly.

The dull color of Sim's face showed the anger in his heart. "That lady, she's there at my house," said he, "and she's going to be left alone there. She's sort of shy. This country's plumb new to her."

"But honest, Sim"—and his neighbor's curiosity now was apparent—"what sort of a looker is she?"

"Prettier'n a spotted pup!" said Sim succinctly.

"She like the country pretty well?"

"Says it's the prettiest she ever seen," replied Sim. "That's what she said."

"And you owe all this to me, come to simmer it down."

"I ain't simmering nothing down," said Sim. "Here's your gate. Down there is mine. Don't none of you go in there until I tell you it's time, that's all."

"Well, I dunno as I care to," replied Wid.

"Better not," said Sim Gage. "I ain't a-going to have that girl bothered by nobody. Of course, you and me both knows we ain't married, and won't never be. It was a housekeeper I was after, and I got one, and a damn good one. But I don't want her bothered by no one fer a while. I've played this game on the level with her so far, anyways, and I allow to play it that way all the way through."

"But now," he added, wincing with pain, "let's cut out all this sort of thing. I believe I got to get to a doctor."

"I'll tell you," said Wid Gardner, "I'll hitch up and take you down to the doctor at the big dam, twenty-five miles below. He's taking care of all the laborers down there— they're always getting into accidents; dynamite, you know. He's got to be a good doctor. I'll take you down."

"Wid," said Sim, "I wish't you would. I don't believe I'll go back home first. She'll be all right there alone, won't she?"

Wid still smiled at him understandingly. "Jealousest man I ever did see! Well, have it your own way. It'll take just so much time anyway—if we get back by nine or ten o'clock to-night we'll be lucky. She'll have to begin sometime to get used to things."

CHAPTER XI

THE COMPANY DOCTOR

The Two Forks, below their junction, make a mighty stream which has burst through a mountain range. Across this narrow gorge which it has rent for itself in time immemorial, the insect, Man, industrious and persevering, has cast a great pile of rock and concrete, a hundred feet high, for that good folk some hundreds of miles away one day may bless the Company for electric lighting. In this labor toiled many man-insects of divers breeds and races, many of them returned soldiers, much as did the slaves of Pharaoh in earlier times. The work was on one of the new government projects revived after the war, in large part to offer employment to the returning men of the late Army.

But Pharaoh had not dynamite or rack-rock or TNT; so that in the total it were safer for an insect to have labored in Pharaoh's time. The Company doctor—himself a returned major—stationed there by reason of the eccentricities of dynamite, rack-rock and other high explosives, was much given to the sport of the angle, and disposed to be irritable when called from the allurements of the stream to attend some laboring man who had undertaken to attach a fuse by means of his teeth, or some such simple process. That is to say, Doctor Allen Barnes was irritable until he had reeled up his line and climbed the bank below the dam site, and betaken himself to the side of the last hospital cot where lay the last victim of dynamic and dynamitical industry. After that he was apt to forget angling and become an absorbed surgeon, and a very able one.

But on this particular day, when word came to him at the stream side that a stranger not of the force had arrived in town with a "bum leg"—so reported the messenger, Foreman Flaherty—Doctor Barnes was wroth exceedingly, for at that moment he was fast in a noble trout that was far out in the white water, and giving him, as he himself would have phrased it, the time of his life.

"Tell him I can't come, Flaherty!" he called over his shoulder. "I'm busy."

"I reckon that's so, Doc," said the foreman. "Why don't you haul him in? That pole of yours ain't no good, it's too limber. If I had him on mine I'd show you how to get him in."

"Oh, you would, would you, dad burn you," remarked Doctor Barnes, who had small love for the human race at many times, and less at this moment. "I wouldn't put it past you. Well, this is my affair and not yours. Who is the fellow, anyhow, and where did he come from, and what does he want? Has he been trying to beat the shot?"

"He ain't on our job," replied the foreman. "Come down from twenty mile up the East Fork. Got kicked by a horse."

"Huh! What's his name? Look at him jump!" remarked the doctor, with mixed emotions and references.

"Sim Gage. Come down with a feller name of Gardner

that lives up in there."

"Oh, above on the East Fork? Say, how's the fishing up there?—Did they say there were any grayling in there?"

"I've saw Wid Gardner lots of times before, and he says a feller can always get a sackful of grayling any time he wants to, in there, come summer time."

"Look at him go! Ain't that fine?" inquired Dr. Allen Barnes. "Did he say they were coming good now, up there? Ain't he a peach?"

"Yes, Wid said the grayling was risin' right good now," said Flaherty. "But this feller, Sim Gage, his leg looks to me like you'd have to cut it off. Can I help, Doc?—I never seen a man's leg cut off, not in my whole life."

"How do I know whether it's got to come off or not, I'd like to know. See that?—Ain't he a darling, now, I'm asking you?"

"He is. Like I was saying, this feller's leg is all swoll up. Leave it to me, I'd say we ought to cut it off right now."

"Well, you go tell him not to cut it off till I get this fish landed," said Dr. Barnes. "Tell him I'll be up there in a few minutes. What's the matter with it, anyhow?"

"Been gone a couple of days," said Flaherty, breaking off twigs and casting them on the current. "Blood poison, I reckon."

"What's that?" The Doctor turned under the spur of his professional conscience. "Oh, well, dang it! Here goes!"

He began to lift up and reel in with all his might, so that

his fish, very much obliged, broke the gear and ran off with joy, a yard of leader attached to his mouth.

"That's the way it goes," said the Doctor. "Get fast to a six-pound brown trout, and along comes a man with a leg that's got to be cut off. Dang such a job anyhow—I will cut his leg off, too, just for this!"

Fuming as usual, he climbed the steep bank below the white face of the dam and crossed the street to his own raw shack, which was office and home alike. He gazed resentfully at his parted leader as he hung up the rod on the nails at the rear of the small porch, and sighing, entered the office for his surgical case.

"Where is that fellow?" he demanded of Flaherty, who had followed him in.

"That's him settin' on the wagon seat up with Wid Gardner, in the road," replied the messenger. "He's got his foot up on the dash board like it was sore, ain't he?"

Grumblingly Dr. Allen Barnes passed on up the road to the wagon where two passengers awaited his coming.

"Are you the man that wants me?" he asked, looking up at Sim Gage.

"Why, yep," said Sim Gage, his face puckered up into his usual frown of perplexity. "I reckon so, Doc. I got my leg hurt."

"Well, come on over to the hospital."

"Hospital? I can't go to no hospital. I can't afford it, Doc."

"Well, I can't cut your leg off right out here in the street, can I, man? I'm offering you the hospital free—the Company takes care of those things. Not that I've got any business taking care of you, but I will."

"Why, this ain't nothing," said Sim Gage, pointing a finger towards his swollen knee, "just a leetle kick of a bronc, that's all. I got to be getting right back, Doc—I ain't got much time."

"It don't take much time to cut off a leg," said Dr. Barnes. "Do it in three minutes." His face, professionally grim, showed no token of a smile.

"Well, I left my folks all alone up there," began Sim.

"You did, eh? Well, they'll be there when you get back, won't they?"

"I dunno, Doc—"

"Well, I don't know anything about it, if you don't. But tell me, how's the fishing up in there? Any grayling?"

"All you want," said Sim Gage. "Come along up any time, and I'll take you out. But no, I guess maybe—"

Dr. Barnes looked at him curiously, and Wid Gardner went on to explain for his neighbor.

"You see, Doc, Sim, he's just newly married," said he, "or else he's going to be right soon. Sim, he's kind of bashful about having you around."

"Thanks! But come—I haven't any time. Come into the office, and we'll have a look at the leg."

Wid drove after the stalking figure, which presently drew

up in front of the little office. In a few moments they had Sim Gage, the injured member bared, sitting up in a white chair in a very white and clean miniature hospital which Dr. Barnes had installed.

"This wound hasn't been cleaned properly," commented the doctor at once. "What did you put on it?"

"Why, whiskey. I didn't have nothing else."

"Try water the next time," said Dr. Barnes with sarcasm. "We'll have to paint it up with iodine now. Lockjaw, blood poison and amputation is the very least that will happen to you if you don't look out."

"Amputation?" Sim turned with curiosity to his neighbor.

"It's where they cut off your leg, Sim," said Wid, explaining.

"Oh, well, maybe we'll save his leg," said Dr. Barnes, grinning at last. "But don't let this occur again, my Christian friend. This will lay you up for two or three weeks the best way it can happen, in all likelihood. Well, I'll swab it out and tie it up, and give you some iodine. Keep it painted. How big do the grayling go up in your country?"

"I've seen plenty over three pounds," said Sim Gage.

"I don't like to doubt your word, my friend, but if you'll show me one three-pound grayling, you won't ever owe me anything for fixing up your leg."

"I sure can, Doc," said Sim Gage. "Grasshoppers is best."

"For you, maybe. If you please, I'll try Queen of the

Waters, or Professor, long-shanked, and about Number 8. And I say again, if you'll put me up to a three-pound grayling I'll cut off your leg for nothing any time you want it done!"

"Well, now," said Sim Gage, his forehead puckering up, "I don't want to put you under no obligations, Doc."

"He won't, neither, Doc," interrupted Wid Gardner, while the surgical dressing was going forward. "There's holes in there twenty feet deep, and I've see two or three hundred grayling in there dang near as long as your arm."

"Ouch, Doc!" remarked Sim Gage, "that yellow stuff smarts."

"It's got to, my man. A couple of days more and you might really have lost that leg, sure enough. I've seen plenty of legs lost, my man. I don't think it'll go much further up—I hope not. But blood poisoning is something bad to have, and I'll tell you that."

"You ain't been in this country long, have you, Doc?" queried Wid Gardner. "You come on up and go fishing with us fellers. A few weeks from now it'll be better. I ain't got no woman at my place, but I can cook some. Sim's got a woman at his."

"What's that?" inquired Dr. Barnes. "Oh, the woman that's waiting? What do you mean about that?"

"Well," replied his patient, his forehead furrowed, "that is, we ain't rightly married yet. Just sort of studying things over, you know, Doc. We're waiting for—well, until things kind of shapes up. You understand, Doc?"

"I don't know that I do," said the Doctor, looking at him

straightly. "You understand one thing—there can't any funny business go on in this valley now. The administration's mighty keen. You know that."

"There ain't, Doc. She's my housekeeper. I'd ask you in all right, only she can't cook, nor nothing."

"A housekeeper, and can't cook? How's that?"

Sim Gage wiped off his face, finding the temperature high for him. "Well," said he, "Wid there and me, we advertised fer a housekeeper. This girl come on out. And when she come she was blind."

"Blind!"

"Blind as a bat. So she says she's fooled me. I sort of felt like we'd all fooled *her*. She's a lady."

"Why don't you send her back, man?" asked the doctor, with very visible disgust.

"I can't. How can I, when she's blind? She wasn't born that way, Doc, far's I can tell, but she was blind when she come out here. Now, leaving her setting there alone, it makes me feel kind of nervous. You don't blame me, now, do you, Doc?"

"No," said Dr. Barnes gravely, "I don't blame you. You people out here get me guessing sometimes. But you make me tired."

He swept a hand across his face and eyes, just because he was tired. "That's all I'm going to do for you to-day, my man," said he in conclusion. "Go on back home and fight out your own woman problems—that isn't in my line."

"She—I reckon she'd be glad to see you—if she could. You see, she's a lady, Doc. She ain't like us people out here."

The physician looked at him with curious appraisal in his eyes, studying both the man and this peculiar problem which all at once had been brought to view.

"A lady?" said he at last, somewhat disgusted. "If she was any lady she'd never have answered any advertisement such as you two people say you have been fools enough to print."

"Look here! That ain't so," said Sim Gage with sudden heat. "That ain't so none a-tall. Now, she is a lady—I won't let nobody say no different. Only thing, she's a blind lady, that's all. She falls over things when she walks. She got her eyes plumb full of cinders on the train, I expect. Cinders is awful. Why, one time when I was going out to Arizony I got a cinder in my eye, and I want to tell *you*—"

"Listen at him lie, Doc!" interrupted Wid Gardner. "He never was nowhere near Arizony in his life. That's his favoright lie. But he's telling you the truth, near as I know it, about that woman. She did come out to be a house-keeper, and she did come out here blind. Now, couldn't she be a lady and that be true?"

"How can I tell?" said Dr. Barnes. "All I know; is that you people came down here and made me break loose from the best fish I've seen since I've been out here. My best fish of a lifetime—I'll never get hold of a trout like that again."

Sim Gage was experiencing at the moment mingled gratitude and resentment, but nothing could quench his own hospitable impulses. "Aw, come on up, Doc," said he, "won't you? We can figure out some way to take care of you right at my place. You and me can sleep in the tent."

"So you live in the tent?" inquired Dr. Barnes.

"Why, of course. She stays in the house. And she's there all alone this very minute."

"Hit the trail, men," said Dr. Barnes. "Go on back home, and stay there, you damn sagebrushers!"

CHAPTER XII

LEFT ALONE

Mary Warren, alone in the little cabin, found herself in a new world whose existence she had never dreamed—that subjective and subconscious land which bridges the forgotten genesis of things to the usual and busy world of the senses, in which we pass our daily lives. Indeed, never before had she known what human life really is, how far out of perspective, how selfish, how distorted. Now, alone in the darkness, back in the chaos and the beginning, she saw for the first time how small a thing is life and how ill it is for the most part lived. A fly buzzed loudly on the window pane—a bold, bronzed, lustrous fly, no doubt, she said to herself, pompous and full of himself—buzzed again and again, until the drone of his wings blurred, grew confused, ceased. She wondered if he had found a web.

The darkness oppressed her like a velvet pall. She strained her eyes, trying in spite of all to pierce it, beat at it, picked at it, to get it from around her head; and only paused at length, her face beaded, because she knew that way madness lay.

Time was a thing now quite out of her comprehension. Night and day, all the natural and accustomed divisions of time, were gone for her. She felt at the hands of her little watch, but found her mind confused—she could not remember whether it was the stem or the hinge which meant noon or midnight.

A thousand new doubts and fears of her newly created world assailing her, she felt rather than saw the flood of the sunlight when she stepped to the door gropingly, and stood, stick in hand, looking out. Yes, that was the sun. But it was hard to reason which way was north, which way lay the east, which was her home.

Home? She had no home! These years, she had known no home but the single room which she had occupied with Annie Squires. And now even that was gone. And even if it were not gone, she had no means of going back to it—her money was almost exhausted. And this black world was not the earth, this new covering of her soul was not life. Oh, small enough seemed Mary Warren to her own self now.

She stumbled back to her seat behind the table, near the bunk, and tried to take up her knitting again. The silence seemed to her so tremendous that she listened intently for some sound, any sound. Came only the twitter of a little near-by bird, the metallic clank of a meadow lark far off across the meadows. They at least were friendly, these birds. She could have kissed them, held them close to her, these new friends.

But why did he not come back—the man? What was going to happen if he did come back? How long would all this last? Must it come to death, or to the acceptance of terror or of shame, as the price of life?

She began to face her problem with a sort of stolid courage or resolution—she knew not what to call it. She was at bay—that was the truth of it. There must be some course of action upon which presently she must determine. What could it be? How could she take arms against her new, vast sea of troubles, so far more great than falls to the average woman, no matter how ill, how afflicted, how unfit for the vast, grim conflict which ends at last at the web?

One way out would be to end life itself. Her instinct, her religious training, her principles, her faith, rebelled against that thought. No—no! That was not right. Her life, even her faint, pulsing, crippled life, was a sacred trust to her. She must guard it, not selfishly, but because it was right to do so. She could feel the sunshine outside, could hear the birds singing. They said that life still existed, that she also must live on, even if there were no sound of singing in her own heart ever again.

Then she must go back to the East, whence she had come?—Even if great-hearted Annie would listen to that and take her back, where was the money for the return passage? How could she ask this man for money, this man whom she had so bitterly deceived? No, her bridges were burned.

What then was left? Only the man himself. And in what capacity? Husband; or what? And if not a husband, what?

. . . No, she resolved. She would accept duty as the price of life, which also was a duty; but she would never relax what always to her had meant life, had been a part of her, the principles ingrained in her teachings and her practices, ever since she was a child. No, it was husband or nothing.

And surely he had been all that he had said he would be. He *was* kindly, he *was* chivalrous, he had proved that. She wondered how he looked. And what had she now to offer for perfection in a man? Was she not reduced to the bargain counter, in the very basement of life? If so, what must be her bargain here?

And then she recalled the refusal of Sim Gage himself to think of marriage. He had said he was not good enough for her. How could she then marry him, even if she so wished? Must she woo him and persuade him, argue with him? All her own virginal soul, all the sanctity of her life, rebelled against that thought also.

Object, matrimony! What a cruel jest it all had been. What a terrible dilemma, this into which it all had resolved itself. Object, matrimony!

So if this man—so she reasoned again, wearily—if this man who had been kind at least, even if uncouth, was willing to take her with all her stories told, and all shortcomings known and understood—if he was willing to take chances and be content—was that indeed the only way out for her, Mary Warren?

What made it all most bitter, most difficult, most horrible for her was the strength of her own soul. Was it the *right* thing to do—was it the courageous and valiant thing to do? Those were the two questions which alone allowed her to face that way for an answer; and they were the very two which drove her hardest. Could she not do much, if in the line of duty? Sacrifice was no new thing for women. . . . And the war! . . . This was not a time for little thoughts.

Such are some of the questions a woman must ask and answer, because she is a woman. They are asked and answered every day of the world; perhaps not often so cruelly as here in this little cabin.

She began, weakly, to try to resign herself to some frame

of mind by which she could entertain the bare, brutal thought of this alternative. She had come more than a thousand miles to meet this man by plan, by arrangement. Oh, no (so she argued), it could not be true that there was but one man for one woman, one woman for a man, in all the world. Annie must have been right. Propinquity did it—was that not why men and women nearly always married in their own village, their own social circle? Well, then, here was propinquity. Object, matrimony! Would propinquity solve all this at last, as though this were a desert island, they two alone remaining? God!

Was it indeed true, asked Mary Warren, in her bitter darkness, that the rude doctrine of material ideas alone must rule the world now in this strange, new, inchoate, revolutionary age? Was it indeed true that sentiment, the emotions, the tenderer things of life, a woman's immeasurable inheritance—must all these things go also into the discards of the world's vast bloody bargain counter?

She remembered Annie's rude but well-meant words, back there where they once crudely struggled with these great questions. "What's the use of trying to change the world, Sis?" she had said. "Something's going wrong every minute of the day and night—something's coming up all the time that ought to be different. But we ain't got nothing to do with running the world—just running our own two lives is enough for us."

Hours or moments later—she could not have told which—she raised her head suddenly. What was it that she had heard? There was a cough, a footfall in the yard.

Oh, then he was coming home! Why not have the whole thing out now, over once and for all? Why not speak plainly and have it done? He had not been so terrible. He was an ignorant man, but not unkind, not brutal.

She felt the light in the door darken, knew that some one was standing there. But something, subconscious, out of her new, dark world—something, she could not tell what—told her this was not Sim Gage.

She reached out her hand instinctively. By mere chance it fell upon the heavy revolver in its holster which Sim had hung upon the pole at the head of her bed. She caught it out, drew back into the room, toward the head of the bed, and stumbling into her rude box chair, sat there, the revolver held loosely in her hand. She knew little of its action.

She heard a heavy step on the floor, that did not sound familiar, a clearing of the throat which was yet more unfamiliar, a laugh which was the last thing needed. This man had no business there, else he would not have laughed.

"Who's there?" she called out, tremulously. "Who are you?" She turned on him her sightless eyes, a vast terror in her soul.

"Good morning," said a throaty voice. She could fairly hear him grin. "How's everything this morning? Where's your man this morning?"

"He's—just across in the meadows—he'll be back soon," said Mary Warren.

"Is that so? I seen him ten miles down the road just a while back. Now, look here, woman—"

He had come fully into the room, and now he saw in her lap the weapon. Half unconsciously she raised it.

"Look out!" he called. "It may be loaded. Drop it!"

"Come a step further, and I'll shoot!" said Mary Warren. And then, although he did not know that she was sightless, he saw on her face that look which might well warn him. Any ruffian knows that a woman is more apt to shoot than is a man.

This ruffian paused now half way inside the door and looked about him. A grin spread across his wide, high-cheeked face. He reached down silently to the stout spruce stick, charred at one end, that stood between him and the stove. Grasping it he advanced on tiptoe, silent as a cat, toward the woman. He was convinced that her sight was poor, almost convinced that she did not see at all, because she made no move when he stopped, the stick drawn back. With a swift sweep he struck the barrel of the revolver a blow so forceful that it was cast quite across the room. He sprang upon it at once.

Mary Warren cried out, drew back as far as she could. The impact of the blow had crushed a finger of the hand that held the weapon. She wrung her hands, held up the bloody finger. "Who are you—what do you want?" she moaned.

"That's what you get when you run against a real one," sneered the voice of the man, who now stood fully within the little room. "Just keep quiet now."

"What do you mean? What are you going to do?" She felt about again for some weapon, anything, but could find nothing.

"That's a purty question to ask, ain't it now?" sneered her assailant. She could catch the reek of raw spirits around him as he stood near by. She shuddered.

"Sim!" she called out aloud at last. "Sim! Sim!"

The name caused a vast mirth in her captor. "Sim! Sim!" he mocked her. "Lot o' help Sim'd be if he was here, wouldn't he? As though I cared for that dirty loafer. He's going to git all that's comin' to *him*. Aw, Sim! He'll leave us Soviet sabcats alone. We're thinkers. We're free men. We run our own government, and we run our own selves, too."

The liquor had made the man loquacious. He must boast. She tried to guess what he might mean.

But something in the muddled brain of the man retained recollection of an earlier purpose. "Stay inside, you!" he said. "I got work to do. If you go outside I'll kill you. Do you hear me?"

She heard his feet passing, heard them upon the scattered boards near the door, then muffled in the grass. She could not guess what he was about.

He went to the edge of the standing grass beyond the dooryard, and began sowing, broadcast, spikes, nails, bits of iron, intended to ruin the sickle blades of the mowers when they came to work. Even he thrust a spike or bolt here or there upright in the ground to catch a blade.

Mary Warren where she sat knew none of this, but she heard a sound presently which she could not mistake—the crackling of fire! The scent of it came to her nostrils. The man had fired the meager remnants of Sim Gage's hay stacks.

She heard next a shot or two, but could not tell what they meant. She could not know that he was firing into the dumb, gaunt cattle which hung about the ricks.

Then later she heard something which caused her very

Emerson Hough

soul to shiver, made her blood run ice—the shrieking scream of a horse in death agony—the hoarser braying of a mule, both dying amid fire! She did not understand it, could not have guessed it; but he had set fire also to the stables. Brutal to the last extreme, he left the animals penned to die in the flames, and laughed at their agony.

Again and again the awful sounds came to her. She was hysterical when she heard his footstep approach once more, shrieked aloud for mercy. He mocked her.

"Stop it! Cut it out, I say. Come on now—do you want to stay here and burn up in the house?"

"I can't see—I'm blind," was all she could manage to say.

"Blind, huh?" He laughed now uproariously. "Well, it's a good thing you was blind, or else you might of seen Sim Gage! Did you ever see Sim? What made you come here? What did you come for?"

"I'm his housekeeper. He employed me—"

"Employed you? For what?—for housekeeping? It looks like it, don't it? Where did you come from, gal?"

"East—Ohio—Cleveland," she spoke almost unconsciously and truthfully.

"Cleveland? Plenty of our people there too still in the iron works. Cleveland? And how come you out here?"

"I'm ill—I'm a blind woman. Can't you leave me alone? Are you any man at all?"

He remained unmoved, phlegmatic. "So? Nice talk about you and Sim Gage! Was you two married? I know you ain't. You come out to marry him, though, didn't you?"

"Yes."

"When?"

"Next week—he's gone for the minister to-day." She said anything, the first thing.

"That's a lie," said the coarse voice of the man she could not see. "I seen him ten mile down toward the dam, I tell you, with Wid Gardner, and Nels Jensen's folks, below, said they was going for a doctor, not a preacher. He wouldn't marry no blind woman like you, no ways."

She sank back, limp, her face in her bloody hands, as she lay against the edge of the bed.

"Come now," said he. "We got no time to waste. We'll see what the other fellers think. Housekeeper—huh! You said you wasn't married to him. You never will be, now."

"You brute!" she cried, with the courage of the cornered thing, the courage of the prisoner bound to the stake for torture. "You brute!"

She could hear him chuckle throatily. "You don't know me—I'm Big Aleck, general of the Soviet brothers in this county." He juggled phrases he never had understood.

"You ought to hang!" she panted. "You will hang, some day."

"You better look a little out, gal, I tell you that. You come along out to the camp, and I'll see how you like that!"

She felt his iron grasp fall upon her wrist. He dragged her

across the floor as though she weighed nothing. She had been wholly helpless, even if in possession of all her faculties and all her senses. He flung her from him upon the grass, laughing as she rose and tried to run, bringing up in the willows, which she could not see. She could hear the flames crackling at the hay ricks on beyond. By this time the sounds from the burning barn mercifully had ceased, but she heard him now at some further work. He was trying to light the battered edge of the door with a match, but it would not burn.

"Where's the oil, gal?" he demanded.

"We've got none," said she, guessing his purpose of firing the house now.

He made no answer but a grunt, and finding the ax at the wood pile nearby, began to hack at the jamb of the door, so that a series of chips stood out from it, offering better food for flames. She heard him again strike a match— caught the faint smell of burning pine.

"Come on!" Again she felt his hand. He dragged her, her feet stumbling in the grass. She could hear horses snorting, so there was some vehicle here, she supposed. He flung her up to the seat, jerked loose the halters, and climbed in as the team plunged forward. Had any one seen the careening wagon, seen the upflung arm of a woman swaying in the grasp of the man who sat beside her in the seat—had any one heard the laugh of the man, the shrieks of the woman, struggling and calling,—he must have thought that two drunken human beings instead of one were endeavoring to show the astonished sky how bestial life may be even here in America in an undone day.

CHAPTER XIII

THE SABCAT CAMP

To Mary Warren's ears, had she struggled in her captor's arms less violently, the sound of the wheels might have changed from the loam of the lane to the gravel of the highway as they passed. But she heard nothing, noted nothing, did not understand why, after a time, the driver pulled up, and with much profanity for his team, descended from his seat. Apparently he fastened the horses near the road. He came back. "Git down, and hurry," said he. "Here's where we change cars."

She heard the grind of a motor's starting crank, the chug of an engine. As its strident whirring continued her captor came again to her side, and with rudeness aided her to the seat of what she took to be a small car. She felt the leap of the car under his rude driving as he turned the gas on full, felt it sway as it set to its pace. She now knew that they were on some highway.

"Now we go better," laughed Big Aleck, his face at her ear. "They can't catch us now. These Johns 'll find what's what, heh? Look yonder—five fires in sight, besides plenty stock bumped off. They'll learn how the free brothers work. If you can't see, you can't tell. All the better!"

She shrank back into the seat, undertaking no reply to his maudlin boastings. She was passing away from the only place in all the world that meant shelter for her now, and already it felt like home, this place that she was leaving.

The car shifted and slowed down, apparently on a less used thoroughfare. "Where are you going?" she cried. "You've left the road!"

Big Aleck laughed uproariously after his fashion. "I should say we have," said he. "But any road's good enough just so it gets us up to our jungle. You don't know what iss a jungle? Well, it's where the sabcat brothers meets all by theirselves on the Reserve."

"Reserve?" asked Mary Warren. "What do you mean?"

"Where the timber is that them army scum is cutting for the Government. Pine, some spruce. This road was made to get timber out. I ought to know about it—I was foreman of the road gang! I know every tree that's marked for the Government. My old bunch of bundle stiffs and before-the-war wobblies is in there now. What chance has them Government cockroaches got against my bullies? Wait till the wheat clocks[1] get started and the clothes[2] begins. We ain't forgot what we knew when they tried to draft us. We're free men now, same as in Russia and Germany."

He laughed again and again at the vast humor of this situation as it lay before him, exulting in the mystification his thieves' jargon would create. His liquor made him reckless.

"It's a rough road, up Tepee Creek," said he, "but nobody comes. This is a Government car—the Cossacks would think I'm going up to work. They got to mark some trees.

I'll mark 'em—so they can tell, when they come to saw 'em, heh?"

He said little more, but one hand cast over her shoulder was his answer to her panting silence, every time she edged over in the impulse to fling herself out of the car. He was a man of enormous strength.

Continually the jolting of the car grew worse and worse. She began to hear the rush of water. Twice she felt the logs of a rude bridge under the wheels as they crossed some stream. They were winding their way up the valley of a stream, into a higher country? Yes. As they climbed now, she could catch the scent of the forest as the wind changed from time to time. The profanity of her captor grew as the difficulty of the trail increased. They were climbing at a gradient as steep as the laboring car could negotiate.

At last, after interminable time, they seemed to strike a sandier soil, more level country—indeed, the trail was following the contour of a high sandy ridge among the pines.

On ahead she heard a shout. "Halt! Stop there! Who are you?"

"Don't shoot, John," replied the driver of the car, laughing. "It's Aleck."

"Well, I'll be damned!" was the reply. "Time you was back, Aleck. Who's that with you?"

"That's a friend of mine I brought along! She's come up to see how us wobblies lives!"

Again his coarse laugh, which made her shudder. Then

more broken laughs, whispered words. She was obliged to take the arm of her rough captor to descend from the car.

"She don't see very well," said Aleck in explanation. "Maybe just as well she don't, heh?"

She stood looking about her vaguely, helpless. She could hear the high moaning of the wind above her, in the tops of pine trees. Some one led her to the front of a tent—she could hear the flapping of the fly in the wind. She sank down by chance upon a blanket roll. Her captor threw down the front flap of the tent. She heard voices of other men. They paid not too much attention to her at first. Big Aleck, their leader, went on with hurried orders.

"We got to get out of here in not more'n an hour or so," said he. "The Johns'll come. I fixed a couple dozen stacks of hay for them."

"See anybody down below, Aleck?" asked a voice which Mary Warren recognized as different from the others she had heard. And then some low question was asked, to which Big Aleck replied.

"Well, I'll take her along with me, when I go out, far as that's concerned," said he. "She says she's Sim Gage's housekeeper! Huh!"

"But suppose she gets away and squeals on us?" spoke a voice.

"She can't get away. Let's go eat."

She was close enough to where they sat eating and drinking to hear all that was said, and they spoke with utter disregard of her presence. She never had heard such language in her life, nor known that such men lived.

Never yet had she so fully taken home to herself the actual presence of a Government, of a country, never before known what threats against that country actually might mean. An enemy? Why, here was the enemy still, entrenched inside the lines of victorious and peace-abiding America—trusting, foolish, blind America, which had accepted anything a human riff-raff sneeringly and cynically had offered her in return for her own rich generosity! Mary Warren began to see, suddenly, the tremendous burden of duty laid on every man and every woman of America—the lasting and enduring and continuous duty of a post-bellum patriotism, that new and terrible thing; that sweet and splendid thing which alone could safeguard the country that had fought for liberty so splendidly, so unselfishly.

"If they ever run across us in here with the goods on us—good-night!" hesitated a voice. "I don't like to carry this here cyanide—we got enough for all the sheep and cattle in Montana."

"Our lawyers'll take care of us if we get arrested," said Big Aleck indifferently.

"Yes, but we mightn't get arrested—these here ranch Johns is handy with rope and lead."

"Ach, no danger," argued Aleck. "It's safer than to blow up a armory or a powder mill, or even a public building—and we done all that, while the war was on. We'll give 'em Force! This Republic be damned—there is no republic but the republic of Man!"

These familiar doctrines seemed to excite the applause usual among hearers of this sort. There was a chorus of approval, so that their orator went on, much inspired.

"People in Gallatin offered a thousand dollars for one man catched putting matches in a threshing machine. Other ranchers was willing to give a thousand if they found out what made their hay get a-fire! Hah! They don't know how we set a bomb so the sun'll start it! They don't think that the very fellers running the threshing machine is the ones that drops the matches in! They don't think that the man running the mowing machine is the one that fixes the sickle bar! They don't think that the man in charge of this here road gang is the one that's a-doctoring trees!

"They're still eating all sorts of things for bread now," he resumed. "Folks in the cities pays more and more. Wheat'll go to four dollars before we're through. We're the farmer's friends, huh? Hay'll be worth fifty dollars a ton in this valley before we're through—but there won't be no horses left to haul it to town! There's thousands of right boes all across the country now. If fourteen thousand iron and steel people was out at one time in Cleveland, what couldn't we do, if we once got a good strike started all across the country, now the war is done? We've made 'em raise wages time and again, haven't we? I tell you, freedom's coming to its own."

Cleveland! Mary Warren pricked up her ears. She had reason; for now the voice went on, mentioning a name which Annie Squires had made familiar—Dorenwald, Charlie Dorenwald, the foreman in the rolling rooms!

"Charlie Dorenwald's the head of that bunch. He's a good man. You know what he pulled in Youngstown."

"Well, I don't know," said one voice, "they lynched a man in Illinois. America's getting lawless! Think about lynching people! It ain't right!"

"There's nothing they won't do," said Big Aleck's voice,

virtuously. "They ask us we shall have respect for a Government that lets people lynch folks!"

"You didn't see any one when you was down in the road, Aleck?" asked some one again, uneasily.

"I told you, no. Well, we got to get to work."

Mary Warren heard them rising from their places. Foot-falls passed here and there, shuffling. The woman could not repress her shuddering. This was Force—unrestrained, ignorant, unleashed, brute Force, that same aftermath Force which was rending apart the world back of the new-dried battlefields of Europe! Order and law, comfort, love, affection, trust—all these things were gone!

What then was her footing here—a woman? Was God indeed asleep? She heard her own soul begging for alleviating death.

Then came silence, except for the airs high up in the sobbing trees. They were gone on their errand. After that,—what?

After a time she heard a sound of dread—the sliddering of a footfall in the sand. She recognized the heavy, dragging stride of the man who had brought her here. He had come back—alone.

Terror seized her, keen and clarifying terror. She screamed, again and again, called aloud the only name that came to her mind.

"*Sim*!" she cried aloud again and again—"*Sim*! *Sim*!"

[1] Wheat clocks: Phosphorus bombs left in wheat or haystacks and fired by the sun.

[2] Clothes: Argot terms for phosphorus, cyanide and other chemicals used in destruction of property or life.

CHAPTER XIV

THE MAN TRAIL

"What do you think of him, Wid?" asked Sim Gage after a time, when they were well on their way homeward in the late afternoon.

"Looks like a good doctor, all right," replied Wid. "Clean-cut and strictly on to his game. I reckon he got plenty practice in the war. I'm sorry neither of us was young enough to git into that war. Your leg hurt much now?"

"Say yes!" replied Sim. "You know, I reckon we didn't get there any too soon with that leg. Fine lot of us, up to my house, huh? Me laid up, and her can't see a wink on earth."

"And yet you said I couldn't come over and see her. So there you are, both alone."

"Well, it's this way, Wid, and you know it," insisted his friend. "The girl is right strange there yet—it's a plumb hard thing to figure out. We got to get her gentled down some. There's been a hell of a misunderstanding all around, Wid, we got to admit that. And we're all to blame for it."

Emerson Hough

"Well, she's to blame too, ain't she?"

"No, she *ain't*! I won't let no man say that. She's just done the best she knew how. Women sometimes don't know which way to jump."

"She didn't make none too good a jump out here," commented his friend. "Has she ever told you anything about herself yet?"

"Not to speak of none, no. She sets and cries a good deal. Says she's broke and blind and all alone. She's got one friend back home—girl she used to room with, but she's going to get married, and so she, this lady, Miss Warren, comes out here plumb desperate, not knowing what kind of a feller I am, or what kind of a place this is—which is both a damn shame, Wid, and you know it. I say I'm up against it right now."

"The real question, Sim, is what are folks going to say? There's people in this valley that ain't a-going to stand it for you and that girl to live there unless you're married. You know that."

"Of course I know that. But do you suppose I'd marry that girl even if she was willing? No, sir, I wouldn't—not a-tall. It wouldn't be right."

"Now listen, Sim. Leave it to me. I'd say that if you ever do want to get married, Sim—and you got to if she stays here—why, here's the one and only chancet of your whole life. Of course, if the girl wasn't blind, she wouldn't never marry you. I don't believe any woman would, real. The way she is, and can't see, maybe she will, after a while, like, when she's gentled down, as you say. It looks like a act of Providence to me."

"Well," said Sim, pondering, "I hadn't just thought of it that way. Do you believe in them things—acts of Providence?"

"I don't believe in nothing much except we're going to get into camp mighty late to-night. It's getting sundown, and I ain't keen to cut wood in the dark."

"I'll tell you what, Wid," said Sim suddenly relenting. "You come on down to our house to-night. I'll introduce you to her after all—Miss Warren. It ain't no more'n fair, after all."

Wid only nodded. They pushed along up the road until finally they arrived, within a few miles of their own homesteads, at the little roadside store and postoffice kept by old Pop Bentley. They would have pulled up here, but as they approached the dusty figure of the mail carrier of that route came out, and held up a hand.

"Hold on, Sim," said he. "I heard at Nels Jensen's place that you had gone down the river. Well, it's time you was gettin' back."

Sim Gage smiled with a sense of his own importance as he took the letter, turning it over in his hand. "What's it say, Wid?" said he.

His neighbor looked at the inscription. "It's for her," said he. "Miss Mary Warren, in care of Sim Gage, Two Forks, Montany."

"Who's it from?" said Sim. "Here's some writing on the back."

"From Annie B. Squires, 9527 Oakford Avenue, Cleveland, Ohio. But listen—"

"That's the girl that Miss Warren told me about!" said Sim. "That's a letter from her. I'd better be getting back."

"I just told you you had," said the mail driver, something of pity in his tone. "I'm trying to tell you *why* you had. Why I brought this letter down is, you ain't *got* no place to get back *to*."

"What you mean?" said Wid Gardner suddenly.

"Hell's loose in this valley to-day," said the mail carrier. "Five fires, when I come through before noon. Wid, your house is gone, and your barn, too. Sim, somebody's burned your hay and your barn, and shot your stock, and set your house afire—it would of burned plumb down if Nels Jensen hadn't got there just in time. They saved the house. It wasn't burned very much anyways, so Nels told me."

Sim Gage and his companion, stupefied, sat looking at the bearer of this news.

"Who done it?" asked Wid Gardner grimly after a time. "That ain't no accident."

"Pop Bentley in here said Big Aleck, the squatter, come up the valley this morning right early—"

"That hellion!" exclaimed Sim. "He's always made trouble in this valley. We seen him down below here, driving a broad-tire wagon."

"Yes, a Company wagon, and a Company team. We found that wagon hitched above your lane, Sim. Your mail box was busted down. There wasn't no Big Aleck around, nor no one else."

"Not no one else?—*No one in the house?*"

"Nels said there wasn't."

"Light down, Sim," said Wid. "Let's go in and talk to Pop Bentley."

Pop Bentley, the keeper of the meager grocery store and little-used post-office, met them with gravity on his whiskered face. He was a tall and thin man, much stooped, who, as far as the memory of man, had always lived here in Two-Forks Valley.

"Well, you heard the news, I reckon," said he to his neighbors. Both men nodded.

"Big Aleck told me he was working on the Government job. He said he was going on up with his team to help finish some roads."

"Well, if it was him," said Wid Gardner, "or any one else, we're a-goin' to find out who it was done this. We been hearing a long while about the free Industrials, whatever the damned Bolsheviks call theirselves. They wander around now and won't settle. Hobos, I call them, no more, but crazy ones. They threatened to burn all the hay in the settlements below, and to wipe out all the wheat crop. Why? They been busting up threshing machines acrosst the range—the paper's been full of it. Why? They've got in here, and that's all about it. Well, fellers, you reckon we're goin' to stand fer this sort of Bolshevik business on the Two-Forks?"

"I say, Pop," broke in Sim Gage to the postmaster, with singular irrelevance at this time, "haven't you got a litter of pups around here somewheres, and a couple hens I can buy? I'm lookin' fer a dog, and things."

"Yard's full of pups, man. If you want one help yourself. But hens, now—"

"Sell me two or three hens and a rooster or so. I promised I'd take 'em home, and I plumb forgot."

Pop Bentley threw up his hands at his feckless neighbor. "You'd better be getting a *place* fer your hens and dogs, seems like."

Sim put a forefinger to his puckered lip. "I don't know as I want to take more'n about one pup now, and three or four hens. I'll fix up the price with you sometime. Yes, I got to be getting home now."

The mail carrier, the postmaster and Sim's friend looked at one another as these details went forward.

"Well," said Pop Bentley, shrugging his bent shoulders, "if you would go away and leave a woman alone in a place like that—"

"What do you mean?" said Sim Gage suddenly.

"Why, that woman ain't *there* no more, you fool. She's gone!"

"Gone? What do you mean?"

"Whoever set fire to your place took her away, or else she's got lost somewheres."

"Gone?" said Sim Gage. "Blind! You, Wid!"—he turned upon his friend half-savagely—"you was talking to me about acts of Providence. There ain't no such thing as Providence if this here's true. Come on—I got to get home."

They did start home, at a gallop, Sim half unconscious of what he did, carrying in his arm an excited puppy, impetuously licking his new master's hands and face. In the bottom of the wagon lay a disregarded sack with a half-dozen fowl, their heads protruding through holes cut for that purpose. Sim never knew how or when they got into the wagon.

At the next gate, that of Nels Jensen's homestead, Sim's neighbor below, the woman of the place came running. "You heard about it?—You're all burned out, both of you."

"Yes, we know," said Wid, nodding. "Tell Nels to come on up to Sim's place early in the morning. We're going to get the neighbors together." Again the tired team was forced into a dull gallop.

They had not far to go. A turn of the road freed them of the screen of willows. There lay before them in the evening light, long prolonged at this season in that latitude, that portion of the valley which these two neighbors owned. For a moment they sat silent.

"Mine's gone," said Wid succinctly. "Not a thing left."

Sim sat clasping the puppy in his arms as he turned to look at his own homestead.

"Mine's gone too," said he. "Barn's burned, and all the hay. House is there, anyhow. Lemme out, Wid."

"No, hold on," said his neighbor. "There's no hurry for me to go home, now that's sure. Your leg's bad, Sim. I'll take you down."

So they drove down Sim Gage's lane between the wire

Emerson Hough

fence and the willows. Sim was looking eagerly ahead. Continually he moaned to himself low, as if in pain. But the hard-faced man on the seat beside him knew it was not in physical pain.

They fastened the team and hurried on about, searching the premises. The barn was gone, and the hay. Two or three head of slaughtered stock lay partially consumed, close to the hay stack. The house still stood, for the dirt roof had stopped the flames which were struggling up from the door frame along the heavy logs.

"The damn, murdering thieves," said Wid Gardner. "Look, Sim—your horse and mule was both killed in there." He pointed to the burned barn. "What *made* them? What do they gain by this? *I* know!"

But Sim Gage was hobbling to his half-burnt home. Gasping, he looked in. It was empty!

"Where's she gone, Wid?" said he, when he could speak. "You reckon Big Aleck—? No. No!"

"Nothing's too low down for him," said Wid Gardner.

There were footprints in the path where the neighbors had stood, but Sim's eye caught others not trampled out, in the strip of sand toward the willows—two footprints, large, and beside them two others, small. The two, old big-game hunters as they were, began to puzzle out this double trail.

"He was a-leading her out this way, Sim," said Wid, pointing. "Look a-yonder, where we come in—them wheel tracks wasn't yours nor mine. Now, look-a-here, in this little open place where the ants has ate it clean— here's her footprints, right here. No use to hunt the creek or the willers, Sim—she's went off in a wagon."

"He took my six-shooter," said Sim, who had hurriedly examined the interior of his home. "Nothing else is gone. Wait while I go git my rifle. It's in the tent."

When he had returned with rifle and belt, Wid turned towards him. "I'll tell you, Sim," said he, "we'll run over to my place and look around, and come back here and eat before it gets plumb dark. I'll saddle up and pass the word."

They climbed back into the wagon seat and once more passed out along Sim Gage's little lane. At the end, where it joined the main road, Wid pulled up.

"Look yonder, Sim!" said he. "There's where that broad-tire wagon was tied."

"The road's full of all sorts of tracks," said Sim, looking down, rifle in hand, from his seat. He carried the puppy again in his arms, and the hens still were expostulating in the bottom of the wagon. "Is them car tracks?"

"A car could be a hundred and fifty miles away by now," said Wid.

They passed on to Wid Gardner's gate. It was wide open. There were wheel tracks there, also, of some sort.

The ruin of this homestead also was complete. The last stack of hay, the barn, house, all, were burned to the ground.

"Well, that's all I want here," said Wid, sighing. "We'll stop at your place for a spell, Sim—that's the best thing we can do."

"But look here!" he went on, his eyes running along the

ground. "Been a car in here—this wasn't a wagon—it was a car! There must of been more'n one of 'em."

"Uh huh," said Sim, climbing down stiffly from the wagon seat now and joining him in the task of puzzling out the trail. They followed it to a place where some ashes had been trodden in the yard. Here the wheels of the car had left their clearest record.

"Not a big one," said Wid. "Ragged tire on the nigh hind wheel. See this?"

They ran the trail on out to the gate, picking it up here and there, catching it plain in the loose sand which covered the gravel road bed.

"Whoever done the work at my place," said Sim, "was drunk. Look how he busted down my mail box."

"Look how this car was running here," assented Wid. "You set here by the gate, Sim, and hold the team. I want to run up the road a piece to where the timber trail turns up the canyon."

"Sure, Wid," said Sim. "I can't walk good."

It was half an hour or more before his friend had returned from his hasty scout further along the road, and by that time it was dark.

"That's where they went, Sim," said Wid Gardner. "I seen the track of that busted tire plain in the half-dried mud, little ways up the trail. Whoever it was done this, has went right up there. When we get a few of the fellers together we'll start. To-morrow morning, early."

"To-morrow!" said Sim. "Why, Wid—"

Wid Gardner laid a hand on his friend's shoulder. "It's the best we can do, Sim," said he.

Without more speech they drove once more along Sim Gage's lane. As they approached the entrance, Sim turned. "Hold up a minute, Wid," said he, "while I look over here where the wagon was tied."

He limped across the road, bent to examine the marks dimly visible in the half darkness.

"Look-a-here," said he, "there's been a car here too—the same car, with the busted tire! They come up in that wagon from my place after they burned me out. They must of taken her out of the wagon and put her in the car, and like you say, they're maybe a couple of hundred miles away by now. Oh, my God A'mighty, Wid, what has you and me done to that pore girl!"

Wid only laid the large hand again on his shoulder. "It'll be squared," said he.

Their rude meal was prepared in silence, and eaten in silence. Sim Gage felt in his pocket, and drawing out the letter he had received, smoothed out the envelope on the table top.

"It's addressed to her, Wid," said he after a time, "and she ain't here."

"I don't see why we oughtn't to open it and read it," said Wid. "Some one'd have to anyhow, if she was here, for she couldn't read, herself."

Sim, by means of a table knife, opened the envelope.

"You read it, Wid," said he. "You can read better'n I can."

And so Wid accepted Sim's conventional fiction, knowing he could neither read nor write.

"Dear Mary," said Anne's letter, "I got to write to you. I wisht you hadn't went away when you did and how you did, for, Mary, I feel so much alone."

"You know when you started out I was joking you about Charlie Dorenwald. I told you, even if you did have an inside chance you maybe might not be married any sooner than I was. That was just a little while ago. So far as it's all concerned you can come right on back. There's nothing doing now between Charlie and I.

"You know he was foreman in the factory. He ought to of had money laid up but he didn't. On Installments I'd soon have got a place fixed up, though Charlie and me was going to fix it up on Installments. But I got to talking with him, right away after you had left, it was all about the war and I said to him, 'Charlie, why didn't you go over?' He says one thing and he says another. Well you know that sort of got me started and at last we had it, and do you know when he got rattled he began to talk Dutch to me? Well, I talked turkey to him. One thing and another went on and Charlie and me we split up right there.

"'I couldn't join the army noways,' he says, 'they wouldn't take me. I had flat feet.'"

"'You got a flat tire, that's what ails you,' I says to him, 'Well now I wouldn't marry you at all, not if you was the last man, which you look to me like you was.'"

"Well, the way he talked, Mary, I wouldn't be surprised if he was married already anyhow. One of the girls said he'd been living with another woman not four blocks off. He ain't hurt none and I don't know as I am neither although of course a girl feels mortified that people think she's going to get married and then she ain't.

"But I'm thinking of you. I've gone back in our old room where it's cheaper and let them take back the Installment furniture. I ain't got a thing to do after hours except read the papers. The country's all stirred up. But anyhow I'm rid of my Dutch patriot. That's why I'm writing to you now.

"I wonder what you're doing out there. Are you married yet? What did he look like, Mary? I know he's a good man after all, kind and chivalrous like he said. If he wasn't you'd be wiring me telling me when you was coming home. I guess you're too happy to write to anybody like me. You'll have a Home of your own.

"And all the time I thought I was stronger than you was and abler to get on and here you are married and happy and me back in the old room! But don't worry none about me—I'll get another job. The most is I miss you so much and you haven't wrote me a word I suppose. When a girl gets married all the girls is crazy to hear all about her and her husband and I haven't heard a word from you.

"Respectfully your friend,"

"Annie Squires."

The two men sat for a time. Wid reached in his pocket for his pipe.

"By God! she come out here maybe to get married, on the level and honest, after a while!" said he. "She'll have to, now!"

Emerson Hough

"That's what I was thinking, Wid," said Sim Gage. "It's—it's chivalerous. We got to find her, now."

CHAPTER XV

THE SPECIES

"Well, pretty one, you got lonesome here all by yourself? So you holler for 'Sim! Sim!'" Big Aleck's voice was close to her as she sat in the tent.

Mary Warren felt about her, back of her on the blankets, stealthily seeking some weapon of defense. She paused. Under her fingers was something which felt like leather. She made no sudden movement, but temporized.

"How could I help it?" she asked.

Always her hand was feeling behind her on the blankets. Yes, there was a holster. It felt familiar—it might be Sim Gage's gun, taken from her at the house. She waited.

"Well, that's too bad you can't see," said Aleck. "You can't see what a fine feller I'd make for you! I'm chief. I'm a big man."

"You're a big coward," said Mary Warren calmly. "What's a blind woman to you? Why don't you let me go?"

"Well, even a blind woman can tell what she's heard," said he thoughtfully. "And then," his coarse voice undertaking a softness foreign to it, "I'm just as tired as Sim Gage was of keeping house alone. I'm a better man than Sim Gage. I'm making plenty of money."

She made no reply, leaned back upon the blanket roll.

"Now, then, gal, listen. I like you. You're handsome—the handsomest gal ever come in this valley. A pretty girl as you shouldn't stay single, and as good a man as me neither. I work on my ranch, but I'm a big man, miss. I'm a thinker, you can see that. I'm a leader of the laboring men. I begun with nothing; and look at me!"

"Well, look at you!" She taunted him. "What would you have been if you hadn't come to America? You'd be shoveling dirt over there at half a dollar a day, or else you'd be dead. You think this is Russia? You call this Germany?"

Pretending to rest her weight on her arm back of her, she felt the touch of leather, felt the stock of the pistol in the holster.

Her tormentor went on. "We don't need no army—we free men can fight the way we are. We'll spoil ten million feet of timber in here before we're through."

"I despise you—I hate you!" she cried suddenly, almost forgetful of herself. "Why do you come to this country, if you don't like it? If you hate America, why don't you go back to your own country and live there? You ought to be hung—I hope to God you will be!"

He only laughed. "That's fine talk for you, ain't it? You'd better listen to what I tell you." He reached out a hand and touched her arm.

With one movement, of sheer instinct, with a primal half-snarl, she swung the revolver out of the scabbard behind her, flung it almost into his face. He cowered, but not soon enough. The shot struck him. He dropped, tried to escape. She heard him scuffling on the sand, fired again and missed—fired yet again and heard him cry out, gasping, begging for mercy.

The range was too short for her to hear the impact of the bullets; she did not know she had struck him with two shots, the second of which had broken his leg and left him disabled. She had shot a man. He was there in front of her, about to die.

"Are you hurt?" she demanded, staring, the revolver in both her hands. "Keep away. I'll kill you!"

"You— Don't shoot again," he cried, as she moved. She could not tell what he meant, what really had happened, except that he was helpless. She rose and fled, groping, stumbling, falling. She could hear him crying out. He did not follow her.

In the forest growth at this altitude the trees stood large, straight and tall, not very close together. The earth was covered with a dense floor of pine needles. As she ran she felt her feet slipping, sinking. Now and again she brought up against a tree. Still she kept on, sobbing, her hands outstretched, getting away farther than would have been possible in denser cover. She felt the sand of the roadway under her feet as her course curved back toward the road, endeavored to follow the trail for a time, but found herself again on the pine needles, running she knew not where or how. She had no hope. She knew she was fleeing death and facing death. Very well, she would meet it further on and in a better guise.

She felt that she was passing down, along the mountain side, advanced more rapidly, stumbling, tripping—and so at last fell full length over a log which lay across her course. Stunned by the impact of her fall beyond and below the unseen barrier, she lay prone and quite unconscious.

At a length of unknown moments, she gained her senses. She sat up, felt about her, listened. There was no sound of pursuit. Only the high wailing of the pines came to her ears.

She could not know it, but the men were not following her. When they heard the sound of three shots ring out, every man busy in his work of sabotage stopped where he was. Was it a surprise? Were officers or the ranchers coming? They scattered, hiding among the trees.

They could hear the bellowing of Big Aleck, beseeching aid. They advanced cautiously, to spy out what had happened and saw him rolling from side to side, striving to rise, falling back. The woman was nowhere visible.

"Who done it, Aleck?" demanded the man next in command, when he had ventured closer. "Did she shoot you?"

Aleck groaned as he rolled over, his face upward. A nod showed his crippled shoulder. His other hand Big Aleck feebly placed upon his hip. They bent over him.

"By God, she got you fair that time!" said one investigator. "She's plugged you twice. She wasn't blind. Where did she go?"

"I don't know where—I heard her run. God, that leg! What will I do? I can't stay here alone!"

"I tell you, you'll have to! If that girl's not blind she'll get out and give this snap away."

"But you can take me out with you, fellers. I can ride." Aleck was pleading, his face gray with pain.

"Worst thing we could do, either for you or for us," replied the other, coldly. "If we got you down to the settlements what could we say? If you was shot once we could call it an accident, but shot twice, and once through the hip from behind—how would that be explained, I'd like to know? Folks would begin to ask too many questions. Besides, they'd ask where that girl was. Then there's the fires you set. No, sir, you stay right here. We other fellers'll get out of here as fast as we can."

"And leave me here?" The terror in Big Aleck's voice had been piteous for any men but these.

"Listen! Before midnight I'll be at the Company dam. I'll tell that new doctor there's been an accident up here in the timber camp. I'll tell him to come up here to-morrow morning sure. When he gets here, you tell him how the accident happened. It's up to you, then. You'll have to pay him pretty well, of course."

"And that reminds me," he went on, "we fellers has got to have the funds, Aleck. We'll need money more'n you will now. Here!"

He stooped over and began to feel in Aleck's coat, drew out a heavy wallet, and began to transfer the bills to his own pocket.

"I'll leave you a hundred and fifty. That's enough," said he. "No telling what we fellers'll have to do before we get out of this. Your getting shot here is apt to blow the whole thing. Did she take the gun away with her?"

Aleck groaned and rolled his head. "I don't know," he said.

Jim Denny was the new leader of the brigand party. "Hell's bells!" said he, impatiently now. "We can't be fooling around—this don't look good to me. Noon tomorrow, anyways, the Doctor ought to be here. As for us, we got to beat it now."

The wolf pack knew no mercy nor unselfishness. Aleck got no more attention from them. There were two cars beside the one which had brought Aleck and Mary Warren up the day before. This last one they left, seeing that the tire was in bad condition. Not one of them turned to say good-by to Aleck as he lay in the tent where he had been dragged.

"Got it right on top the hip bone," said one man. "She busted him plenty with that soft-nose."

"And served him right," said Jim Denny, the new leader, grumbling. "Aleck has never been looking for the worst of it, any way of the game. If he had left that woman down below where she belonged, we wouldn't be in this fix. I tell you them ranchers'll be out in a pack after us, and the only thing we can do is to pull our freight good and plenty right now."

The whir of the engine drowned conversation. An instant later the two carloads of banditti were passing down around curve after curve of the sandy road. Mary Warren, still dazed, and dull where she lay, heard them go by. Yonder then, lay the trail—but could she know which way? If she turned her head she would lose the direction. She kept her eyes fixed upon the last point of the compass from which she had heard the car distinctly, and taking the muzzle of the revolver in her hand, endeavored to scratch a mark in the sand to give her the direction later by the sense of touch. She laid the pistol itself at the upper end of the little furrow, pointing toward the road which she had left. Sinking down, she resigned herself to what she felt must soon be the end.

The chill of the mountain night was coming on. The whispering in the pines grew less. Vaguely she sensed that the sun was low, that soon twilight would come. She had no means of making a fire, had no covering, no food. Simply a lost unit of one of the many species inhabiting the earth, surviving each as it may, she cowered alone and helpless in the wilderness.

The hush of the evening came. The pines were silent. There was only one little faint sound above her—in some tree, she thought. It was made by a worm boring under the bark, seeking place for the larvae which presently it would leave, in order that its species might endure. A small sound, of no great carrying power.

CHAPTER XVI

THE REBIRTH OF SIM GAGE

Neither Sim Gage nor his neighbor slept to any worth that night. At times one would speak, but they held no discussion. Wid Gardner, in an iron wrath, was thinking much.

Sim Gage lay with his eyes opened toward the rude ceiling. In his heart was something new. Hitherto in all his life he had never quarreled with fate, but smiled at it as something beyond his making or his mending. He was one of the world's lost sheep, one of the army of the unhoping. The mountains, the valleys, the trees, had been enough for him, the glint of the sun on the silver gray of the sage yonder on the plains. He had been content to spend his life here where chance had thrown him. But now—and Sim Gage himself knew it—something new had been born in Sim Gage's heart. It troubled him. He lay there and bent his mind upon the puzzle, intensely, wonderingly.

It had been bravado with him up to the time that he knew this girl was coming out. After that, curiosity and a sense of fair play, mingled, had ensued. Then a new feeling had come after he had met the girl herself—pity, and remorse in regard to a helpless woman. Sim Gage did not know the dangerous kinship that pity holds. He knew no proverbs and no poetry.

But now, mixed also with his feeling of vague loss, his sense of rage, there was now, as Sim Gage realized perfectly well, a new and yet more powerful emotion in his soul. He was not the same man, now; he never again would be. Pity and propinquity and the great law had done their work! For the first and only time in all his life Sim Gage was in love!

Love dareth and endureth all things, magnifies and lessens, softens and hardens, loosens and binds, establishes for itself new worlds, fabricates for itself new values, chastens, humbles, makes weak, makes strong. Sim Gage never before had known how merciless, how cruel all this may be. He was in love. With all his heart and life and soul he loved *her*, right or wrong. There had been a miracle in Two-Forks Valley.

The two men were astir long before dawn. Wid Gardner first kicked off his blankets. "I'll find me a horse," said he. "You git breakfast, Sim, if you can." He went into the darkness of the starlit morning.

Sim Gage, his wounded leg stiff and painful enough, crawled out of his bunk—the same where She but now had slept—and made some sort of a light by means of matches and a stub of candle; found a stick and made some shavings; made shift to start a fire. With a hatchet he found on the floor he hacked off more of the charred woodwork of his own door-frame, seeing that it must be ruined altogether. It was nothing to him what became of this house. The only question in his mind was, Where was She? What had happened to Her?

His breakfast was that of the solitary man in such

surroundings. He got a little bacon into a pan, chipped up some potatoes which he managed to pare—old potatoes now, and ready to sprout long since. He mixed up some flour and water with salt and baking powder and cooked that in a pan.

The odors of the cooking brought new life into the otherwise silent interior of Sim Gage's cabin. Sim felt something at his feet, at his leg. It was the Airedale puppy which he had left curled up all night at the foot of his bed. The scent of the meat now had awakened him, and he was begging his new master for attention.

Sim leaned down stiffly to pat him on the head, gave him a bit of food. Then he bethought him of the sack of fowls which he had entirely forgotten—found them luckily still alive in the wagon bed, cut off the sacking around them, and drove them out into the open to shift for themselves as best they might. But the little dog would not be cast off. He followed Sim wherever he went, licked his hand. That made him think how She would have petted the puppy had She been there. He had got the dog for Her.

By the time he had the meal ready Wid Gardner was back leading a horse. There was no saddle at either ranch now, but Wid searched around and found a bit of discarded sack, a piece of rope near the burned barn.

"I'll ride down the valley," said he after the two had eaten in silence. "Wait till I ride down to Jensen's. He'll come along."

"Well, hurry back," said the new Sim, with a resolution and decision in his voice which surprised his neighbor. "I can't very well go off alone. Send word down to the dam. We got to clean out this gang."

"Yes," replied Wid, "they'd better look out who's working on the dam. It ain't all soldiers. You can't tell a thing about where this is going to run to—they might blow out the dam, for all you can tell. They ain't up in there for no good,—after the timber, likely. I wonder how many there is of them."

"I don't care how many there is," said Sim Gage simply.

Early as Gardner was, he was not the only traveler on the road. As he approached Nels Jensen's gate he saw below that place on the road the light of a car traveling at speed.

He slid off his horse, tied the animal, and stood, rifle in hand, directly in front of the approaching vehicle.

"Halt!" he cried, and flung up his left hand high, the rifle held in his right, under his arm pit.

It was no enemy who now slowed down the car and cut out the lights. A voice not unfamiliar called out, "What's wrong with you, man? What do you want? You trying to hold me up?"

"Is that you, Doc? No one passes here. What are you doing up here?" Wid walked up to the edge of the car.

"I'm on a call, that's what I'm doing up here," replied Doctor Barnes. "Have you heard anything about an accident up on the Reserve?"

"Accidents a-plenty, right around here. I don't know nothing about the Reserve. Who told you?"

"A man, last night late. Said there was a man hurt up in the timber camp, for me to go up fast as I could. Tree fell on him. They left him up there alone, because they couldn't bring him out."

"That so?" commented Wid Gardner grimly.

—"So that elected me, you see. Every time I try to get a night's sleep, here comes some damn sagebrusher and wants me to come out and cure his sick cow, or else mamma's got a baby, or a horse has got in the wire, or papa's broke a leg, or something. Damn the country anyhow! I wish I'd never seen it. I'm a doctor, yes, but I'm the Company doctor, and I don't have to run on these fool trips. But of course I do," he added, smiling sunnily after his usual fashion. "So I come along here. And you hold me up. What do *you* want?"

"I want you to wait and come in and see Nels Jensen with me, Doc," said Wid Gardner. "Hell's to pay."

"What's wrong?" Doctor Barnes' face grew graver.

"We don't know what. When Sim and me come home, some one had been here when we was gone. Sim's barn is burned, and all his hay, and all mine, and my house—I haven't got lock, stock nor barrel left of my ranch, and nothing to make a crop with."

"What do you think?" asked Doctor Barnes gravely.

"We don't know what to think. It's like enough a hold-on from that old Industrial work—they been threatening all down the valley, since times are hard and wages fell a little after the war work shut down. There was some hay burned down below there. Folks said it was spontaneous combustion, or something—said it got hot workin' in the stacks. I ain't so sure now. It's them old ways. As if they ever got anything by that!"

Dr. Barnes puckered his lips into a long whistle. "I wonder if there's any two and two to put together in *this* thing!" said he. "I came up here to get that poor devil out of the woods. But who can tell what in the merry hell has really happened up there?"

"We got to go and see," said Wid Gardner. "You know that woman?"

The doctor nodded.

"She's gone too. Whoever it was took her off in a car from up at the head of Sim Gage's lane."

Doctor Barnes got down out of the car, and the two walked through Nels Jensen's gate. Jensen was afoot, ready for the day's work. He agreed that one of his boys would carry the news to the Company dam.

"Better give us a little something to eat along with us, Karen," he said to his wife. He took down his rifle, and looked inquiringly at Doctor Barnes. "Have you got an extra gun?" asked the latter. Jensen nodded, finding the spare piece near at hand.

Very little more was said. They all walked out into the morning, when the red ball of the sun was coming up above the misty valley.

"Go on ahead in the car," said Wid. "I'll bring my horse."

They met at Sim Gage's half-burned home. Sim himself hobbled out, rifle under one arm and the little Airedale under the other, the latter wriggling and barking in his delight. The purr of a good motor was soon under them. In a few moments they were out of Sim Gage's lane and along the highway as far as the point where the Tepee

Creek trail turned off into the mountains.

"Wait here, Doc," said Wid, "Sim and me want to have a look—we know the track of that car that done the work down here."

But when they bent over the trail, they saw that it was different from what it had been when they left it the night before! Wid cursed aloud, and Sim Gage joined him heartily.

"It's wiped out," said Sim. "Some one's been over this trail since last night. This car ain't got no busted tire."

"That may be the very man that came down and called me!" exclaimed Doctor Barnes.

"I heard him when he went down the road," nodded Nels Jensen—"last night. I'll bet that's the same car. I'll bet it come down out of the mountains."

They passed on up the creek valley toward the Reserve far more rapidly than the weaker car of Big Aleck had climbed the same grade the day previous, but the main body of the forest lay three thousand feet above the valley floor, and the ascent was so sharp that at times they were obliged to stop in order to allow the engine to cool.

"What's that?" said Sim Gage after a time, when they had been on their way perhaps an hour up the winding canon, and had paused for the time. "Smoke? That ain't no camp fire—it's more."

They made one or two more curves of the road and then got confirmation. A long, low blanket of smoke was drifting off down the valley to the right, settling in a gray-blue cloud along the mountain side. The wind was from left to right, so that the smoke carried free of the trail.

"She's a-fire, boys!" exclaimed Wid. "We better git out of here while we can."

"We ain't a-going to do nothing of the sort," said a quiet voice. Wid Gardner turned to look into the face of Sim Gage. "We're a-going right on up ahead."

Wid Gardner looked at Doctor Barnes. The latter made his answer by starting the car once more. Although they did not know it, they now were approaching their journey's end. They could not as yet see the swift advance of the fire from tree to tree, because the wind as yet was no stronger than the gentle air of morning; could not as yet hear any roar of the flames. But they saw that now, on these mountain slopes before them, one of the most valuable timber bodies in the state was passing into destruction.

"God damn their souls!" said Wid Gardner fervently. "Wasn't it enough what they done to us already?"

"Go on, Doc." It was Sim's voice. Wid Gardner knew perfectly well what drove Sim Gage on.

But the car soon came to a sudden halt. A couple of hundred yards on ahead lay an open glade. At the left of the trail stood a great wall tent.

In an instant, every man was out of the car, the three ranchmen, like hounds on the scent, silently trotting off, taking cover from tree to tree. A few moments, and the four of them, rifles at a ready, had surrounded the tent. As they closed in, they all heard a high, clear voice—one they would not have suspected Sim Gage to have owned—calling out: "Throw up your hands, in there!"

Actually, Sim Gage was leader!

There came an exclamation in a hoarse and broken voice. "Who are you? Don't shoot—I surrender."

"How many are there of you?" inquired Doctor Barnes.

"It's me—Big Aleck—I'm shot—I'm dying—Help!—Who is it?"

"Come out, Aleck!" called the high and resolute voice of Sim Gage—"Come on out!"

"I can't come out. I'm shot, I tell you."

Then Sim Gage did what ordinarily might not have been a wise thing to do. Without pause he swept aside the tent flap with the barrel of his rifle, and stepped in, quickly covering the prostrate figure that lay on the bloody blankets before him.

Big Aleck was able to do more than move. He raised one hand, feebly, imploring mercy.

"Come out, damn you!" said Sim Gage, his hand at the dollar of the crippled man. He dragged his prisoner out into the light and threw him full length,—mercilessly— upon the needle-covered sand.

The crippled man began to weep, to beg. It was small mercy he saw as he looked from face to face.

"That's my man," exclaimed Doctor Barnes. "But it's not any accident with a tree. That's gun shot!"

"Who done that work down below?" demanded Sim of the prostrate man. "Where is she? Tell me!" His voice still rang high and imperative.

Big Aleck shivered where he lay. Now he too saw the flames on ahead in the woods.

"Who set that fire?" demanded the Doctor suddenly. "Whose work was that?"

"It was sabcats!" said Big Aleck, frightened into an ingenious lie. "They was in here. I'm the government foreman. I don't know how they got in or got out. They must of set a 'clock' somewhere for to start it."

"Who do you mean—sabcats?" demanded Doctor Barnes. The other three stood coldly and implacably staring at the crippled man.

"I caught them in here—I'm in charge of this work, you see. I tried to stop them. They shot me and left me here. They said they'd send a doctor."

"I'm the doctor," replied the medical man, who stood looking at him. "Where is that woman?"

Big Aleck rolled his head. "I don't know. I don't know nothing. I'm shot—I'm going to die."

"We've got to get out," said Doctor Barnes. "Boys, shall we get him into the car?"

"No!" said Sim Gage, sharply. "I won't ride with him. *Where is she*?" He stepped close up to Big Aleck, pushing in front of the others. "You know. Damn you, tell me!"

"Keep him away!" yelled Big Aleck. "He's going to kill me!" He tried to get on his elbows, his hands and knees, but could not, broken down as he was. He was abject—an evil man overtaken by an evil fate.

"Where is she?" repeated Sim Gage. "Tell me!"

"I tell you I don't know. She ran off, that way."

"That's the car that brung her up!" said Wid Gardner, motioning toward the ragged tire of the rear wheel. "See that tire, Sim? That's the car! She's been here."

"Go see if you can git the trail, Wid," said Sim Gage to his friend. "Quick!"

Sim himself passed for a moment, hurriedly, to the car which had brought his party up. He had left the little dog tied there, but now heard it whining, and stopped to loosen it. It ran about, barking. Head down, Sim Gage stumbled off, following a trail which he half thought he saw, but he lost it on the pine needles, and came back, bitter of heart, once more to face the man who lay helpless on the ground—the man who now he knew was his enemy, not to be forgiven or spared.

"Where is she?" he said to Aleck once more. "It was her trail, I know it. Tell me the truth now, while you can talk."

"You was follering right the way she went, far as I know," moaned Aleck. "How kin I tell where she went, after I was shot?"

"After you was shot? Who shot you? *Did she*?"

"I told you who shot me. It was them fellers."

"Then why didn't they kill you, if they wanted to? They *could* of finished you, couldn't they? Where's my six-shooter, Aleck—you took it outen my house, and you know you did."

He stepped back into the tent and began to kick around among the blankets. "There's nothing here excepting your own rifle." He came out, unloaded the gun, smashed the lever against the nearest tree.

"You won't never need no gun no more," said he.

"I'll have to look after him, now," said Doctor Barnes, stepping forward. He had stood looking at the crippled man, his own hands on his hips. "He's bad off."

"Keep away—don't you touch him!" It was still the new voice of Sim Gage that was talking now, and there was something in his tone which made the others all fall back. All the time Sim Gage's rifle was covering the writhing man.

"I tried to save her," whimpered Big Aleck now.

"You lie! Why did you bring her up here then? Why didn't you leave her there—she didn't have to come." Sim Gage still was talking now sharp, decisive. "Where is she now?"

"Good God, man, I told you I didn't know. How do I know which way she'd run? She said she was blind—but I don't believe she was."

"*Why* don't you?" demanded Sim Gage. "*Because she could shoot you*?—Because she *did* shoot you, twice? What made her? Where's my gun? Did she take it with her after she shot you?"

The sweat broke out now on the gray and grimed forehead of the suffering man. "I won't tell you nothing more!" he broke out. "What right you got to arrest me? I ain't committed no crime, and you ain't got no warrant. I want a lawyer. I want this doctor to take care of me. I got money to get a lawyer. I don't have to answer no questions you ask me."

"You say she went over that way?" Sim's finger was pointing across the road in the direction of the fire.

"I told you, yes," nodded Big Aleck. And Sim Gage's own knowledge gained from the last direction of the footprints confirmed this.

"Blind—and out all night in these mountains!" he said, his voice shaking for the first time. "And then comes that fire. You done that, Aleck—you know you done it."

"I told you I didn't know nothing," protested the crippled man, who now had turned again upon his back. "I ain't a-goin' to talk. It was them fellers."

"Some things you'd better know," said Sim Gage, suddenly judge in this court, suddenly assembled. "Some things I know now. You come down to my house your own self. It was you set my barn a-fire and burned my house and my hay, and killed my stock. It was you carried that girl off. I know why you done it, too. You wasn't fighting that bunch in here—they was with you. You was all on the same business, and you know it. You made trouble before the war, and you're making it now, when we're all trying to settle down in the peace."

He was beginning to tremble now as he talked. "Didn't she shoot you?—Now, tell me the truth."

"Yes!" said the prisoner suddenly, seeing that in the other's eyes which demanded the truth. "She did shoot me, and then ran away. She took your gun. But I didn't set the fire. Honest to God, I don't know how it got out. I swear—oh, my God—have mercy!"

But what he afterward would have sworn no man ever knew. There was a rifle shot—from whose rifle none of the four ever could tell. It struck Big Aleck fair below the eyes, and blew his head well apart. He fell backward at the door of the tent.

They turned away slowly. Just for an instant they stood looking at the sweeping blanket of smoke. They walked to the car, paying no further attention to the figure which lay motionless behind them. The fire might come and make its winding sheet.

It was coming. Wid Gardner lifted his head. "Wind's changing," said he. "Hurry!"

They headed down the trail as fast as might be.

"*Wait*, now, Doc!" said Sim Gage, a moment after they started. "Wait now!"

"What's up?" said Doctor Barnes. "Look at that smoke."

"Where's that little dog, now? We've forgot him."

He sprang out of the car, began stumbling back up the trail, his own leg dragging.

"Cut off the car!" he called back. "I can't hear a thing."

As he stood there came up to him from the mountain side a sound which made him turn and plunge down in that direction himself. It was a shot. Then the bark of the Airedale, baying "treed."

The dog itself, keen of nose, and of the instinct to run almost any sort of trail, even so very faint as this on which it was set, had in part followed out the winding course of the fleeing girl after Sim Gage himself had abandoned it, thinking it had been laid on that trail. And now what Sim saw on ahead, down the hill, below the trail, was the figure of Mary Warren herself, sitting up weakly, gropingly, on the log over which she had fallen the night before—beneath which, like some animal, she had cowered all that awful night on the heap of pine needles which she had swept up for herself!

A cry broke from Sim Gage's lips. She heard him and herself called out aloud, "Sim! Sim! Is it you? I knew it was you when the dog came!"

And then, still shivering and trembling with fear and cold and exhaustion, Mary Warren once more lost all sense of things, and dropped limp. The little dog stood licking at her hands and face.

Here was work for Doctor Barnes after all. He took charge. The four of them carried the woman up the hill to the car. He had restoratives which served in good stead now.

"Poor thing!" said he. "Out all night! It's just a God's mercy she didn't freeze to death, that's all."

He himself was wondering at the extraordinary beauty of this woman. Who was she—what was there in this talk that two ranchmen had made, down there at the dam? Why, this was no ordinary ranchwoman at all, but a woman of distinction, one to attract notice anywhere.

Mary Warren at last began to talk,—before the smoke cloud drove them down the trail. "I heard a shot," said she, turning a face toward them. "Who was it? I didn't signal then, for I didn't know. I waited. Then the dog came."

No one answered her.

"That must have been what brought me to. It sounded up the hill. Where—where is he?"

They did not answer even yet, and she went on.

"Who are you all?" she demanded. "I don't see you, of course." She was looking into the face of Doctor Barnes who bent above her, his hand on her pulse.

"I'm Doctor Barnes," said he. "I work down at the Company's plant at the big dam. You are Miss Mary Warren, are you not?"

She nodded. "Yes."

"I won't introduce these others, but they're all friends—we all are."

She was recognizing the voice, the diction of a gentleman. The thought gave her comfort.

"What's that smoke?" she said suddenly, herself catching the scent pervading the air.

"The whole mountain's afire," said Sim Gage. "We got to hurry if we get out of here."

"I know—it was those people!—Where is that man? You found him?"

The voice of Doctor Barnes broke in quickly. "He'd been

hurt by a tree—we had to leave him because he was too far gone, Miss Warren," said he. "We couldn't save him. He couldn't answer any questions—not even a hypothetical question—when we tried him. But now, don't try to talk. He's got what he had coming, and he'll never trouble you again."

"Whose little dog is this?" she asked suddenly, reaching out a hand which the young Airedale kissed fervently. "If it hadn't been for that little dog, you'd never have found me, would you? You couldn't have heard me call. I would not have dared to shoot. Whose little dog?"

"It's yours, ma'am," said Sim Gage. "And I got four hens."

CHAPTER XVII

SAGEBRUSHERS

Nels Jensen reached his home late in the afternoon, his face grave and his tongue more than usually tight. His wife, Karen, looked at him for some time before she spoke.

"Find anything, up in?"

He nodded quietly.

"Doctor get to that sick man?"

"He wasn't sick," rejoined Nels. "Tree fell on him."

"What you do with him?"

"Died before we come out. Whole woods was afire up in there."

"I see the smoke a while back," said she unemotionally, nodding and gazing out of the window toward the distant landscape. "Died, did he? Did you bring him down?"

"The wind has changed," said Nels sententiously. "Before night, won't be nothing to bring down. We left him in his tent."

"Who set that fire, Nels?" she demanded of her husband after a time.

"The same people that burned out Sim Gage and Wid Gardner. All of 'em had cleared out but that one."

"How about that woman, Nels?"

"We brung her down with us. She'd spent the night in the woods alone. Doctor's got her in bed over at Sim's place now." He turned his heavy face upon her frowningly, apparently passing upon some question they earlier had discussed. "I say it's all right, Karen, about her."

"Well, are they going to be married?" she demanded of him. "That's the question. Because if they ain't—"

"If they are or they ain't," said Nels Jensen, "she's not no common folks like us."

"A lady—huh!"

"Yes, if I can tell one. Such being so, best thing you can do, Karen, is to get some eggs together, and like enough a loaf of bread, and go over there right soon."

"If they wasn't *going* to be married," began Karen, "people in here wouldn't let that run along."

"Karen," said her husband succinctly, "sometimes you women folks make me tired. Go on and get the eggs."

"Oh, all right," said his wife; and already she was reaching for her sunbonnet. When she and her sturdy spouse had made their way by a short cut across the fields to Sim Gage's house, Karen Jensen had melted, and was no longer righteous judge, but simply neighbor.

"Where is she?" she demanded imperiously of Wid Gardner, whom she found standing outside the door.

Wid nodded toward the interior of the half-ruined cabin. As she passed in she saw Doctor Barnes, sitting on a box, quietly watching the pale face of a woman, young, dark-haired, flushed, her eyes heavy, her hands spread out piteously upon the blanket covering of the rude bunk bed. Karen's first quick glance assured her that this young woman was all that Nels Jensen had called her—a lady. She looked so helpless now that the big ranchwoman's heart went out to her in spite of all.

"You'd better get right out, Doctor," said she; and that gentleman followed her orders, exceeding glad to welcome a woman in this womanless wreck of a home.

Doctor Barnes stood outside, hands in pocket, for a time looking across the meadows lined with their banks of willows, silvering as usual in the evening breeze. "Come here," said he at length to the three men. They all followed him to one side.

"Now, Gage," said he, "I want you to tell me the truth about how this woman came out here."

Wid Gardner, taking pity on his friend, told him instead, going into all the details of the conspiracy that had now proved so disastrous. Doctor Barnes frowned in resentment when he heard.

"She's got to go back East," said he, "as soon as she's able to travel."

"That's what I think," said Sim Gage slowly. "It's what I told her. But she always said she didn't have no place to go back to. She could stay here as long as she liked, but now I ain't got much."

"But it can't run on this way, Gage," said Doctor Barnes. "That girl's clean as wheat. Something's got to be done about this."

"Well, good God A'mighty!" said Sim Gage, "ain't that what I know? If only you'll tell me what's right to do, I sure will do it. In one way it ain't just only my fault she come out here, nor it ain't my fault if she don't go back."

Doctor Barnes engaged for some time in breaking up bits of bark and casting them from his thumb nail. "Have you ever had any talk with her about this?" said he.

"Some," said Sim honestly; "yes, some."

"What was it?"

"She told me, when she answered that ad, she was getting plumb desperate, account of her eyes. She was out of work, and she was broke, and she didn't have no folks on earth, and she'd lost all her money—her folks used to be rich, I reckon, like enough. That's the only reason she answered that fool ad about me being in the market, so to speak, fer a wife. That's how she come out. She must of been locoed. You cain't blame *her*. She was all alone in the whole world, but just one girl that knowed her. We got a letter from that girl—I got it here in my pocket. We opened it and read it, Wid and me did, yesterday. Her name's Annie Squires. But she's broke too, I reckon. Now what are we a-goin' to do?"

"Have you ever talked the whole business over—you

two—since she came out?"

"Doc," said Sim Gage, "I told you, I tried my damnedest, and I just couldn't. I says to myself, lady like she was, it wouldn't be right fer a man like me to marry her noways on earth."

"And what did she say?"

Sim Gage began to stammer painfully. "I don't know what she would say," said he. "I ain't never asked her none yet."

"Well, I reckon you'll have to," said Doctor Barnes slowly, after a long time in thought; "if she lives."

"Lives? Doc, you don't mean to tell me she's that sick?"

"She isn't trying to fight very hard. When your patient would rather die than live, you've got hard lines, as a doctor. It's hard lines here more ways than one."

"Die—her!—What would *I* do then, Doc?" asked Sim Gage, so simply that Doctor Barnes looked at him keenly, gravely.

"It's not a question about you, you damn sagebrusher," said he at last, gently. "Question is, what's best for her. If I didn't feel such a woman was too good to be wasted I'd say, let her go; ethics be damned out here. If she gets well she'll have to decide some time what's to do about this whole business. That brings you into the question again. It was a bad bet, but deceived as she was, she's put herself under your protection. And mine!"

"You see," he added, "that's something that really doesn't come under my profession, but it's something that's up to every decent man."

Mrs. Jensen came to the door, broom in hand. "You, Sim," said she, "come in here!" She accosted him in hoarse whispers when he had obeyed.

"Look-a-here at this place!" said she. "Is this where a hog or a human has been living? I've got things straightened around now, and don't you dare muss 'em up. When that pore girl is able to get around again I'm a-going to take her and show her where everything is—she'll keep this house better blind than you did with your both eyes open. I've got a aunt been blind twenty year, and she cooks and sweeps and sews and knits as good as anybody. She'll do the same way. She's a good knitter, I know. The pore child."

Sim reached out a hand gently to the work which he found lying, needles still in place, on the table where Mary Warren had left it the day before.

"She'll learn soon," said Karen Jensen. "Ain't she pretty enough to make you cry, laying there the way she is." The keen gray eyes of Karen Jensen softened. "She's asleep," she whispered. "Doctor doped her."

"If only now," said Sim Gage, frowning as usual in thought, "if only I could get some sort of woman to come here and stay a while, until she gets well. It ain't right she should be in a place like this all alone."

"You pore fool," said Karen Jensen, "did you think for a minute I'd go away and leave that girl alone with you? Go out and get some wood! I'm a-going to get supper here. Tell Nels he can go back home after supper, and him and Minna and Theodore 'll have to keep house until I get back. The pore thing—you said she was right blind?" she concluded.

"Plumb blind," said Sim Gage. "What's more, she can't see none a-tall. It ain't no wonder she's scared sick."

"I'm mighty glad you're a-goin' to get supper here to-night," he continued. "I'm that rattled, like, I couldn't make bread worth a damn."

He edged out of the cabin and communicated his news. "Mrs. Jensen says she'll take care of her till she gets better," he said.

"That's the best thing I've heard," commented Doctor Barnes. "That'll help. I'll stay here to-night myself. Gardner, can you run my car down to the dam?"

"I might," said Wid. "I never did drive a car much, but I think I could. Mormons does; and I've had a lot to do with mowing machines, like them."

"Well, get down to the dam and tell the people I can't be back until to-morrow afternoon. Here's where I belong just now. Where do I sleep, Gage?"

"Out here in the tent, I reckon," replied Sim, "though most all my blankets is in there on the bed. Maybe I kin find a slicker somewheres. Wid, he ain't got nothing left over to his place, neither."

"Don't bother about things," said Nels Jensen. "I'll go over and bring some blankets from my place. The woman'll take care of that girl until she gets in better shape."

Doctor Barnes looked at them all for a time, frowning in his own way. "You damn worthless people," said he with sudden sheer affection. "God has been good to you, hasn't he?"

"Now, ain't that the truth?" said Sim Gage, perhaps not quite fully understanding.

CHAPTER XVIII

DONNA QUIXOTE

At ten of the following morning Mrs. Jensen had finished "redding up," as she called it, and had gone out into the yard. Doctor Barnes, alone at the bedside of his patient, was not professionally surprised when she opened her eyes.

"Well, how's everything this morning?" he said quietly. "Better, eh?"

She did not speak for some time, but turned toward him. "Who are you?" she asked presently.

"Nobody in particular," he answered. "Only the doctor person. I was up in the mountains with you yesterday."

"Was it yesterday?" said she. "Yes, I remember!"

"What became of him?" she asked after a time. "That awful man—I had it in my heart to kill him!"

Doctor Barnes made no comment, and after a while she went on, speaking slowly.

"He said so many things. Why, those men would

do anything?"

"He'll not do any more treason," said Doctor Barnes.

"What do you mean?"

"A tree fell on him. I got there too late to be of any use."

"He's dead?"

"Yes. Don't let's talk of that."

"I've got to live?"

"Yes."

"Who are you?" she inquired after a time. "You're a doctor?"

"I'm your sort, yes, Miss Warren," said he.

"A gentleman."

"Relative term!"

"You've been very good. Where do you live?"

"Down at the Government dam, below here. I'm the Company doctor."

"Well, why don't you go? Am I going to live, or can I die?"

"What brought you out here, Miss Warren," said he at last. "You don't belong in a place like this."

"Where then do I belong?" she asked. "Food and a

bed—that's more than I can earn."

"Maybe we can fix up a way for you to be useful, if you don't go away." He spoke so gently, she began to trust him.

"But I'm not going away. I have no place to go to." She smiled bitterly. "I haven't money enough to buy my ticket back home if I had a home to go to. That's the truth. Why didn't you let me die?"

"You ought to want to live," said Doctor Barnes. "The lane turns, sometimes."

"Not for me. Worse and worse, that's all. . . . I'll have to tell you— I don't like to tell strangers, about myself. But, you see, my brother was killed in the war. We had some money once, my brother and I. Our banker lost it for us. I had to work, and then, after he went away, I began to—to lose my eyes."

"How long was that coming on?"

"Two years—about. The last part came all at once, on the cars, when I was coming out. I've never seen—him—Mr. Gage, you know. I don't know what he looks like."

"They call him Sim Gage."

She remained silent, and he thought best to add a word or so, but could not, though he tried. Mary Warren's face had colored painfully.

"I suppose they've told you—I suppose everybody knows all about that—that insane thing I did, coming out here. Well, I was desperate, that's all. Yet it seems there are good people left in the world. You are all good people. If only I could see; so I could tell what to do. Then maybe I could earn my living, someway—if I have to live.

"Good-hearted, isn't he—Mr. Gage?" She nodded with a woman's confident intuition as she went on. "He didn't cast me out. What can I do to repay him?"

He could make no answer.

"Little to give him, Doctor—but of course, if he could—in any sort of justice—accept—accept—"

Doctor Barnes suddenly reached out a hand and pushed her hair back from her forehead. "I wouldn't," said he. "Please don't. Take things easy for a little while."

She turned her dark and sightless eyes upon him. "No!" said she. "That isn't the way we do in my family. We don't take things easy."

"Has he said anything to you?" asked Doctor Barnes after a long time. "I have very much reluctance to ask."

"He's too much of a man," she said. "No, not yet. It was a sort of bargain, even if we didn't say so outright. 'Object, matrimony!' I came out here with my eyes open. But now God has closed them. . . . Will you tell me the truth?"

"Yes."

"Does he—do you think he—"

"Cares for you?"

"Yes!"

Doctor Barnes replied with extreme difficulty. "We'll say

he does care—that he cares immensely."

She nodded. "I wanted to be fair," said she. "I'm glad I can talk to some one I can trust."

"What makes you think you can trust me?" blustered Doctor Barnes. "And you're so Puritan foolish, you're going to marry this man? You think that is right?"

"He took me in, when I deceived him. I owe my life to him. He's never once hinted or laughed since I came here. Why, he's a gentleman."

She turned her head away. "Perhaps he would never know," she added.

"Something to take on," commented Doctor Barnes grimly.

"I'd try very hard," she went on. "I'd try to do my best. Mrs. Jensen says I could learn a great many things. She has an aunt that's—that has lost her eyesight. It may be my place in the world—here. I want to carry my own weight in the world—or else I want to die."

"He seems hard to understand—Mr. Gage," she went on slowly, the damp of sheer anguish on her forehead now at speaking as she never could wish to speak, thus to a stranger, and of the most intimate things of a gentle-woman's life. "As though I didn't know he couldn't ever really love a woman like me! Of course it isn't right either way. It's awful. . . . But I'd do my best. Life is more of a compromise than I used to think it was. But someway, out here—I'd be shut in forever here in this Valley. No one would ever know. It—it wouldn't seem so wicked, some way? It's the end of the world, isn't it, to-day? Well, then—"

"I'm trying my best," said Doctor Barnes after a time, "to get at the inside of your mind."

She lay for a time picking at the nap of the rough blanket—there were no pillow slips and no pillows. At length she turned to him, her eyes wet.

"It's rather hard for a man to understand things like these—hard for a woman to explain them to a stranger she's never seen," said she. "But there wasn't ever any other man. I'm not here on any rebound. It's reason—it's duty. That's all. They keep telling us women we must reason. My brother was all I had left. You see, he didn't have a good foot—he was lame. That was why we lived together so long, and—and there was no one else. And then—you know about my eyes? Of course I didn't know I was going to be quite blind when I started out here. If I had, I should have ended it all."

"You're a good man, Doctor," said she presently, since he made no answer. "You didn't tell me your name?"

"My name is Allen Barnes. I've been down at the dam for quite a while. I'm only around thirty yet myself. I don't know a lot."

"Tell me about the country—it's very beautiful, isn't it?"

"Yes, very beautiful."

"And the people?"

"If you don't marry Sim Gage they'll tar and feather you. If you do, they'll back-bite and hate you. If you get in trouble they'll work their fingers to the bone to take care of you."

"There was another thing," she resumed irrelevantly, "I thought it was a *sacrifice*, my coming out here to work. I thought I ought to make it. You see, I'm the only one left of all my family. I couldn't count much anyway."

"Donna Quixote!" broke out Allen Barnes.

"Oh, I suppose," said she, smiling bitterly. "I suppose that, of course."

"This is a terrible thing! I don't believe I can make you change."

"No, I suppose not," said she. "My brother went to France, crippled as he was. Do you suppose my duty's going to frighten me? You were in the army?"

"Yes," said he. "Mustered out a major. Medical Corps. In over a year—I saw the last days—before Metz and the armistice. I'm a doctor, but they crowd me into the service again now, because they think I'll be safe and useful here. But from what you know about things going on in this country, you know there's danger for any big public work like that plant. Our country's not mopped up, yet—though it's going to be! There must be some reason for suspicion at Headquarters—I think we all might guess why from the doings of the last day or so in here."

"I'm glad," said she. "That makes me feel much better. I shall be sorry to have you go away. But you'll not be so far. And you were in the war?"

"A little." He laughed, and Mary Warren tried to laugh. Then, hands in pockets, and frowning, he left her, and walked apart in the yard for a time.

Sim Gage, his face puckered up, was wandering

aimlessly, shovel in hand, in the vicinity of the burned barn, engaged in burying his dead cattle. He had relapsed as to his clothing, and was clad once more in his ancient nether garments. His arms were bare, his brick-red shoulders showed above a collarless and ragged flannel shirt. His face, unreaped, was not lovable to look on. When Doctor Allen Barnes saw him, he walked away, his head forward and shaking from side to side. He did not want to talk with Sim Gage or any one else.

CHAPTER XIX

THE PLEDGE

Wid Gardner, by some miracle of self-confidence, did prove able to drive a car in some fashion, for he made the round trip to the dam in good enough time. But he had had his trip for nothing; for Doctor Barnes now made sudden and unexplained resolution not to remain longer at Sim Gage's ranch. After his departure in his own car, Wid Gardner approached Sim as he stood, hands in pockets, in his door yard.

"Well," said he. And Sim, in the succinct fashion of the land, replied likewise, "Well"; which left honors even conversationally.

"How's things down below?" asked Sim presently.

"Sort of uneasylike," replied Wid. "News had got down there that something's wrong. Company of soldiers is expected any day from Kansas. This here Doc Barnes is the main guy down there, a Major or something. They're watching the head engineer for the Company, I believe. No one knows who's who. A heap of things has happened that oughtn't to happen, but looks like Washington was getting on the game.

Emerson Hough

"Well, I got to go over home and look around," he concluded. "We've got to do some building before long—you got to get up another house and barn, and so have I."

"I don't see why," said Sim Gage bitterly. "I ain't got nothing to put into a barn, ner I ain't got no cows to feed no hay to neither. I could of sold the Government plenty hay this fall if I'd had any, but now how could I, without no horses and no money to get none? I'm run down mighty low, Wid, and that's the truth. Mrs. Jensen can't stay along here always, though Lord knows what we would a-done if she hadn't come now. One thing's sure—*She* ain't a-goin' to stay here lessen things straightens out. You know who I mean."

Wid nodded, his face grave under its grizzled stubble. "Yes," said he.

"Say," he added, suddenly. "You know that letter we got fer her? Now, if that girl that wrote it, that Annie Squires, could come out here and get into this here game, why, how would that be? You reckon she would?"

"Naw, she wouldn't come," said Sim Gage. "But, say, that reminds me—I never did tell *her* about that letter."

"Better take it in to her," said Wid, turning away.

He walked towards the gate. After Sim had seen him safely in the distance he went with laggard step toward the door of his own home.

Mary Warren was not asleep. It was her voice, not loud, which greeted his timid tapping at the half-burned door frame.

"Come in. Who is it?"

"It's me, ma'am," said he; and entered a little at a time.

He might have seen the faint color rise to her cheek as she drew herself up in bed, to talk with him. Her face, turned full toward him, was a thing upon which he could not gaze direct. It terrified him with its high born beauty, even as he now resolved to "look right into her eyes."

"You've not been in to see me, Mr. Gage," said she at length, bravely. "Why didn't you come? I get awfully lonesome."

"Is that so?" said he. "That's just the way I do."

"It's too bad, all this awful trouble," said she. "I've been what they call a Jonah, don't you think, Mr. Gage?"

"Oh, no, ma'am!"

"It was very noble of you—up there," she began, on another tack. "You saved my life. Not worth much."

She was smiling cheerily as she could. Sim Gage looked carefully at her face to see how much she knew.

"Doctor Barnes told me that that man, the one that took me away, was hurt by a tree; that you got there too late to save him. But to think, I'd have shot that man. I *did* try to shoot him, Mr. Gage!"

"Why, *did* you, ma'am?" said Sim Gage. "But then, it would of been a miracle if you had a-hit him, your eyes being poor, like. I reckon it's just as well you didn't."

"Won't you sit down?" She motioned her hand vaguely. "There's a box right there."

"How do you know, ma'am?"

"Oh, I know where everything is now. I'm going to learn all about this place. I can do all sorts of things after a while—cook and sweep and wash dishes and feed the chickens, and—oh, a lot of things." It was well enough that he did not see her face as she turned it away, anxious to be brave, not succeeding.

"That there looks, now, like you'd moved in," said Sim Gage. "Looks like you'd come to stay, as the feller says." He tried to laugh, but did not make much of it; nor did she.

"Oh, I forgot," he resumed suddenly, bethinking himself of the errand which had brought him hither. "I got a letter fer you, ma'am."

"A letter? Why, that's strange—I didn't know of any one—"

"Sure, it's fer you, ma'am. It's from Annie Squires."

"Annie! Oh! what does she say? Tell me!"

Sim had the letter opened now, his face puckered.

"Why, nothing very much, ma'am," said he. "I can't exactly see what it says—light's rather poor in here just now. But Wid, he read it. And she said it was all right with her, and that she was back in her little room again. I reckon it's the room where you both used to live?"

"She isn't married! What did she say?"

"No'm, not married. That's all off. Her feller throwed her down. But she says she wants you to write to her right away and tell her—now—tell her about things—you know—"

"What does she say?—Tell me *exactly* what she said."

"One thing-"—he plunged desperately—"she said she was sure you was happily married. And she wanted you to tell her all about your husband. But then, good God A'mighty! she didn't know!"

"Well," said Mary Warren, her blood high in her face, "I'll have to tell her all about that, won't I? I'll write to her at once."

"You'll write to her? What?"

—"And tell her how happy I am, how fortunate I've been. I'll tell her how you took me in even though I was blind; how you saved my life; how kind and gentle you've been all along, where you might have been so different! I'll tell her how fine and splendid it's been of you to take care of a sick, blind, helpless girl like me; and to—to—give her a man's protection."

He was speechless. She struggled on, red to the hair.

"You don't know women, how much they want a strong man to depend on, Mr. Gage; a man like you. Chivalrous? Why, yes, you've been all of that and more. I'll write to Annie and tell her that I'm very happy, and that I've got the very best—the very best—*husband*—in all the world. I'll tell her that? I'll say that—that my *husband*—"

He heard her sobbing. He could endure no more. Suddenly he reached out a hand and touched hers very gently.

"Don't, ma'am," said he. "Fer God's sake don't cry."

It was some time after that—neither could have told how long—that he managed to go on, his voice trembling. "Do you *mean* that, ma'am? Do you mean that, real and for sure? You wouldn't joke with a feller like over a thing like that?"

"I'm not joking," said she. "My God! Yes, I mean it."

His hand, broad, coarse, thick-fingered, patted hers a hundred times as it lay upon the blankets, until she got nervous over his nervousness.

"It's too bad I ain't got no linen sheets," said he suddenly. "But them blankets is eleven-pound four-points, at that. Of course, you know, ma'am," said he, turning towards her, his voice broken, his own vague eyes wet all at once, "you *do* know I only want to do whatever is the best fer you, now don't you?"

"Of course. I do believe that."

"And it *couldn't* run on this way very long. Even Mrs. Jensen wouldn't stay very long. Nobody would come. They'd like enough tar and feather you and me, people in this Valley, if we *wasn't* married. And yet you say you've got no place to go back to. You talk like you was going to tell her, Annie Squires, that you was married. She supposes it *now*, like enough. If there was any way, shape or manner you could get out of marrying me, why of course I wouldn't let you. But what else is there we can do?"

"Some time it would come to that," said Mary Warren, trying to dry her eyes. "It's the only way fair to us both."

"Putting it that way, now!" said Sim Gage, wisely, "putting it *that* way, I'm here to say I ain't a-scared to do *nothing* that's best fer you. And I want to say right now and here, I didn't mean no harm to you. I swear, neither Wid nor me ever did dream that a woman like you'd come out here—I never knew such a woman as you was in the whole *world*. I just didn't *know*—that was all. You won't blame me too much fer gettin' you here into this awful place, will you?"

"No, I understand," said she gently. "I think I know more about you now than I did at first."

"I ain't much to know, ma'am. But you—why, if I studied all my life, I wouldn't begin to know you hardly none at all." She could not doubt the reverence of his tone, could not miss the sweetness of it. No; nor the sureness of the anchorage that it offered.

"If this is the way you want it," he went on, "I'll promise you never to bother you, no way in the world. I'll be on the square with you, so help me God! I'll take care of you the best way I can, so help me God! I'll work, I'll do the best I can fer you; so help me God!"

"And I promise to be faithful to you, Sim Gage," said she, using his common name unconsciously now. "I swear to be true to you, and to help you all I can, every way I can. I'll do my duty—my *duty*. Do you understand?"

She was pale again by now, and trembling all through her body. Her hands trembled on the blankets. It was a woman's pledge she was giving. And no man's hands or lips touched hers. It was terrible. It was terrible, but had it not been thus she could not have endured it. She must wait.

"I understand a heap of things I can't say nothing about, ma'am," said Sim Gage. "I'm that sort of man, that can't talk very much. But I understand a heap more'n I'm going to try to say. Sometimes it's that way."

"Sometimes it's that way," said Mary Warren, "yes. Then that's our promise!"

"Yes, it's a promise, so fer as I'm concerned," said Sim Gage.

"Then there isn't much left," said she after a time, her throat fluttering. She patted his great hand bravely as it lay upon the blankets, afraid to touch her own. "The rest will be—I think the rest will be easier than this."

"A heap easier," said he. "I dreaded this more'n I would to be shot. I wanted to do the right thing, but I didn't know what *was* right. Won't you *say* you knowed I wanted to do right all the time, and that I just didn't *know*? Can't you see that I'm sorry I made you marry me, because it wasn't no way right? Can't you see it's only just to get you some sort of a home?"

"I said *yes*, Sim Gage," said Mary Warren.

"Yes?" A certain exultation was in his voice. "To *me*? All my life everything's been *no* to me!"

She laid her hand on his, pity rising in her own heart. "I'll take care of you," said she.

"I was scared from the first of any woman coming out here," said Sim Gage truthfully. "But whatever you say goes. But our gettin' married! When?"

"The sooner the better."

They both nodded assent to this, neither seeing the other, for he dared not look her way now.

"I'll go down to the Company dam right soon," said he. "Ministers comes in down there sometimes. Up here we ain't got no church. I ain't been to church—well, scarcely in my whole life, but sure not fer ten years. You want to have it over with, don't you, ma'am?"

"Yes."

"That's just the way I feel! It may take a week or so before I can get any minister up here. But I hope you ain't a-goin' to change?"

"I don't change," said Mary Warren. "If I promise, I promise. I have said—yes."

"How is your bad knee?" she asked after a time, with an attempt to be of service to him. "You've never told me."

"Swoll up twict as big as it ought to be, ma'am. But how come you to think of that? *You* mustn't mind about me. You mustn't never think of me a-tall."

"Now," he continued a little later, the place seeming insufferably small to him all at once, "I think I've got to get out in the air." He pushed over his box seat with much clatter as he rose, agony in every fiber of his soul.

"I suppose you could kiss me," said Mary Warren, hesitatingly. "It's—usual." She tried to smile as she turned her face toward him. It was a piteous thing, a terrible thing.

"No, ma'am, thank you. I don't think I will, now, but I thank you just the same. You see, this ain't a usual case."

"Good-by!" said Mary Warren to him with a sudden wondering joy. "Go out and look at the mountains for me. Look out over the valley. I wish I could see them. And you'll come in and see me when you can, won't you?"

She was talking to the empty room, weeping to an empty world.

CHAPTER XX

MAJOR ALLEN BARNES, M.D., PH.D.— AND SIM GAGE

Sim Gage's reflections kept him wandering about for the space of an hour or two in the open air.

"I'll tell you," said he, after a time to Mrs. Jensen, who once more had cared for their household needs, "I reckon I'll go on down to the dam, on the mail coach this evening. You go in and tell her, won't you? Say I can't noways get back before to-morrow. I got to see about one thing and another. She'll understand."

Therefore, when the mail wagon came down the valley an hour later, Sim Gage was waiting for it at the end of his own lane. He had meantime arrayed himself cap-a-pie in all the new apparel he recently had purchased, so that he stood now reeking of discomfort, in his new hat, his new shoes, his tight collar. Evidently something of formal character was in his plans.

It was well toward midnight when the leisurely mail wagon arrived at the end of its semi-weekly round and put up at the Company works. At that hour the company doctor was not visible, so Sim found quarters elsewhere. It was a due time after breakfast on the following morning before he ventured to the doctor's office.

Doctor Barnes himself was engaged in bringing up his correspondence. He was his own typist, and at the time was engaged in picking out letter after letter upon a small typewriter with which he had not yet acquired familiarity. He was occupied with two letters of importance. One was going to a certain medical authority of the University from which he himself had received his degree. It contained a certain hypothetical question regarding diseases of the eye, upon which he himself at the time did not feel competent to pass.

The second letter was one to his new Chief, an officer of the reclamation engineers, at Washington. He wore again to-day the uniform of a Major of the Army. The wheels of officialdom were revolving. The public quality of this enterprise was well understood. That lawless elements were afoot in that region was a fact also well recognized. To have this dam go out now would be an injury to the peace measures of the country. Soldiers were coming to protect it, and the soldiers must have a commander. In the hurried times of war, when there was not opportunity always for exactness, majors were made overnight when needful out of such material as the Government found at hand. It might have used worse than that of Allen Barnes to-day and here.

"Oh, there *you* are," said he at length, turning around and finding Sim Gage standing in the door. "What brought you down here? Anything gone wrong?"

"Well, I ain't sure, Doc," said Sim Gage, "but like enough. One thing, my knee hurts me considerable." In reality he was sparring for time. "But you're dressed up for a soldier?"

"Yes. Sit down there on the operating chair," said Doctor Barnes, tersely. "We'll look it over. Anything happen to it?"

"Why, nothing much," said Sim. "I hurt it a little when I was getting in the mail wagon yesterday evening—busted her open. So last night, when I was going to bed, I took a needle and thread and sewed her up again."

"What's that? Sewed it up?"

"Yes, I got a needle and some black patent thread. Do you reckon she'll hold all right now, Doctor?"

Doctor Barnes was standing, scissors in hand, about to rip open the trouser leg.

"No, you don't!" said Sim. "Them's my best pants. You just go easy now, and don't you cut them none a-tall. Wait till I take 'em off."

The doctor bent over the wounded member. "You put in a regular button-hole stitch," said he, grinning, "didn't you? About three stitches would have been plenty. You put in about two dozen—and with black thread! Like enough poisoned again."

"Well," said Sim, "I didn't want to take no chances of her breaking open again."

The doctor was busy, removing the stitches, and with no gentle hand this time made the proper surgical suture. "Leave it alone this way," said he, "and mind what I tell you. Seems like you can't kill a man out in this country. You can do things in surgery out here that you wouldn't dare tackle back in France, or in the States. I suppose, maybe, I could cut your head off, for instance."

"I wish't you would," said Sim Gage. "She bothers me sometimes."

After a pause he continued, "I been thinking over a heap of things. You see, I'm busted about flat. If I could go on and put up some hay, way prices is, I could make some money this fall, but them damn robbers has cleaned me, and I can't start with nothing. And I ain't got nothing. So there I am."

He vouchsafed nothing more, but had already said so much that Doctor Barnes sat regarding him quietly.

"Gage," said he after a time, "things might be better in this valley. I know that you'll stick with the Government. Now, listen. I'm going to have practical command here from this time on. This is under Army control. I'm going to run a telephone wire up the valley as far as your settlement. I'll appoint you a government special scout, to watch that road. If these ruffians are in this valley again we want to catch them."

"You think I could be any use that way, Doc?" said Sim.

"Yes, I've got to have some of the settlers with me that I can depend on, besides the regular detail ordered in here."

"Would I be some sort of soldier, too, like?" demanded Sim Gage. "I tried to get in. They wouldn't take me. I'm— I'm past forty-five."

"You'd be under orders just like a soldier."

"Would I have any sort of uniform, like, now?"

Doctor Barnes sat thinking for some time. "No," said he. "You have to pass an examination before you really get into the Army; and you're over age, you and Wid, both of you. But I'll tell you—I'll give you a hat—you shall have a hat with a cord on it, so you'll be like a soldier. We'll have a green service cord on it,—say green with a little white in it, Sim Gage? Don't that make you feel as if you were in a uniform?"

"Now that'd sure be fine, Doc, a hat like that," said Sim. "I sure would like that. And I certainly would try to do what was right."

Doctor Barnes, still sitting before the little white operating table where his surgical instruments lay, was looking thoughtful. "In all likelihood I shall have to put a corporal and four men up at your place. That means they'll have to have a house. I can commandeer some of the teams down here, and some men, and they'll all throw in together and help you build an extra cabin. You and they can live in that, I suppose?"

"I reckon we could," said Sim Gage. "That'd be fine, wouldn't it?"

"And as those men would need horses for their own transport, they'd need hay. We'd pay you for hay. I don't see why we couldn't leave one wagon and a team at least up there, to get in supplies. That would help you in getting things started around on your place again, wouldn't it?"

"Would it, Doc?" said Sim Gage, brightening immensely. "It would raise a *load* offen me, that's what it would! Right now, especial." He cleared his throat.

"That there brings me right around to what I come down here to talk about," said he with sudden resolution. "For instance, there was a letter come to her up there—from back where she lived—from Annie Squires. So her and me got to talking over that letter, you see."

"What did Annie Squires say, if it's any of my business?" said the Doctor, looking at him steadily.

"Well, I was just talking things over, that way, and we allowed that maybe Annie Squires could come out here—after—well, after the *wedding*, you see."

It was out! Sim Gage wiped off his brow.

"The wedding?"

"Why, one thing and other, her and me got to talking things over. Things couldn't run on; so we—we fixed it up."

"Gage," said Doctor Barnes suddenly, "I've got to talk to you."

"Well, all right, all right, Doc. That'll be all right. I wish't you would."

"See here, man. Don't you realize what that woman is? She's too good for men like you and me."

"Yes, Doc. But I wouldn't never raise hand nor voice to her, the least way in the world. I allowed she could live along as my housekeeper, but seems not. You can shoot me, Doc, if you don't think I'm a-doing the right thing by her in every way, shape and manner."

"She's too *good*—it's an impossible thing."

Sim Gage's face was lifted, seriously. "Doc, you know mighty well that's true, and so do I—she's plumb too good for me. But it ain't me done all the thinking."

"Didn't you ask her about it?"

"It kind of come around."

Doctor Barnes rose and paced rapidly up and down within the narrow confines of his office. "You *do* love her, don't you?"

Sim Gage for the first time in his life felt the secret quick of his simple, sensitive soul cut open and exposed to gaze. Not even the medical man before him could fail of sudden pity at witnessing what was written on his face—all the dignity, the simplicity, the reticence, all the bashfulness of a man brought up helplessly against the knife. He could not—or perhaps would not—answer such a question even from the man before him, whom he suddenly had come to trust and respect as a being superior to himself.

But Allen Barnes was the pitiless surgeon now. "I don't care a damn about you, of course, Gage. You're not fit for her to wipe her shoes on, and you know it. But *she* can't see it and doesn't know it. If she could see you—what do you suppose she'd think? Gage—*she mustn't ever know*!"

Sim Gage looked at him quietly. "Every one of them words you said to me, Doc, is plumb true, and it ain't enough. I told her my own self, that first day, and since then, it was a blessing she was blind. But look-a-here, I reckon you don't understand how things is. You say you're going to build a house up there, and help me get a start. That's fine. Because hers is the other one, my old house. I wish't I could get some sheets and pillow cases down here while I'm right here now—I'd like to fix her up in there better'n what she is. I'd even like to have a tablecloth, like. But you understand, that's for *her*, not me.

That's *her* house, and not mine. She can't see. It's a God's blessing she can't. And what you said is so—she mustn't *ever* know, not now ner no time, what—Sim Gage really is."

Doctor Barnes' voice was out of control. He turned once more to this newly revealed Sim Gage, a man whom he had not hitherto understood.

"Marriage means all sorts of things. It covers up things, begins things, ends things. That's true."

"It ends things for her, Doc—it don't begin nothing fer me, you understand. It is, but it isn't. I'd never step a foot across that door sill, night or day—you understand that, don't you? You didn't think *that* for one minute, did you? You didn't think I was so low-down I couldn't understand a thing like *that*, did you? It's because she's blind and don't know the truth; and because she's plumb up against it. That's why."

"Oh, damn you!" said Doctor Barnes savagely. "You understand me better than I did you. Yes—it's the only way."

"It sure is funny how funny things get mixed up some-times, ain't it, Doc?" remarked Sim Gage. "But now, part of my coming down here was about a minister."

"Well," said Doctor Barnes, desperately, feeling that he was party to a crime, "it's priest day next Sunday. We have five or six different sorts of priests and ministers that come in here once a month, and they all come the same Sunday, so they can watch each other—every fellow is afraid the other fellow will get some souls saved the wrong way if he isn't there on the job too. Listen, Gage— I'll bring one of these chaps—Church of England man, I reckon, for he hasn't got much to do down here—up to your ranch next Sunday morning. We've got to get this over with, or we'll all be crazy—I will, anyhow. When I show up, you two be ready to be married.

"Does that go, Sim Gage?" he concluded, looking into the haggard and stubbly face of the squalid-figured man before him.

"It goes," said Sim Gage.

CHAPTER XXI

WITH THIS RING

It was the Sabbath, and the summer sun was casting its southering light even with the eaves of Sim Gage's half-ruined house. It was high noon.

High noon for a wedding. But this was a wedding of no pomp or splendor. No bell summoned any hither. There was no organ peal, nor maids with flowers and serious faces to wait upon the bride; no processional; no aisles fenced off with bride's ribbon; no audience to crane. In the little room stood only a surpliced priest of the Church of England. The witnesses were Nels Jensen and Karen, his wife, back of whom was Wid Gardner, near to him Doctor Barnes. Those made all present, now at high noon. And Sim Gage, trembling very much, stood at the side of a bed where Mary Warren lay propped up in the blankets to speak her wedding words.

"Dearly beloved, we are gathered together," began the holy man; and so the ceremony went on in the lofty words which some inspired man has written for the most solemn of all ceremonies.

"Dearly beloved . . . Dearly beloved!

"Who giveth this woman in marriage?" went on the deep voice of the minister at last, himself strangely moved. Indeed, it had only been after a long consultation with Doctor Barnes that he had been willing to go on with this ceremony. "Who giveth this woman in marriage?"

Sim Gage had no idea of the marriage ceremony of the Church of England or of any other church. As for Doctor Barnes, the matter had been too serious for him to plan details. But now, seeing the exigency, he stepped forward quickly and offered himself as the next friend of Mary Warren, orphaned and friendless.

The ceremony went on until it came to that portion having to do with the ring—for this was Church of England, and full ceremony was used.

"With what token?" began the voice of the man of God. Sim Gage's eyes were raised in sudden question. Neither he nor Doctor Barnes, quasi best man, had ever given thought to this matter of the ring. But again Doctor Barnes was able to serve. Quickly he slipped off the seal ring from his own finger and passed it to Sim Gage. The gentle hand of the churchly official showed him how to place it upon the finger of Mary Warren, who raised her own hand in his.

So finally it was over, and those solemn ofttimes mocking words were said: "Whom God hath joined together let no man put asunder!" And then the surpliced minister of the church prayed God to witness and to bless this wedding of this man and this woman; that prayer which sometimes is a mockery before God.

There was at least one woman to weep, and Karen Jensen wept. She left the place and ran out the door into the open sunlight, followed soon by her husband and Wid Gardner.

Sim stood for a moment undecided. He did not stoop even now to greet his wife with that salutation usual at this moment. The group at the bedside broke apart. The bride, white as a ghost, dropped back on her blankets. It was a godsend that at this instant Tim, the little dog, broke in the door, barking and overjoyed, welcoming the company, and making a diversion, which saved the moment.

Sim bent and picked up the little animal.

"He's glad," said he. With a vague and gentle pat of the blankets in the general direction of Mary Gage, his wife, he turned, head bent, and tip-toed out into the sunlight.

Karen Jensen interrupted any conversation, having dried her tears. "Come on back in five or ten minutes," she said. "I'll have the wedding breakfast ready. I've baked a cake."

When they had eaten of the cake, which they all agreed was marvelous, the minister gladly repacked his vestments in his traveling bag preparatory to his journey back with Doctor Barnes. He turned, after a gentle handshake, saying: "Good-by, Mrs. Gage." Sim Gage, bridegroom, suddenly flushed dark under his brick-red skin at hearing these words.

Karen Jensen finished her labors attendant upon the wedding breakfast, and made ready for her own departure. Wid Gardner likewise found reason for a visit to his own homestead. Mary Gage was left alone, and ah! how white a bride she was.

Sim Gage stood outside his own door, looking at the departing figures of Nels and Karen Jensen crossing the meadow toward their home; turning to catch sight of Wid, though the latter was no longer visible. In desperation he looked upon a sky, a landscape, which for the first time in all his life seemed to him ominous. For the first time in his life Sim Gage, sagebrusher, man of the outlands, felt himself alone.

CHAPTER XXII

MRS. GAGE

Ten days after the wedding at Sim Gage's ranch, the mistress of that establishment, sitting alone, heard the excited barking of the little dog in the yard, and the sound of a motor passing through the gate. Instinctively she turned toward the window, as the car stopped. She heard a voice certainly familiar and welcome as well.

"Well, how do you do this morning? And how is every-thing?" It was Doctor Barnes saluting her. He came up to the unscreened window where she stood, and stood there for a time with one or other like remark, before he passed around the house and came in at the door.

"You're alone?" said he.

"Why, yes, Mr. Gage has gone over to Mr. Gardner's. They're getting out some building material."

"Mrs. Jensen gone home too?"

"Oh, yes. I'm mistress of the house. I wonder how it looks?"

"You'd be surprised!" said Doctor Barnes, cryptically.

He sat down, hat on knee, silent for a time, musing, looking at the pathetically beautiful face of the woman before him.

"You'd never get any of your own philosophy second hand," said he at length.

She smiled faintly. "No, I'm not given to hysteria, if that's what you want to say."

"Women do strange things. But not your sort—no."

"You don't call this strange—what I've done?"

"No, it was inevitable—for you."

She seated herself on the bed, hands in lap. How fine it was to hear a voice like his, to meet a brain like his, keen, broad, educated, here in this place!

"No, you've not read books to get your own philosophy of life. So you can reason about things."

"I don't think you're very merciful to me," said Mary Gage.

"Why, yes. God has shut your eyes to our new and distracted world. This new world?—you ought to be thankful that you cannot see it. I wish I did not have to see it. But you don't want to hear me talk? You don't want philosophizing? I'm afraid I'm not very happy in my philosophy after all."

He rose, hands in pockets, and tried to pace up and down the narrow little room.

"Don't move the chairs, please," said she. "I know where

they all are now."

He laughed, and again seated himself.

"You know why I've come up? I suppose Sim has told you that we're going to have a soldier post here in your yard?"

"Yes, I was glad of that—it seemed like company."

"It will make you feel a great deal safer. And did your husband tell you that I'm going to be a person of conse-quence now? I'm a Major again, not just plain doctor."

"There must have been reason. The Government is alarmed?"

"Yes. Our chief engineer Waldhorn—well, he's still a German-American, to put it mildly. Told me three times he had bought fifteen thousand dollars' worth of Liberty Bonds. I fear German-Americans buying bonds! And I know Waldhorn's a red Socialist—Bolshevik—if they make them."

"If they doubt him, why don't they remove him?"

"If he knew he was suspected—bang! up might go the dam. I hardly need say that you're to keep absolutely quiet about all this. I tell you because I can trust you. As for me, I'm a pretty busy little doctor right now—cook and the captain bold, and the mate of the Nancy brig. Within a week we'll have a telephone line strung up here. My men will be here to-morrow morning to begin work with the building. Suppose I had a chance to get you a woman companion out here. Would you be glad?"

"Please don't jest."

"Well, I've sent for your old friend, Annie Squires!" said she.

"Annie! Why—no! She wrote to me—"

"Yes, I know. And I wired her. She's coming on out. She has left Cleveland to-day. I'm going to meet her myself at the station, and bring her out. If she can cook she can get on the pay roll. Odd, how you two came to meet—"

—"Why, cook?—work?—of course Annie could! Of course—she'd be happy. She's alone, like myself—but not married."

"And she'll find you happily married, as she said in the letter. You are happily married? I beg your pardon, but he's—he's been considerate?"

"More. Chivalrous. He wrote me at first that I might expect to find a 'chivalrous ranchman, of ample means.' That's true, isn't it?"

For a long time he sat silent. "Yes," said he, "I believe I'll say that's true!

"You think this Annie person can cook?" he added.

"Of course! Oh, do you suppose she *really* is coming?"

"If I'm going to be a Major again I'm going to have plenary powers!"

"Well, Major," she smiled slowly at last, "you seem to have a way of ordering things! Tell me about yourself. I mean about you, yourself, personally. I've no way of getting the commonest notion of people any more. It's very, very hard."

He went on quickly, warned by the quiver of her lips. "All right," said he. "I'll fill out my questionnaire. This registrant is Barnes, Major Allen, age thirty-one, Medical Corps, assigned to special service Engineers' detail, power dam of the Transcontinental Light and Power Company; graduate of Johns Hopkins; height eleven feet five inches—you see, I've felt all of that tall ever since I got to be a Major. Eyes, gray; hair, sandy. Mobility of chest, four and a half inches. Features, clean-cut and classical. Good muscular development. Stature, erect and robust. Blood pressure, 128. Pulse, full and regular. Habits, very bad. Three freckles on left hand."

"Dear me!" she said, smiling in spite of all, and thus evincing definitely a certain dimple in her left cheek which now he noticed in confirmation of his earlier suspicion. "Bad habits?"

"Well, I smoke, and everything, you know. Majors have to be regular fellows."

"You're rather pleasant to talk to!"

"Very!"

"You know, you seem rather a manny sort of man to me—do you know what I mean?"

"I'm glad you think so."

"And I owe you a great deal, Major—or—Doctor."

"Please don't make yourself a continuous trial balance all the time. Don't be thinking of sacrifices and duties—isn't there some way we can plan just to get some plain joy out of life as we go along? I believe that's my religion, if I've got any."

"I often wish I could see the mountains," said she, vaguely.

He rose suddenly. "Come with me, then! I'll take you out into the sunlight. I'll tell you all about the mountains. I'll show you something of the world. I couldn't live out here if it wasn't for the sheer beauty of this country. It's wonderful—it's so beautiful."

"What was it you put down by the door as you came in?" she asked of him curiously.

He turned to her with like curiosity. "How do you know?" said he. "Are you shamming? That was my fishing rod and my fish basket I put down there; but I didn't think you'd know anything about it."

"I'm beginning to have abnormally acute senses, I suppose. That's necessity."

"Nature is a very wonderful old girl," said Doctor Barnes. "But come now, I'm going to ask you to go down to the stream with me and have a try about those grayling. I told Sim Gage I was going to some time, and this will be about my last chance. If we have any luck I'll show you there's something in this country beside bacon and beans."

"I'd love to," said Mary, eagerly. "Why, that'll be fine!"

She rose and went directly to her sunbonnet, which hung upon a nail in the wall—the sunbonnet which Mrs. Jensen had fashioned for her and promised her to be of much utility. But she stumbled as she turned.

"I can tell where the window is, and the door," said she, breathlessly. "I miss the reading most of all—and friends. I can't see my friends."

"Well, your friends can see you, and that's much of a consolation," said Major Allen Barnes. "I stare shamelessly, and you never know. Come along now, and we'll go fishing and have a bully time."

He took her arm and led her out into the brilliant sunlight, across the yard, across the little rivulet which made down from the spring through the thin fringe of willows, out across the edge of the hay lands to the high, unbroken ridges covered with stubby sage brush which lay beyond between the meadows and the river. The little Airedale, Tim, went with them, bounding and barking, running in a hundred circles, finding a score of things of which he tried to tell them.

It was no long walk, no more than a half mile in all, but he stopped frequently to tell her about the country, to explain how blue the sky was with its small white clouds, how inviting the long line of the mountains across the valley, how sweet the green of the meadows and the blue-gray of the sage. She was eager as a child.

"The river is that way," said she after a while.

"How do you know?"

"I can feel it—I can feel the water. It's cooler along the stream, I suppose."

"Well, you've guessed it right," said he. "There's going to be quite a world for you, so don't be discouraged. Yes, that's the river just ahead of us—my word! it's the prettiest river that ever lay out of doors in all the world."

"I can hear it," said she, pausing and listening.

"Yes—that's where it breaks over a little gravel bed up

yonder, fifty yards from us. And here, right in front of us, we are at the corner of the bend, and it's deep—twelve feet deep at least. And then it bends off to the left again, with willows on this side and grassy banks on the other side. And the water is as clear as the air itself. You can see straight down into it.

"And look—look!" he said, as he stood with her, catching her by the wrist at the brink. "Down in this hole, right before us, there's more than a million grayling—there's four hundred billion of them right down in there, and every one of them is eight feet long! Sim Gage was right—I'll bet some of them do weigh three pounds. It must be right in the height of the summer run. What a wonderful country!"

"Here, now," he went on, "sit right here on the grass on my coat. Lie down, you Tim! That's right, boy—I can't stand this any longer—I've got to get busy."

Hurriedly he went about jointing his rod, putting on the reel, threading the line through the guides, while she sat, her hand on the dog's shaggy head.

She felt something placed in her lap. "That's my fly hook," said he. "I'm asking you to look at it. Hundreds of them, and no two alike, and all the nineteen colors of the rainbow. I'm going to put on this one—see—it's dressed long and light, to look like a grasshopper. Queen of the Waters, they call it."

"Listen!" said she suddenly, raising a finger. "What was that?"

"What was it? Nothing in the world except the biggest grayling I ever saw! He broke up there just at the head of the pool where the water runs deep under the willows, just off the bar. If I can get this fly just above him—wait now—sit perfectly still where you are."

He passed up the stream a few paces and began to cast, measuring the distance with the fly still in the air. She could hear the faint whistle of the line, and some idea of what he was doing came to her. And then she heard an exclamation, synchronous with a splash in the pool.

"Got him!" said he. "And he's one sockdollager, believe me! We've got hold of old Grandpa Grayling now—and if things just hold—"

"Here," said he after a while. She felt the rod placed in her hand, felt a strenuous tugging and pulling that almost wrenched it away.

"Hold tight!" said he. "Take the line in your left hand, this way. Now, if he pulls hard, ease off. Pull in when you can—not too hard—he's got a tender mouth. Let him run! I want you to see what fun it is. Can't you see him out there now, jumping?"

Tim, eager for any sport, sprang up and began to bark excitedly. Her lips parted, her eyes shining, sightless as they were, Mary faced toward the splashing which she heard. She spoke low, in a whisper, as though afraid of alarming the fish. "Where is he?" she said. "Where did he go?"

"He's out there," responded her companion, chuckling. "He's getting rattled now. Don't hold him too tight—that's the idea—work him along easy now. Now shorten up your line a little bit, and sit right where you are. I'm going to net him. Lift the tip of the rod a little, please, and bring him in toward you."

She obeyed as best she could. Suddenly she heard a splash, and felt a flopping object placed, net and all, directly in her lap. With eagerness she caught it in her hands, meeting Tim's towsley head, engaged in the same errand, and much disposed to claim the fish as all his own.

"There's Grandpa!" said Doctor Barnes. "I've lost my bet to Sim Gage—that fellow will go over three pounds. I didn't know there was such a grayling in the world."

"And now tell me," said he, as she felt him lift the fish from her lap, and with woman's instinct brushed away the drops of water from her frock, "isn't life worth living after all, when you have a day like this, and a sky such as we have, and sport like this?"

He looked at her face. There was less droop to the corners of her mouth than he ever had seen. There was a certain light that came to her features which he had not yet recognized. She drew a long breath and sighed as she dropped her hands into her lap. "Do you suppose we could get another one?" said she.

He laughed exultantly. "I should say we could! Just sit still where you are, and we'll load up again."

As a matter of fact the grayling were rising freely, and in a moment or so he had fastened another which he added to the one in the basket. This one she insisted that he land alone, so that he might have all the sport. And thus, he generously sharing with her, they placed six of the splendid fish in the basket, and he declared they had enough for the time.

"Come," said he, "we'll go back now."

She reached out a hand. "I want to carry the fish," said she. "Let me, please. I want to do something."

He passed the basket strap over her shoulder for her, Tim following on behind, panting, as guardian of the spoils. "You're a good sport," said Major Barnes. "One of the best I ever saw, and I saw a lot of them over there."

She was stumbling forward through the sage as best she might, tripping here and there, sweeping her skirts now and again from the ragged branches which caught against them. He took her hand in his to lead her. It lay light and warm in his own—astonishingly light and warm, as suddenly he realized. She had pushed the sunbonnet back from her forehead as she would have done had she been desirous of seeing better. He noted the color of her cheeks, the regularity of her features, the evenness of her dark brows, the wholly pleasing contour of her figure, as she stumbled bravely along at his side.

"You're fine!" he repeated, suddenly. "You're fine! I expect to see you live to bless the day you came here. I expect to hear you say yet that you're *glad* you're alive— not alive just because it was your duty to live. Don't talk to me any more about duty."

He was striding along excitedly. "Not too fast!" she panted, holding fast to his hand.

And so they came presently to the cabin door again, and saw Sim Gage perched high on a load of logs, coming down the lane.

"I'm going to put the new cabin for the men right over there," said Doctor Barnes. "And when Annie Squires comes—why, we're going to have the grandest little ranch here you ever saw. And, of course, I can telephone up every once in a while."

"Telephone?" said she vaguely. "Then you won't be coming up yourself?"

CHAPTER XXIII

THE OUTLOOK

Doctor Barnes was making ready to depart when Sim Gage came in at the gate with his load of logs. They exchanged greetings, Sim regarding his visitor rather closely.

"We've just got back from fishing," said Doctor Barnes.

"Yes, I seen you both, down in the medders."

"We had one grand time, brother. Look here." He opened the lid of his basket.

"All right," said Sim. "We'll cook 'em for supper. Some folks like 'em. There's need for about everything we can get. I reckon God's forgot us all right."

"Cheer up!" rejoined his guest. "I was just thinking God was in His heaven to-day. Well, thank you, old man, for that fishing. That's the finest grayling water in the whole world. I've lost my bet with you. May I come up again some time?"

"Yes," said Sim Sage, "sometimes,—when you know I'm around. Come again," he added, somewhat formally, as they shook hands. "I'll be around."

He turned toward his house as soon as he saw the car well off in the lane. He found his wife sitting with her face turned toward the window.

"He's just about going around the corner now," said she, following the sound of the car. And then, presently, "And how are you, sir? You've been gone a long while."

Sim had seated himself awkwardly on a chair, his hat on his knee. "Have a good time down in the medder?" he asked presently. "He told me you was fishing."

"Oh, yes, and we caught some whoppers too. They'll be good to eat, I'm sure."

"Yes, I expect you'll like them." He seemed for some reason less than ordinarily loquacious, and suddenly she felt it.

"Tell me," said she, turning squarely towards him with a summoning of her own courage. "Why are you away all the time? It's been more than a week, and I've hardly seen you. You're away all the time. Am I doing wrong in any way?"

"Why, no."

"I don't mean to cry—it's just because I'm not used to things yet. It's hard to be blind. But—I meant all I said— then. Don't you believe me?"

"I know you did," said he, simply. But still the awkward silence, and still her attempt to set things more at ease.

"Why don't you come over here close to me?" said she,

with an attempt dutiful at least. "How can I tell anything about you? You've never even touched me yet, nor I you. You've never even—I've never had any real notion of how you look, what you are like. I never saw your picture. It was an awful thing of me to do."

"Are you sorry?"

"But any woman wants to see her husband, to know what he is, what he looks like. I can't tell you how I wonder. And I don't seem to know—and can't learn. Tell me *about* yourself, won't you? What sort of looking man are you? What are you like?"

"I ain't like nothing much," said Sim Gage. "I ain't much for looks. Of course, I suppose women do kind of want to know what men folks is like, that way. I hadn't thought of that, me being so busy—and me being so pleased just to look at you, and not even thinking of your looking at me." He struggled in saying these words, so brave for Sim Gage to venture.

"Yes? Can't you go on?"

"I ain't so tall as some, but I'm rather broad out, and right strong at that. My eyes is sort of dark, like, with long lashes, now, and I got dark hair, in a way of speaking— and I got good features. I dunno as I can say much more." Surely he had been guilty of falsehood enough for one effort. But he did not know he lied, so eager was he to have favor in her eyes.

"That's fine!" said she. "I knew all along you were a fine-looking man—the Western type. We women all admire it, don't you know? And I'd like to see you in the Western dress too. I always liked that. But, tell me, what can you do? What do you do? Do you read out here much? Do you have anything in the way of music? I used to play the piano a little."

Sim moved about awkwardly on his chair. "I ain't got around to getting another pianny since I moved in here. Maybe we can, some day, after the hay gets turned. I used to play the fiddle some, but I ain't got no fiddle now, neither. Some play the fiddle better'n what I do. A mouth harp's a good thing when you're alone a good deal. Most any one can play a mouth harp some. Lots of fellers do out here, nights, of winters."

"Is there anything else you can do?" she asked, bravely, now. The utter bleak barrenness of the man and his life came home to her, struggling with her gratitude, her sense of duty.

He thought for a time before he spoke. "Why, yes, several things, and I'm sorry you can't see them things, too. For instance, I can tie a strong string around my arm, and bust it, just doubling up my muscle. I'm right strong."

"That's fine!" said she. "Isn't it odd? What else, then?" She smiled so bravely that he did not suspect. "Mayn't I feel the muscle on your arm?"

Hesitatingly, groping, she did put out her hand. By chance, as he shifted back, afraid of her hand, it touched the coarse fabric of his shirt sleeve. Had it fallen further she might have felt his arm, bare; might have discovered the sleeve itself to be ragged and fringed with long-continued use. But she did not know.

"Oh, you're just in your working clothes, aren't you?" she said. "So this is the West I used to read about," she said musing. "Everything Western—even the way you talk. Not like the people back East that I used to know. Is every one out here like you?"

"No, not exactly, maybe," said he. "Like I said, you'd get tired of looking at me if that's all there was to do."

She broke out into laughter, wholly hysterical, which he did not in the least understand. He knew the tragedy of her blindness, but did not know that he himself was tragic.

"You are odd," said she. "You've made me laugh." She both laughed and wept.

"You see, it's this way," he went on eagerly. "It's all right in the summer time, when you can get out of doors, and the weather is pleasant, like it is now. But in the winter time—*that's* when it gets lonesome! The snow'll be eight feet deep all around here. We have to go on snow shoes all the winter through. Now, if we was shut in here alone together—or if you was shut in here all by yourself, and still lonesomer, me being over in the other house mostly—the evenings would seem awful long. They always used to, to me."

She could not answer at all. A terrible picture was coming before her. He struggled on.

"If that Annie Squires girl came out here, she'd be a lot of help. But how can you tell whether she'd stay all winter? That's the trouble with women folks—you can't tell what they'll do. She wouldn't want to stay here long unless she was settled down some way, would she? She ain't married, like you, ma'am. She might get restless, like enough, wouldn't she?"

"I don't know," said Mary Gage, suddenly turning away. She felt a vast cloud settling down upon her. Ten days? She had been married ten days! What would ten years mean?

"I wish I didn't have to think at all," said she, her lips trembling.

"So do I, ma'am," said Sim Gage to his lawful wedded wife with engaging candor. "I sure do wish that."

CHAPTER XXIV

ANNIE MOVES IN

The hum of a motor at the gate brought Mary Gage to the window once more, the third morning after Doctor Barnes' visit. It was Doctor Barnes now, she knew. She could not see that he now helped out of the car a passenger who looked about her curiously, more especially at the figure of Sim Gage who, hands in pockets, stood gazing at them as they drove into the yard.

"Listen," said Doctor Barnes under his breath to the young woman, "that's the man—that's Sim Gage. Don't show surprise, and don't talk. Remember what I've told you. For God's sake, play the game!"

Sim Gage slowly approached the car, and the doctor accosted him. "This is Miss Squires, Mr. Gage," said he, "the young woman we have been expecting."

"Pleased to meet you," said Sim, after the fashion of his extremest social formality. And then, in a burst of welcome, "How'd you like it, coming out?"

"Fine!" said Annie, dusting off her frock. "Lovely."

She paid no attention to Sim Gage's words, "Go right on

in. She's anxious to see you," but hurried on, muttering to herself, "Ain't it the limit? And her blind!"

She stopped for an instant at the door, staring into the dim interior, then with a cry rushed in. Mary, stone blind, stood staring, trembling. The two met in swift embrace, mingled their tears.

"Oh, Mary, it can't be!" said Annie after a time. "It will get well, won't it? Say, now—your eyes will come back, won't they? How did you get here—what did you do? And you're married!"

"Yes," said Mary Gage, "that's true."

"Oh, then," said Annie Squires, pulling herself together with resourcefulness, "that was your husband out in the yard, that fine-looking man! I was in such a hurry. You lucky thing! Why didn't you tell me more about him, Mary? He has such a pleasant way. I don't mind men being light complected, or even bald. He's fine!"

"I think so," said Mary. "You like him?"

"Why, how could any one help liking him, Sis?" demanded Annie, choking. "Of course. So this is where you live?"

"Yes, this is my home," said Mary Gage. "And then you're not disappointed in him? I'm so glad! I've never seen him—my husband. You're joking about the color of his hair, of course."

"You'll have to help yourself, Annie," she went on, having no reply. "I'm not of much use. I've learned a few things and I help a little. You can see about everything there is, I suppose, at one look. Isn't it nice?"

　　　　　Emerson Hough

"Couldn't be better," said Annie Squires, again choking back her tears. "You certain are the lucky kid. And he— he married you after he saw you was blind?"

"It was a strange thing for a man to do," said Mary Gage, slowly. "Yes,—but fine."

"I'm glad you've done so well. This will settle a heap of things, won't it, Mary?"

"Some things."

The step of Doctor Barnes was heard at the door. Mary Gage called out, asking him to come in. Some talk then followed about the domestic resources of the place, in which Annie was immediately interested.

"But I've got four hens," said Mary Gage, smiling.

"Well, it seems to be a right cheerful, friendly sort of place, don't it?" said Annie after a while, "where they come in and kill the cattle and horses and burn the house, and run away with people!" She was looking at the burned door jamb of Sim Gage's cabin as she spoke. Doctor Barnes had told her the story of the raid.

"Who's *that* coming in?" she remarked after a time, having caught sight through the window of an approaching figure.

"That's your neighbor, Wid Gardner," said Doctor Barnes.

"He's taller than some," said Annie after a time. "Gee, ain't he plain! And ain't he sunburned!"

Wid Gardner himself presently approached the door, to be suddenly taken aback when he met the somewhat robust and blooming young person who had just arrived.

"You've knew Mrs. Gage for some time?" he managed to say at last, to make conversation, after he also had declared himself pleased to meet the newcomer.

"Lived together for years," said Annie. "Only real pal I ever had. I took care of her the best I knew how. I'm going to keep on." A certain truculence was in her tone.

Wid Gardner and Annie Squires soon found themselves together and somewhat apart, for she beckoned him to meet her outside the cabin.

"Say, Mister," said she to him suddenly, "tell me,—are you the man that wrote them letters to us girls? I know he never done nothing like that." She indicated Sim Gage, who stood staring vacuously at her trunk, which still stood upon the ground near the car.

Wid Gardner flushed deeply. "I ain't saying one way or the other," said he. "But I know the letters went, all right. Like enough we both ought to of been shot for it."

"You know it, and you said it!"

"But now, Miss Squires," he went on, "we didn't ever really suppose that anybody would answer our fool letters. We never did realize that a girl would actual be so foolish, way that one was."

"Fine business, wasn't it, you men—to treat a good clean girl like that! Look at that!" Again she indicated Sim Gage, withering contempt in her tone.

"Who's going to run this place?" she demanded. "She can't."

"I dunno," said Wid Gardner vaguely. "You won't be going back right away, will you?"'

"Not any quicker'n God'll let me!" said Annie Squires. Which struck poor Wid silent.

Doctor Barnes and Sim had passed to the other side of the premises, where the little group of men who had come in the day previous, and had pitched their tent in the yard, were engaged in laying up the logs of the cabin which was to be the quarters of the men stationed here. There were a half dozen of them in all, a corporal, four privates, and a carpenter impressed from the Company forces to supervise the building.

"In a week you won't know the place, Sim," said the doctor. "They'll run this house up in jig time. With two bunk rooms and a dining room and a kitchen, there'll be plenty of room. I'll see that it's furnished. Gardner can stay here until he gets time to build on his own place. That girl that came out with me is a good sort, as big-hearted as they make them. It's a godsend, her coming out. She told me she could cook, and would be glad to have a job. If your wife can keep busy, it will be all the better for them both."

"But now, I told you I'd put you on the pay roll, Gage," he concluded. "I want you to act as a scout here, to keep watch on this road and the cross road into the Reserve. When I was in town I got you a hat—regulation O. D.,— with a green cord around it, as I told you. Go on over to the car and get it—it's yours."

Sim walked slowly over to the car and peered in at the new head gear. He took it up gingerly by the rim, regarding the green cord with curiosity. Half reverently he placed it on his head. A vast new pride came to him at that moment. Never before had he taken on any badge of authority, known any sort of singling out or distinction in all his drab, vague life. No power ever had sent to him a parchment engraved "placing special confidence in your loyalty and discretion." But even his mind divined that now in some way he did represent the authority and government of his country, that some one had placed confidence in his loyalty and discretion. If not, why this green cord on his hat?

"When you wear that, Gage," said Doctor Barnes sharply to him, "you button up your shirt and roll down your sleeves, do you understand? You shave and you wash clean every morning. You comb your hair and keep it combed. If I'm cast away as Major of this desert island out here I'm going to be the law and the gospel. And the first thing, Sim Gage, that a soldier learns is to be neat. Think of that cord on your hat!"

"Doc," said Sim Gage, "that's just what I am a-thinking of."

"Well, I've got to go on back to the dam. I suppose those two women can take care of themselves somehow now."

"I wish't you wouldn't go away," said Sim uneasily. "One woman is bad enough—but now there's two of them."

"Two won't be as much trouble as one," said Doctor Barnes.

As he turned he saw standing in the door a figure which to him suddenly seemed pathetic. It was Mary Gage. She was looking out now vaguely. He did not even go over to say good-by.

In the meantime Annie Squires, not backward in her

relations with mankind, again engaged Wid Gardner in conversation as they stood at the edge of the yard, and Wid's downcast head bespoke his lack of happiness at what he heard.

"I never in all my born days saw a joint like this," said Annie, her dark eyes snapping. "It ain't fit for cowboys—it ain't fit for nobody. Her *married* to him! And how on earth are we going to keep it from her? If she ever knew—my God! it would break her heart—she'd kill herself now if she knew the truth. Man, you don't know that girl—you just think she's a common, ordinary woman, don't you? You can't understand a woman like that, you people. She just thought it was her duty to get married. Her *duty*—do you get me?—her *duty*! It's a crime when a woman like that gets that sort of bugs in their nut. Well, what could I do? I figured if she could marry and get a good home it would be the best thing for her. Do you know what us two girls done?—we flipped a copper to see which one of us should have the chance. Wasn't that a fine thing to do? Well, she won—and look at that!"

She again pointed to Sim Gage, who stood hands in pocket, looking after Doctor Barnes' departing car. "Look at him! Is he human or ain't he? He ain't got but one gallus, and I bet he ain't been shaved for a week. His clothes may fall off him any minute. He's past forty-eight if he's a day. Say, man, leave me take the ax and go kill that thing right away! I got to do it sometime. Do you get me?"

"Yes," said Wid Gardner, somewhat agitated, "yes, there's a heap of truth in what you say. There ain't no use in me denying not a single thing. All I got to say is we didn't never mean to do what this here has turned out to be. But now you've come out here, too, and in some ways it makes it harder to keep things quiet. You don't look to me like you was easy to be right quiet. What are you going to do about it your own self?"

"I've told you what I'm going to do about it. Just as soon as the Lord'll let us, I'm going to take her out of here. Do you think I'm one of them sort that'll set down and let the world walk over me, and say I like it? Oh, no, not sister Annie! I ain't blind."

"Say, Mister," said she a moment later as he maintained disconsolate silence, "they call you Wid. What's your real name?"

"My name is Henry," remarked her companion. "They only call me Wid for short."

"Huh! Well, now, Henry, go get some wood for supper. Cut it short enough so the door'll shut tight. And fetch in another pail of water—water's apt to get bad, standing around that way. And while you're out along this little creek pull some of this water cress and bring it in—didn't you know it's good to eat? And, Henry, if you've got any cows, you see that one of them is brought over here, and a churn—we got to have some butter. We got to get a garden started even if it is a little bit late. And, Henry, listen, them hens got to have some kind of a door to their coop—they're just walking around aimless. And I want you to get a collar for that little dog—I'm going to see if I can learn it to lead Mary around. There's a heap of things have got to be done here. How long you been living here yourself?"

"Why, I don't live here a-tall," said Wid, aghast at the new duties which seemed to be crowding upon him. "That's my place over there acrosst the fence. I just strolled over in here to-day. They burned me out."

"You two was neighbors, huh? And I suppose you both set around and figured out that fine little game about advertising for a wife? Well, you got one, anyway, didn't you?"

"Well, this ain't my place—Sim lives here."

"You don't suppose I'd ask him to do anything, do you?" said Annie Squires. "He's no good. I tell you he'll be playing in luck if I don't break loose and read the law to him."

"Well, now," said Wid, apologetically, "I wouldn't start any too strong right at first. There ain't nothing he wouldn't do for her—nothing in the whole, wide world."

"But now, about you," he added—"I'm glad you've come. It looks sort of like you was going to move in, don't it?"

"You've said it," said Annie.

Wid Gardner looked at her curiously, and meekly went about his new duties regarding wood and water.

CHAPTER XXV

ANOTHER MAN'S WIFE

Revolution, and not less, had occurred within a month at Sim Gage's ranch. This was not so much evidenced by the presence of a hard-bitten corporal and his little army of four men; nor so much more by the advent of Annie Squires; neither was it proved by the new buildings that had risen so quickly; nor by the appearance of new equipment. It was not so much in the material as in the intangible things of life that greatest change had come.

Karen Jensen smiled now as she talked with her new friend, Annie Squires. Even Mary Gage, for some reason, had ceased to weep. But the main miracle was in the instance of Sim Gage himself.

Perhaps it was the hat which did it, with its brave cord of green, humblest of all the insignia of those who stand at the threshold of the Army. To Sim's vague soul it carried a purpose in life, knowledge that there was such a thing as service in the world. Daily his face now was new-reaped, his hands made clean. He imitated the erectness and alertness of these young soldiers whom he saw, learned the jerk of the elbow in their smart salute. Enriched by a pair of cast-off breeches, and the worn leggins thereto, he rode now with both feet in the stirrups and looked square between his horse's ears. Strong as are many lazy men, not cowardly, and therefore like many timid men, he rode straight, with his campaign hat a trifle at one side, like to the fashion of these others.

And he wished that She might see him now, in his new uniform. He wondered if she knew how much larger and more important a man he was now. Into the pleached garden of his life came a new vision of the procession of the days; and he was no longer content. He saw the vision of a world holding the cares and duties of a man.

That this revolution had come to pass was by reason of the presence of this blind woman who walked tap-tapping, led by a little dog; a blind woman who for some reason had begun to smile again.

As for Doctor Barnes, he had been the actual agent, to be sure. This new order of things was the product of his affirmative and initiating mind. Mary Gage, consciously or unconsciously, within a few weeks, learned his step as surely as his voice, could have told you which was his car had a dozen come into the yard at the same time. Therefore, on this certain morning, she knew his voice, when, after stopping his car in the dooryard, he called out to the men before he approached the door of her own home. It was then that Mary Gage did something which she never yet had done when she had heard the step and voice of her lawful lord and master—something she had not done since her arrival here. Blind, she turned unconsciously to the mirror which she knew Annie had hung on the wall! She smoothed back her hair, felt for the corners of her collar to make it neat. She really did not know that she did these things.

She was young. Life was still buoyant in her bosom, after all, and far more now than at any time in her life. New graciousness of face and figure began to come to her. Well-being appeared in her eye and her cheek. The clean air of this new world had done its work, the actinic sun had painted her with the colors of the luckier woman, who expects to live and to be loved. It was a lovely face she might have seen in yonder mirror—a face flushed as she heard this step at the door.

"Greetings and salutations!" said he as he entered. "Of course you know who I am."

"I'm trained in hide-and-seek," said she. "Sit down, won't you?"

He tossed his hat on the table. "Alone?" he asked.

"I always am. Annie is busy almost all day, over at the soldier house, you know."

"I suppose he is up in the hills to-day?"

She knew whom he meant. "Yes. Annie tells me he goes up every other day to look around. I should think he would be afraid."

"Annie told you?—doesn't he tell you what he does?"

"No. Sometimes in the evening he comes in for a moment."

"Well, of course," he went on, "in my capacity as Pooh Bah, Major and doctor too, I've got to be part medico to take care of the poor devils who blow off their hands or drop things on their feet, or eat too much cheap candy at the store. How is Sim's knee by this time?"

"He limps a little—I can hear it when he walks on the

boards. Annie says that Wid Gardner says that Sim says that his leg's all right." She smiled, and he laughed with her.

"That's fine. And how about Madam herself, Mrs. Gage?"

She shivered. "I wish you wouldn't call me that. It—well, don't, please. Let's not ever joke."

"What shall I call you?"

"I don't know. What's *wrong* here, Doctor?" She faced him now.

He evaded. "I was wondering about your health."

"Oh, I'm very well. Sometimes my eyes hurt me a little, as though I felt more of the light. Subjective, I suppose."

She could not feel him look at her. At length, he spoke, quietly. "I've some news for you, or possible news. It has very much to do with your happiness. Tell me, if it were in my power to give you back your eyes, would you tell me to do that?"

"My eyes? What do you mean? To see again?"

"If I gave you back your sight, I would be giving you back the truth; and that would be very, very cruel."

He saw the fluttering of her throat, the twitching of the hands in her lap, and so hurried on.

"Listen! There's a chance in a hundred that your sight can be restored. My old preceptor writes me, from what I've told him, that there is about that chance. If it did succeed—"

"Then I'd see again!"

"Yes. So you would be very unhappy."

"You say a thing like that!"

He winced, flushed.

"You come here now with hopes that you ought not to offer, and you qualify even that! Fine—fine! You think I can stand much more than I have?"

Still the trembling of her hands, the fluttering at her throat. He endured it for a time, but broke out savagely at last. "You'd be perfect then—as lovely as ever any woman—why, you're perfect now! And yet without that one flaw where would you be? You'd not be married then, though you are now."

"Go on!" she said at length, coldly.

"You don't know one of us here except that girl, Annie, as different from you as night is from day. You don't know about the rest of us. You only think about us, imagine us—you don't see us, don't know us. Ah, God! If you only could! But—if you did!"

The last words broke from him unconsciously. He sat chilled with horror at his own speech, but knew he had to go on.

"I am going to do what shall leave us both unhappy as long as we live. I'll give you back your eyes if I can."

"I am helpless." She spoke simply.

"Yes! Why, if I even look at you, I feel I'm an

eavesdropper, I'm stealing. You can't see in my face what your face puts there—you can't see my eyes with yours. You can't understand how you've made me know things I never did know until I saw you. Why, cruel? yes! And now you're asking me to be still more cruel. And I'm going to be."

"Don't!" she broke out. "Oh, God! Don't! Please—you must not talk. I thought you were different from this."

"And yet you have asked me a dozen times what's wrong here. Why, everything's wrong! That man loves you because he can see you—any man would—but you don't love him, because you *haven't* seen him. You're not a woman to him at all, but an abstraction. He's not a man to you at all, but an imagination. *That's* not love of man and woman. But when you have back your eyes,—*then* you're in shape to compete with the best women in the world for the best man in the world. That's love! That's marriage! That's right! Nothing else is."

He paused horrified. Her voice was icy. "I asked you what was wrong here. I begin to see now. You spoke the truth—everything is wrong."

"You'll hate me all your life and I hate myself now as I never have before in my life—despise myself. What a mockery we've made of it all. God help those who see!"

She sat silent for a very long time. "You say I shall be able to see him—my husband?"

"Yes, I think so," he said.

"And you also?"

"No! Him, but not me. You never will. I'll be an imagination forever. You'll never see me at all."

"Under what star of sadness was I born?" said Mary Gage, simply. "What a problem!"

"Good-by," he replied. "I don't need to wait."

She held out her hands to him, gropingly. "Going?"

"Yes. I'm coming back, week after next, to get you. I'll not talk this way ever again. Don't forgive me—you can't.

"You'll have to go down to our hospital, perhaps for a couple of weeks," he concluded.

He stepped from the room so silently, passed so quickly on the turf, that she was not sure he had gone. He never saw her hands reach out, did not hear her voice: "No, no! I'll not go! Let me be as I am!"

CHAPTER XXVI

THE WAYS OF MR. GARDNER

Two figures stood regarding Doctor Barnes as his car turned into the willow lane out-bound for the highway.

"Why didn't he say good-by, anyways, when he left?" commented Wid, turning to Annie Squires. "Went off like he'd forgot something."

"That's his way," replied Annie, rolling down her sleeves. They had met as she was passing from the barracks cabin. "He's a live wire, anyways. God knows this country needs them."

"Why, what's the matter with this country?" demanded Wid mildly. "Ain't it all right?"

"No, it ain't. Till I come here it was inhabited exclusively with corpses."

"Well, then?"

"And since then, if it wouldn't of been for the Doctor yonder, you and Sim Gage would be setting down here yet and looking at the burned places and saying, 'Well, I wonder how that happened?'"

"Well, if you didn't like this here country, now what made you come here?" demanded Wid calmly and without resentment.

"You know why I come. That lamb in there was needing me. A fine sight you'd be, to come a thousand miles to look at! You and him! Say, hanging would be too good for him, and drowning too expensive for you."

"Oh, come now—that's making it a little strong, now, Miss Annie, ain't it? What have I done to you to make you feel that way? *I* ain't ever advertised for no wife, have I? Comes to that, I can make just as good bread as you kin."

"Huh! Is that so!"

"Yes, and cook apricots and bacon, and fry ham as good as you can if there was any to fry. Me, I'd be happy if they wasn't no women in the whole wide world. They're a damn nuisance, anyways, ask me about it."

He was looking out of the corner of his eye at Annie, witnessing her wrath.

"The gall of you!" exclaimed Annie, red of face and with snapping eye. "Oh, they're damn nuisances, are they? Well, then, I'll tell you. I fixed your socks up last night for you. Holes? Gee! Me setting in there by a bum lamp that you had to strike a match to see where it was. Never again! You can go plumb to, for all of me, henceforth and forever."

"I ain't never going to wear them socks again," said Wid calmly. "I'm a-going to keep them socks for soovenirs. Such darning I never have saw in my born days. If I couldn't darn better'n that I'd go jump in the creek. I didn't ask you to darn them socks noways. Spoiled a perfectly good pair of socks for me, that's what you done."

The war light grew strong in Annie's eyes. "You never did need but one pair anyways, all summer. Souvenirs! Why, one pair'd last you your whole life. I suppose you wrop things around your feet in the winter time, like the Rooshians in the factory. Say, you're every way the grandest little man that ever lived alone by hisself! Well, here's where you'll get your chance to be left alone again."

"You ain't gone yet," said Wid calmly.

"What's the reason I ain't, or won't be?"

"Well," said Wid Gardner, reaching down for a straw and moving slowly over toward a saw horse that stood in the yard, "like enough I won't let you go."

"What's that you say?" demanded Annie scoffingly. None the less she slowly drew over to the end of another saw horse and seated herself. "I'll go when I get good and ready."

"Of course, you can't tell much about a woman first few weeks. They put on their best airs then. But anyways, I've sort of got reconciled to seeing you around here. I had a po'try book in my house. Like it says, I first endured seeing you, and then felt sorry for you, and then—"

"Cut out the poetry stuff," said Annie. "It ain't past noon yet."

"I ain't had time to build my own house over yet. Pianny and all gone now, though."

"Gee, but you do lie easy," said Annie. "You're the smoothest running liar I ever did see."

"And all my books and things, and pictures and dishes."

"All of your both two tin plates, huh?"

"And my other suits of clothes, and my bedstead, and my dewingport, and everything—all, all gone, Miss Squires!"

"Is that so! Oh, sad! sad! You must of been reading some of them mail order catalogues in your dreams."

"And my cook stove too. I've just been cooking out in the open air when I couldn't stand your cooking here no more—out of doors, like I was camping out."

"If any sheep herder was ever worse than you two, God help him! You wasn't one of you fit for her to wipe a foot on,—that doctor least of all, that got me out here under pretences that she was married happy. And I find her married to that! I wish to God she could see all this, and see you all, for just one minute. Just once, that's all!"

"Yes," said Wid Gardner, suddenly serious. "I know. There ain't nothing I can do to square it. But all I've got or expect to have—why, it's free for you to take along and do anything you can for her and your own self, Miss Annie, if you want to, even if you do go away and leave us.

"But look at my land over there." He swept a long arm toward the waving grasses of the valley. "I've got my land all clear. She's worth fifty a acre as she lays, and'll be worth a hundred and fifty when I get water out of the creek on to her. I got three hundred and twenty acres under fence. I been saving the money the Doc's paying me here.

"Say," he added, presently, "what kind of a place is that

Niagry place I been reading about? Is it far from Cleveland?"

"Not so very," replied Annie to his sudden and irrelevant query.

"It's a great place for young married folks to go and visit, I reckon? I was reading about in a book onct, before my books was burned up. Seems like it was called 'A Chanct Acquaintance.' Ever since, I allowed I'd go to Niagry on my wedding journey."

"Well," said Annie, judicially, "I been around some, what with floor-walkers and foremen and men in the factory, but I'm going to say that when it comes to chanct acquaintances, this here place has got 'em faded for suddenness! Go on over home and rub your eyes and wake up, man! You're dopy."

"No, I ain't," said Wid. "I'm in a perfectly sane, sound and disposin' mind. You're getting awful sun-burned, but it only makes you good-lookinger, Miss Annie.

"But now lemme tell you one thing," he went on, "I don't want to see you making no more eyes at that corporal in there. Plenty of men in the Army has run away and left three, four wives at home."

"I don't care nothing about no man's past," said Annie. "They all look alike to me."

"Well, I can't say that about you. Some ways you're a powerful homely girl. Your hair's gettin' sunburned around the ends like Karen Jensen's. And your eyes—turn around, won't you, so I kin remember what color your eyes is. I sort of forgot, but they ain't much. Not that I care about it. Women is nothing in my young life."

"Huh! you're eighty if you're a day."

"It's the way I got my hair combed."

Extending a strong right arm she pushed him off the end of the saw horse. He rose, dusting his trousers calmly. "Oh, dear, I didn't think so much sinfulness could be packed in so young a life! But say, Annie, what's the use of fooling? I got to tell you the truth about it sometime. Like on my flour sack: 'Eventual, why not now?' And the plain, plumb truth is, you're the best as well as the pertiest girl that ever set a foot on Montana dirt."

Annie's face was turned away now.

"Your hair and eyes and teeth, and your way of talking, and your way of taking hold of things and making a home—haven't you been making a home fer all of us people here? I told you I'd have to tell the truth at last. Besides, I said I was to blame for everything that's gone wrong here. I was. But I'll give you all I am and all I got to square it, anyways you like."

"Well, anyways," said Annie Squires, drawing a long breath, "I think if you took on something, you'd see it through; and you wouldn't pass the buck if you fell down."

"That's me," said Wid.

"I get you," said Annie.

"You said that to me right out here in broad daylight, in presence of witnesses, four hens and a dog."

"I said I understood you. That was all."

Wid Gardner turned to her and looked her squarely, in the eyes. "Not appropry to nothing, neither here nor there, ner bragging none, I'm able to put up as much hay in a day as any two Mormons in the Two Forks Valley. In the hay fields of life, it's deeds and not words that counts. I read that in a book somewheres."

"Say," he went on, suddenly, "have you noticed how perty the moonlight is on the medders these nights? You reckon it shines that same way over at Niagry?"

Annie did not answer at the instant. "Well," said she at last, "in some ways this country is a lot like Cleveland. Go on over to your own house, if you've got one, and don't you never speak to me again, so long as you live."

"Well, anyways," said Wid, chuckling, "you didn't really call me a sheep man. But listen—I've told you almost the truth about everything. Now I got to be going."

"I was *afraid* you'd be making some break," said Annie Squires. "I was *expecting* you'd do some fool thing or other. I almost *knew* you'd do it. But then—"

"Yes; and but then?"

"But then—" concluded Annie.

CHAPTER XXVII

DORENWALD, CHIEF

Mary Gage, sitting alone in her cabin, could hear the hum of voices as Wid Gardner and Annie Squires talked together in the open sunlight. Presently she heard the footfall of Annie as she came to the door.

"Well, Sis," said that cheerful individual, "how are you getting on?"

"Couldn't you come in for a while, Annie? I'm very lonesome. What were you talking about?"

"I just told that man out there I'm going to take you back home."

Mary Gage sat silent for a time. "We'll have to get a better solution than that."

"It's a fine little solution you've got so far, ain't it now?" commented Annie. "Highbrows always have to lean on the lowbrows, more or less. You listen to me."

"Sometime, I suppose," she went on after a moment's pause, "I'll have to talk right out with you. For instance, you being a farmer's wife! Now, as for me, I was raised on a farm. When I was ten years old I was milking five cows every day. When I was twelve I was sitting up at night knitting socks for the other kids. That was before I got the idea of going to the white lights after my career. Well, it's lucky I met you, like enough. But me once talking of getting married to Charlie Dorenwald! I should admire to see him, me handy to a flat iron."

"But, Annie, I'd die if it wasn't for some one to help me all the time. Some pay for that with money. How can I pay for it at all? Tell me, Annie." She turned suddenly. "If I—if I could get my eyesight back again, what ought I to do?"

"I wouldn't talk about that, Sis, if I was you. But just wait, there's some one coming—it's him."

Mary could hear Sim Gage's rapid step as he came around to the door, pausing no more than to throw down his horse's bridle over its head.

Sim Gage was excited. "Where's the Doc?—he been here this morning?"

"He went away less than an hour ago," replied Mary Gage. "How long was it, Annie? Why?"

"Well, I got to go down to the dam. Something up in the hills I don't like."

"Not those same men?" Mary Gage's face showed terror.

"I don't know yet. Two cars was in camp on the creek, half way up towards the Reserve. I seen 'em and sneaked back."

"Telephone down, why don't you?"

"I hadn't thought of that," said Sim. "I ain't used to them things. Say, Miss Squires, supposin' you see if you can get the doctor down at the dam?"

But when Annie tried to use the telephone her ring sounded idle and vacant in the box. The instrument was dead.

"Out of order!" said Annie, "right when you want it. When you want to make a date the girls says, 'Party's line's out of order.' Of course it is!"

"Well, then I'll have to start down right away. I got to see the Doc about this. I hate to leave you alone."

"Let him go," said Annie to Mary Gage. "The soldiers 'll be back for supper pretty soon."

"I've got to go over to Wid's," said Sim; "got to get another horse."

He turned and left the room without more word of parting than he had shown of greeting. He walked more alertly than ever he had in his life.

He found Wid Gardner and told his news. His neighbor listened to him gravely.

"It may be only some people in there fishing," said Wid, "but it's no time to take chances. You say the wire's down? That looks so bad, I reckon you'd better ride on down. How far have you rode today?"

"Round thirty, forty miles."

"Forty more won't hurt you none," said Wid. "The roan bronc can stand it. I'll go on over and tell the women folks not to be afraid."

"Gee, but this is some quiet place!" said Annie Squires, as the two women sat alone in nervous silence. "You can cut it with a knife, can't you?"

"Did you say Mr. Gardner was coming over here before long?" asked Mary. "Annie, I'm so afraid!"

"Hush, Sis! It's like enough only a scare. I wish't that doctor man had stayed. But tell me, was he saying anything to you about your eyes?"

"Yes."

"What?"

"He said he was coming up here in a week or two to take me down to the hospital. He said he thought perhaps he could save my eyes! Oh, Annie, Annie!"

"Hush, Sis! I told you to forget it. You mustn't hope—remember, you *mustn't* hope, Mary, whatever you do."

"No, I mustn't hope. I told him I wouldn't go."

"Some folks is grand little jokers. Women can't help stringing a man along, can't they? Of course you'll go."

She cast her arms about Mary Gage, and held her tight. "You poor kid!" said she. "You get your eyes first, and let's figure out the rest after that. You make me tired. Cut out all that duty and sacrifice stuff. Live and get yours. That's the idea!"

"Now, you sit here." She rose and placed a comforting hand on Mary's shoulder. "Just keep quiet here, and I'll go out and see if I can call Henry Gardner. He seems to me like a man that wouldn't scare easy. I'll go as far as the fence and yoo-hoo at him. I'll be right back."

But Annie Squires did not come back for almost an hour. Wid Gardner, coming across lots by the creek path, found Mary Gage alone, and sat with her there in an uneasiness he could not himself conceal, wondering over the girl's absence. Mary was well-nigh beside herself when at length they heard Annie coming rapidly, saw her at the door.

"Get back in!" she said. "Sit down, both of you! Wait, now—Listen! Who do you think I found right out here, almost in our very yard, Mary?"

Panting, she seated herself, and after a time began more coherently. "I'll tell you. I just walked out to the gate, and says I to myself, I'll yoo-hoo so that Mr. Gardner can hear over there and come on down. So I yoo-hooed. Did you hear me?"

Wid shook his head. "I didn't hear nothing."

"Well, I heard some one holler back, soft-like, 'Yoo-hoo!' It didn't sound just right, so I walked on a little more. 'Yoo-hoo!' says I. Then I seen a man come out of the bushes. I seen it wasn't you, all right. He come on right fast, and Mary—I couldn't of believed it, but it's the truth. It was Charlie—Charlie Dorenwald! I couldn't make no mistake about them legs.

"When I seen who it was I turned around to run. I was scared he'd shoot me. He hollered at me to stop, and I stopped. He come after me and caught me by the arm, and he laughs. I was scared silly—silly, I tell you. He laughs some more, and then he sobers down to solid talk.

"'Why, Charlie,' says I, 'it can't be you. I'm so glad.' I allowed the best thing was to jolly him along. I knew he'd make trouble. I wanted a chance to think."

"We stood out there so close I could see the cabin all the time—and we talked. That fellow couldn't help bragging about himself. He was half loaded. Says I to him, 'What made you come out here, Charlie? To find me?'"

"'Yes,' says he. 'I knew you was here.'"

"'How did you know it?' I asked him."

"'That's a good question,' says he. 'Haven't I got plenty people working for me that could tell me where you was, or anything else I wanted to know? The free brothers work together.'"

Wid Gardner's eyes were full on her. He did not speak.

"So we turned and moved further up the lane then," went on Annie. "I kept on asking him how he come here. I told him I'd been too proud to send for him. But now he'd come, how could I help loving him all over again!"

"You didn't mean that," said Wid quietly.

"How much do you think I'd mean it? That Dutch snake! Listen— He told me more than the papers ever told. He told me he'd been a sort of chief there in Cleveland right along, along in the war, and after peace was signed. He pulled off some good things, so he said, so they sent him out here. He was after me. Folks, that man took himself apart for me. He made me promise to go along with him, all dolled up, and in our own car!"

"You ain't going," said Wid, quietly.

"One guess! But there'll be trouble. I've only told you a little part of it that that fellow spilled to me. Dorenwald's nutty over these things. He tells what the German Socialists will do when they get to America. He says this is the world revolution,—whatever he means. Oh, my God!"

Annie began to weep in a sudden hysteria.

"Which way did that man go from here?" she heard Wid Gardner's voice at length.

"I don't know. He said he had a man with him, a 'brainy-cat,' he called him, to lecture in halls. He made me promise to be out there at the gate at sun-up to-morrow morning to go away with him. I'd have promised him anything. I'm awful scared. Why don't the men come back?"

Annie Squires was sobbing now. "And this was our country. We let them people in. I know it's true, what he said. And I told him that at sun-up—"

"Don't bother about that," said Wid Gardner quietly. "Now you two set right here in the house," he added, as he rose and picked up the rifle he saw hanging on its nails. "I'm going out and lay in the willers along the lane a little while, near the gate. I can hear you if you holler. I think it's best for me to go out there and keep a watch till the fellers come back. Don't be a-scared, because I'll be right there, not far from the gate."

He stepped out, rifle in hand. The two women sat alone, shivering in nervous terror, starting at every little sound.

They sat they knew not how long, before the clear air of the moonlight night was rent by sharp sounds. A single piercing shot echoed close at hand; scattering shots sounded farther up the lane; then many shots; and then came the sound of a car passing rapidly on the distant highway.

CHAPTER XXVIII

A CHANGE OF BASE

The roan horse which Sim Gage rode was in no downcast frame of mind, but he himself, engrossed with his errand, did not at first notice that it was the same half wild animal with which he had had combat at an earlier time. He fought it for half an hour or more down a half dozen miles of the road, but at length the brute made matters worse by picking up a stone, and going dead lame, so that any great speed was out of the question.

Night was falling now across the winding trail which passed along the valley lands and over the shoulders of the mountains. It was wild country even yet, but beautiful as it lay in the light of the fading day. Sim Gage had no time to note the play of light or shadow on the hills. He rode. It was past midnight when he swung off his now meek and wet-sided horse, cast down the bridle rein, and went in search of Doctor Barnes.

The latter met his caller with the point of an electric torch at the door.

"Oh, it's you, Gage?" said he. "Come in."

Sim Gage entered and seated himself, his hurt leg stiffly

before him on the floor. Briefly as he could, he told the reason of his errand and the reason for his delay.

"Leave your horse here," said Doctor Barnes, already preparing for his journey. "We'll take my car."

A half hour later the two were again en route. The head light of the car, swinging from side to side around the steep and unprotected curves of the mountain slopes, showed the rude passageway, in places risky enough at that hour and that speed. At that latitude the summer nights are short, and their journey was unfinished when the gray dawn began to turn to pink upon the mountain tops. In the clearer light Doctor Barnes saw something which caused him to pull up.

"There's the wire break," he exclaimed. "Look here."

They both left the car and approached the nearest pole. It bore the fresh marks of a linesman's climbing irons. "Professional work. And that's a cut with nippers—not a break. Keep away from the free end, Gage's, it's probably a live wire. You're right. That gang is back in here again. But tell me, what's that?—Do you smell anything?"

Sim Gage nodded. "Smoke," said he.

As the light grew stronger so that the far slopes of the mountain were visible they saw the proof. Smoke, a heavy, rolling blanket of smoke, lay high over the farther summits.

"Damn their souls!" said Doctor Barnes fervently and tersely. "They've set the forest afire again."

A half hour later they swung into the ranch yard. The call of "Halt!" came, backed by a tousled head nestled against the stock of a Springfield which protruded from a window.

"Advance, friend!" exclaimed the corporal when he got his countersign, and a moment later met his Major in the dooryard. They were joined by Wid Gardner, who rose from the place where he had sat, rifle across his knees, most of the night crouched against the end of the cabin.

"We've got him in here," said the Sergeant, leading the way to the barracks door.

"Got what?"

"The one we shot. He's deader'n hell, but I thought you might like to look through his pockets."

Wid Gardner unemotionally accompanied them into the room of the barracks where, on a couple of boards, between two carpenter's trestles, lay a long figure covered with a blanket.

"Scout Gardner got him last night about nine o'clock, sir," said the Sergeant; "out in the lane behind the gate. Called to him to halt, and he didn't stop."

"He didn't have no chanct to halt," said Wid Gardner calmly. "I hollered that to him after I had dropped him. He wasn't the one I was after, neither."

"The rest of them got away," went on the Sergeant. "We heard the shot when we was just coming down the road. We come on to the head of the lane and heard brush breaking. They was trying to get to their car, down a little further. They whirled and came back through us in the car, and we shot into them, but I don't know if we got any of 'em, the horses was pitching so. They went back up the trail, or maybe up on the Reserve road—I dunno. We come on down here to get orders."

Doctor Barnes slipped back the blanket. There was revealed the thin, aquiline face of a man dressed in rather dandified clothing. There were rings on both hands, a rather showy but valuable stickpin in the scarf. The hands were not those of a laboring man. At the bridge of the nose a faint depression showed that he wore eyeglasses. His complexion was blond, and his eyes, open now only to a slit, might also have been light in color. There was on his features, indefinably foreign, the stamp not to say of birth so much as of education. The man apparently once was used to easy if not gentle ways of life.

"Tell me how it happened," said Doctor Barnes to Gardner, who stood by.

"She can tell you more'n I can," said Wid—"Miss Squires. This ain't the feller. The real one that I want she used to work with—he was foreman back East in the shops where she worked. His name was Dorenwald. She promised to meet him out there at sun-up this morning. I went out last night to see what I could see. I found this feller. He was coming down the trail. I waited till he got clost enough— about forty yard. Onct was enough."

"How many cars did you see?" Doctor Barnes demanded of the sergeant.

"One."

"Gage says he saw two."

"The other may be back in the hills yet."

"Well, here's work! Tell me, Gardner, is there any way

those people can get out on the other side of the Reserve, down the West Fork? You know the backwater above the little dam, two miles below the big dam? Most of the timber we intended to float out that way, to the mill at the little dam. They may have gone on across in there.

"Now, Corporal, leave McQueston and two men here. I want the rest of you with me—we'll go up in the hills with my car. McQueston, take one man and go and fix the break in the line three miles down the road. We'll either come back in my car or send it back to you somehow. The fire may block us. Get your men ready. March!"

It was anxious enough waiting at the ranch, but the wait might have been longer. It was not yet eleven o'clock when the two women heard the hum of the heavily loaded car and saw the men climb out again. It was Doctor Barnes who came to the cabin.

"It's no use," said he. "The fire has cut off the Tepee Creek trail. The best fir is gone, and there's no hope of stopping the fire now. If they took their car up, they must have left it in there—some of them went back up the trail. They may be over on the West Fork; and if they've got there, they've got a shorter route down to the dams than around by the Valley road."

He turned now to Mary Gage more specifically. "We've got a company of troops down there to guard the big dam. It's safer there than it is here. What do you think of going back now, to stop until this row is over? We can take better care of you there than we can here."

She sat for a moment, her face turned away.

"Will you come?" he repeated.

"One guess!" said Annie Squires for her. "In a minute!"
And by that time she was throwing things into the valises.

CHAPTER XXIX

MARTIAL LAW

The entire flow of the greater of the Two Forks streams lay harnessed at last, after years of labor and an expenditure of millions. For twenty miles there lay a lake where once a clear, gravel-bottomed stream had flowed above the gorge of the mountain canyon. The gray face of a man-made wall rose sheer a hundred feet above the original bed of the stream, leaving it in part revealed; and this barrier checked and stayed the once resistless flood against which an entire mountain range had proved inefficient. Presently for hundreds of miles each way the transmission lines would carry out power to those seeking light, to those employing labor; and the used water would irrigate lands far below.

Allied with this unit of the great dam was a lesser dam operating a mill plant on the other Fork. Down this stream ship timbers once had come. The camp of the reclamation engineers and construction men lay upon a bench or plateau which once formed the bank of the stream upon that side, now about half way up to the top of the great dam. The road running up and down the valley ascended from this plateau to a sufficient elevation to surmount the permanent water level above the upper dam. On the opposite side rose a sheer and bare rock running

Emerson Hough

two-thirds up to the top of the mountain peak which here had shouldered its way down as though in curiosity to look at the bottom of the gorge itself. The great dam was anchored to the rock face on that side, and it was there that the chutes and wells for the turbines were located, as well as the spill gates which now were in temporary service. A wide roadway of cement, with vast buttresses on each side, ran along the top of the dam and looked down upon the abrupt surface of its lower face. Here, and there, at either side of the dam, and at the original stream level, stood low buildings of stone, to house the vast dynamos or care for other phases of the tremendous industrial installation of the National Government.

Here and there were stationed the armed guards, in the uniform of the Army. They did sentry-go along the dam-top, and patrolled or watched the lower levels of the works below the dam. They patrolled also the street and the road above and below the camp.

Well paid human labor had erected this great dam, mixed with the returned soldiers and a small per cent of labor sometimes sullen, with no affection for its work. In time among such as these came agents of a new and vast discontent, some who spoke of a "rule of reason," meaning thereby the crazed European rule of ignorant selfishness, others who spoke of "violence" as the only remedy for labor against capital. With what promises they deluded labor, with what hopes of any change, with what possibilities of later benefits, with what chimeras of an easier, unearned day, it matters not. They found listeners.

Against these covert forces working for the destruction of our civilization, our Government developed an unsuspected efficiency, sometimes through its department of justice, sometimes through a vast and silent civilian body of detectives working all over the country and again through its franker agencies of the military arm. Thus that able engineer who had built the great power dam here at the Two Forks—a man who had built a half score of railroads and laid piers for bridges without number, and planned city monuments, with the boldest and most fertile of imaginations, Friedrich Waldhorn his name, was a graduate of our best institutions and those of Germany— long since had been watched as closely as many another of less importance in charge of work remotely or intimately concerned with the country's public resources.

Waldhorn—before the war an outspoken Socialist and free-thinker—may have known that he was watched— must have known it when a young medical officer given military duties quite outside his own profession, was put over him in authority at the scene of his engineering triumph, and at precisely the time of its climax. But the situation for Waldhorn was this, that if he resigned and left the place he would only come the more closely under immediate espionage. Whatever his motives, he remained, sullen and uncommunicative.

Meanwhile the little camp sprawled in the sun, scattered along the plateau on the side of the mountain gorge. Crude, unpainted, built of logs or raw boards, it lay in the shadow for the greater part of the day, deep down in the narrow cleft of the mountains, far out in the wilderness. The great forest deepened and thickened, back of it, forty miles into the high country.

Those who lived here in the canyon could not as yet understand the nature of the thin blue veil which today obscured their scanty sunlight, did not know that each minute of day was destroying trees which had cost a thousand years to grow, which never in the knowledge of man might be replaced. But when the party of Major Barnes came down from Sim Gage's ranch, questions were answered. The forest had been fired again. The soldiers swore the silent soldier oath of revenge.

Doctor Barnes did not pause even to help the women out of the car. He hurried to the long, screened gallery in front of the residence and office of Waldhorn, chief engineer.

Waldhorn met him at the door, well-fed, suave, polite, a burly man, well-clad and bearing the marks of alertness and success. Always of few words, he scarcely more than spoke at present, his mildly elevated eyebrows making inquiry of the dusty man before him.

"Yes, Doctor, or—ah, Major?" he said, smilingly, insulting.

"Call it Major!" snapped Barnes. "I've come to tell you that I want your house."

"Yes? When?"

"In two minutes."

"Why?"

"I want it for Government uses. A patient of mine has come down here to stay a while—wife of one of my scouts."

"Well, now, my dear Major, I would not like to interfere with your private graft in the practice of medicine in any way. But I'm engineer in charge of this work, I fancy."

"Fancy something else while the fancying's good. Go on over to that little log house, Waldhorn. You'll live there until we send you out."

"Send me out! What do you mean, sir?"

"This camp is under martial law. You're under arrest, if you like to call it that way."

"You're going to arrest me? Why—what do you mean?"

"Call it what you like. But move, now, and don't waste my time."

"I beg pardon," drawled Waldhorn, smiling with a well-concealed sneer, "but isn't this a trifle sudden? I'm willing to give up my place to the ladies, of course, my dear Major, but I must ask some sort of explanation as to this other procedure. Martial law? What is your authority?"

"Call it Jehovah and the Continental Congress, my dear chap," said Doctor Barnes, likewise drawling. "I'll take that up after a while. I'm in charge here. If you go over there quietly to that other house it may look like an act of courtesy. If you don't—it might be called an act of God. Come, hurry—I can't talk here any longer."

Waldhorn saw two troopers coming at a fast walk from across the street, saw that the eyes of Doctor Barnes watched his hand carefully. Therefore, as though easily and naturally, he leaned with both his own hands above his head resting against the jamb of the door.

"I suppose I'll have to charge this up to the fact that I'm of German descent," said he. "I can't help that. I've lived here thirty years. I'm as good a citizen as you, but I'll have to submit. Be sure I'm going to take this up in the courts."

"Old stuff. Take it up where you damn please," said Barnes sharply. "I'm as good an American as you are, too, even if my parents were *not* born in Germany. Step outside."

He motioned to his men. "McQueston," he said, "watch him until I come out."

"You're not going into my private rooms?—I forbid that. I'll never forget that, you upstart!"

Doctor Barnes smiled. "I'll try to fix it so you won't." He stepped on in across the gallery.

Waldhorn looked from the face of one to that of the other private soldier who stood before him, and saw the cold mask not only of discipline, but of more. Under their charge he marched over to the log building indicated, and slammed the door behind him. The men stood one on each side, out of range of the window.

Doctor Barnes was angry and frowning when he went back to the car to drive it down to the door of the new quarters which had just been vacated.

"Gee, Doc, you look sore," said Annie Squires casually. "Say, where do you get the stuff you're pulling in here, anyway?"

"Never mind! You go in there and clean up the rooms and make a place for Mrs. Gage. You'll find everything for cooking and housekeeping. Don't touch anything else. I'm taking his Chink over to my place."

"Are you going there with the women?" he inquired, turning to Sim Gage.

Sim colored. "No. Wid and me'll be over with the soldiers. We're going to stick together."

"Better bunk in my shack, then. Go over to the barracks, both of you, and get rifles and an extra pistol each. I want both of you on patrol."

"You see," he explained, as he drew the two apart, "we don't know what those anarchist ruffians up there may do. They may drop down here by either fork any time, day or night."

He spoke briefly also to Mary Gage before he handed her in at the door of her new domicile:

"Sim and Wid both think that only one car went back up the road above the ranch. That means that the other car is up in the mountains between the Two Forks, probably in the Reserve. For a time there probably won't anything happen. You mustn't be scared—we're just taking the proper precautions now. This is very valuable Government property."

"Are we at the dam here?" asked Mary Gage. "I can hear the water—it's very heavy, isn't it?"

"It never stops. We don't hear it, because we're used to it—I don't think it will bother you very long. We'll try to make you comfortable."

He turned, offering her his arm, on which he placed her hand. He was a trifle surprised to see that Sim Gage without a word had passed to the other side of his wife, also giving her an arm. He walked along slowly and gravely, limping, silent as he had been all the afternoon, but made no sign of his own discomfort, indeed did not speak at all.

"Both of you are fit for the hospital. Well, all right, it may be a good place for you after all." As he spoke, frowning,

Doctor Barnes stood back and allowed Annie to lead Mary Gage into the vacated rooms of the chief engineer.

"Doc, what did you mean when you said that there just now?" asked Sim Gage, when they turned back from the door. "About her and the hospital?"

"I've brought her down here, Sim," said Doctor Barnes directly, "principally because, with her consent and yours, I want to see if I can't do something for her eyes."

"Her eyes! Why—what do you mean?"

"There's one chance in a hundred that she'll see again."

Doctor Allen Barnes, his face unshaven, dirty, haggard, a man looking neither major nor physician now, turned squarely to the man whom he addressed. "I don't know for sure," said he, "but then, it may be true."

"Her eyes?—Her eyes!"

Doctor Barnes felt on his arm as savage a grip as he ever had known. Sim Gage's face changed as he turned away.

"Good God A'mighty! If she could *see*!" His own face seemed suddenly pale beneath its grime.

CHAPTER XXX

BEFORE DAWN

A day passed, two, and three. Nothing came to break the monotony at the big dam. Donkey engines screamed intermittently. Workmen still passed here or there with their barrows. Teams strained at heavy loads of gravel and cement. The general labor in the way of finishing touches on the undertaking still went on under the care of the foremen, monotonously regular. No one knew that Waldhorn, chief engineer, was a prisoner under guard.

Mary Gage was more ignorant than any prisoner of what went on about her. A hard lot, that of waiting at any time, but the waiting of the newly blind—there is no human misery to equal it. It seemed at times to her she must go mad.

She recognized the footfall of Doctor Barnes when one morning she heard it on the gallery floor inside the slamming screen door. "Come in," she said, meeting him. "What is it?"

He entered without any speech, cast himself into a chair. She knew he was looking at her steadfastly.

"Well," said she, feeling herself color slightly. Still he did not answer. She shifted uneasily.

"What are you doing?" she demanded, just a trace of the personal in her tone.

"Eavesdropping again. Staring. This is the day when I say good-by to you. I've come to say my good-by now."

"Why should it be like that?" she asked after a time.

"Will you be happy?"

She did not answer, and he leaned forward as he spoke.

"You left a happy world behind you. Do you want to see this world now, this sordid, bloody, torn and worn old world, so full of everything but joy and justice? Do you want to see it any more? Why?"

"It is my right to see the world," said Mary Gage simply. "I want to see life. There's not much risk left for me. But you talk as though things were final."

"I'm going away. Let's not talk at all."

For a long time she sat silent.

"Don't you think that in time we forget things?"

"I suppose in ten years I will forget things—in part."

"Nonsense! In five years—two—you'll be married."

"So you think that of me?" said he after a time. "Fine!"

"But you have always told me that life is life, you know."

"Yes, sometimes I have tried my hand at scientific reasoning. But when I say ten years for forgetting anything, that's pathological diagnosis, and not personal. I try to reason that time will cure any inorganic disease just as time cures the sting of death. Otherwise the world could not carry its grief and do its work. The world is sick, near to death. It must have time. So must I. I can't stay here and work any more. If you can see—if you get well and normal again—I'll be here."

She looked at him steadily. He wanted to take her face between his hands.

"Oh, I'll not leave here until everything is right with your case. There's good excuse for me to go out. It will be for you the same as though we had never met at all."

"That's fine of you! So you believe that of me?"

"Why not? I must. You're married. That's outside my province now. I've just come to tell you now that I don't think we ought to wait any longer about your eyes. We'll try this afternoon, in our little hospital here. I wish my old preceptor were here; but Annie will help me all she can, and I'll do my very best."

"I'm quite ready."

"I don't know whether or not to be glad that you have no curiosity about your own case," he said presently.

"That only shows you how helpless I am. I have no choice. I have lost my own identity."

"Didn't your doctor back in Cleveland tell you anything about what was wrong with your eyes?"

"He said at first it was retinal; then he said it was iritis. He didn't like to answer any questions."

"The old way—adding to all the old mummeries of the most mumming of all professions—medicine! That dates back to bats' wings and toads' livers as cure for the spleen. But at least and at last he said it was iritis?"

"Yes. He told me that I might gradually lose one eye— which was true. He thought the trouble might advance to the other eye. It came out that way. He must have known."

"Perhaps he knew part," said Doctor Barnes. "You had some pain?"

"Unbearable pain part of the time—over the eyes, in the front of the head."

"Didn't your doctor tell you what iritis meant?"

"No. I suppose inflammation of the eyes—the iris."

"Precisely. Now, just because you're a woman of intelligence I'm going to try to give you a little explanation of your trouble, so you will know what you are facing."

"I wish you would."

"Very well. Now, you must think of the eye as a lens, but one made up of cells, of tissues. It can know inflammation. As a result of many inflammations there is what we call an exudation—a liquid passes from the tissues. This may be thin or serum-like, or it may be heavier, something like granulations. The tissues are weak—they exude something in their distress, in their attempt to correct this condition when they have been inflamed.

"The pupil of your eye is the aperture, the stop of the lens. That is the hole through which the light passes. Around it lie the tissues of the iris. In the back of the eye is the retina, which acts as a film for the eye's picture.

"Now, it was the part of the eye around that opening which got inflamed and began to exude. Such inflamm- ation may come from eye-strain, sometimes from glare like furnace heat, or the reflection of the sun on the snow. Snow-blindness is sometimes painful. Why? Iritis.

"In any case, a chronic irritation came into your case some time. Little by little there came a heavy exudation around the edges of the inflamed iris. It was so heavy that we call it a 'plastic' exudation. Now, that was what was the technical trouble of your eye—plastic exudation.

"This exudation, or growth, as we might call it, went on from the edges of the iris until it met in the middle of the pupil. Then there was spread across the aperture of your lens an opaque granulated curtain through which light could not pass. Therefore you could not see. The plastic exudation had done its evil work as the result of the iritis—that is to say, of the sufferings of the iris."

"I begin to understand," said Mary Gage. "That covers what seemed to happen."

"It covers it precisely, for that is precisely what did happen. It was not cataract. I knew, or thought I knew, that it was not from retinal scars due to inflammation in the back of the eye. It was just a filling up of the opening of the eye.

"So I know you lost sight in that last eye little by little, as you did in the other. You kept on knitting all the time. On your way out you struck the glare from the white sands of the plains in the dry country. At once the inflammation finished its exudation—and you were blind."

She sat motionless.

"Sometimes we take off the film of a cataract from the eye; sometimes even we can take out the crystalline lens and substitute a heavy lens in glasses to be worn by the patient."

"But in my case you intend to cut out that exudation from the pupil?"

"No. I wish we could. What we do is to cut a little key-hole aperture, not through the pupil, but at one side the pupil. In other words, I've got to make an artificial pupil—it will be just a little at one side of the middle of the eye. You will hardly notice it."

"But that will mean I cannot see!"

"On the contrary, it will mean that you can see. Remember, your eye is a lens. Suppose you put a piece of black paper over a part of your lens—paste it there. You will find that you can still make pictures with that lens, and that they will not be distorted. Not quite so much illumination will get into the lens, but the picture will be the same. Therefore you will see, and see finely.

"Now, you must not be uneasy, and you must not think of this merely as an interesting experiment just because you have not heard of it before. My old preceptor, Fuller of Johns Hopkins, did this operation often, and almost always with success. He could do it better than I, but I am the best that offers, and it must be done now.

"There is a very general human shrinking from the

thought of any operation on the eye—it is so delicate, so sensitive in every way, but as a matter of fact, science can do many things by way of operation upon the eye. If I did not think I could give you back your sight, you may be sure I should never undertake this work to-day. The operation is known technically as iridectomy. That would mean nothing to you if I had not tried to explain it.

"Of course there will be wounds in the tissues of the iris which must be healed. There must not be any more inflammation. That means that for some time after the operation your eyes must be bandaged, and you will remain in absolute darkness. You will have to keep on the bandages for a week or more—you understand that. If after hearing this explanation you do not wish to go forward, this is the time to let me know."

"I am quite ready," said Mary Gage. "As though I could ever thank you enough!"

"Let me remain in your memory, as a picturesque and noble figure, my dear lady! Think of me as a Sir Galahad, which I am not. Picture me of lofty carriage and beautiful countenance, which is not true. Imagine me as a pleasing and masterful personality in every way—which I am not. You will not meet me face to face."

"I've been praying for my sight when it didn't seem to be any use to have faith in God any more. If I should get back my eyes I would always have faith in prayer. But—the other day you told me I'd not be married, then! May not a blind woman be a married woman also?"

"No! Not if she never saw her husband. How could she ever have chosen, have selected? How could either her body or her soul ever have seen?"

She rose before him suddenly. "You say that!" She choked. "You say that, who helped put me where I am! And now you say you are going away—and you say that's all wrong, my being married! What do you mean?"

"If I gave you back your eyes and your life, isn't that something?"

"Why, no! A fight which isn't fought is worse than defeat. But you're talking as though you really meant to go away and leave me—always!"

"Yes. I've come to say good-by—and then to operate. Two this afternoon. Annie will come for you. I have told her what to do."

"And my husband?"

"Said he couldn't stand it to see you hurt. Said he would stand outside the door, but that he couldn't come in. Said he would be right there all the time. There's a great man, Mrs. Gage."

"And you are a very wise man, are you not!" said she suddenly, smiling at him slowly, her dark eyes full upon him.

"What do you mean?"

"Oh, so much you know about life and duty and the rights of everybody else! If I had my eyes, I'd not be married! Did you ever stop to think what you have been taking into your own hands here?"

"Go on," said he. "I've got it coming."

"Well, one thing you've forgotten. I've been a problem

and a trouble and a nuisance—yes. But I'm a woman! You treat me as though I were a pawn, a doll. I'm tired of it. I ought to tell you something, for fear you'll really go away, and give me no chance."

"I ought to have as much courage as you're showing now." He smiled, wryly.

"Then, if you have courage, you ought to stay here and see things through. You tell me this is right and this is not right—how do you know? I owe you very much—but ought you to decide everything for me? Let me also be the judge. If there's any problem in these matters, anything unsaid, let's face it *all*. Cut into my eyes, but don't cut into my soul any more. If you gave me back my sight, and did not give me back every unsettled problem, with all the facts before me to settle it at last, you would leave me with unhappiness hanging over me as long as ever I lived. Not even my eyes would pay me for it."

She rose, stumbling, reaching out a hand to save herself; and he dared not touch her hand even to aid her now.

"Oh, fine of you all," she said bitterly. "Did the Emperor of Prussia ever do more? You, whom I have never seen in all my life! Any situation that is hard here for you—take it. Haven't I done as much? If there's any other fight on ahead unsettled for you, can't you fight it out? Can't you give me the privilege—since you've been talking of a woman's rights and privileges—to fight out my own battles too—to fight out all of life's fights, even to take all of its losses? I'd rather have it that way. That means I want to see you, who you are, what you are, whether you are good, whether you are just, whether you are light, whether—"

"You have a keen mind," said he slowly. "You're telling

Emerson Hough

me to stay here. If we could meet face to face as though you never had been blind—why, then—I might say something or do something which would make you feel that I believed you never had been married. I have told you that already."

"Yes! Then surely you will not go away. Because you have brought up a problem between you and me—Aren't we big enough to fight that out between us? Ought we not? Give me my eyes! Give me my rights!

"Why, listen," she went on more gently, less argumentatively, "just the other day, when we were talking over this question about my eyes, I called out to you when you went away, and you did not hear me. I said No; I would not take my eyes from you and pay the price. I said it would be sweeter to be blind and remain deceived. But that's gone by. I've been thinking since then. Now I want it all—all! I want all the fight of it, all the risk of it. Then, after I've taken my chance and made my fight, I want all the joy of it or all the sorrow of it at the end! I want life! Don't you? I've always had the feeling that you were a strong man. I don't want anything I haven't earned. I'll never give what hasn't been earned. I won't ever pray for what isn't mine."

"Now I'm ready," she repeated simply. "I can't talk any more, and you mustn't. Good-by."

She felt her hand caught tight in both of his, but he could not speak to his hand clasp. "At two!" was all he managed to say.

And so, in this far-off spot in the wilderness, the science of to-day, not long after two by the clock, had done what it might to remedy nature's unkindness, and to make Mary Gage as other women. When the sun had dropped back of its shielding mountain wall, Mary Gage lay still asleep, her eyes bandaged, in her darkened room. Whether at length she would awaken to darkness or to light, none could tell. Allen Barnes only knew that, tried as never he had been in all his life before, he had done his surgeon's work unfalteringly.

"Doc," said Sim Gage tremblingly, when they met upon the gravel street in the straggling little camp, each white-faced from fatigue, "tell me how long before we'll know."

"Three or four days at least. We'll have to wait."

"You're sure she'll see?"

"I hope so. I think so."

"What'll she see first?"

"Light."

"Who'll she see first, Doc—Annie, you reckon?"

"If she asks for you, let her see you first," said Doctor Barnes. "That's your right."

"No," said Sim Gage, "no, I don't think so. I think she'd ought to see you first, because you're the doctor. A doctor, now, he ain't like folks, you know. He's just the doctor."

"Yes, he's just the doctor, Gage, that's all."

He left Sim Gage standing in the road, looking steadfastly at the door.

CHAPTER XXXI

THE BLIND SEE

To those waiting for the threatened attack upon the power dam, the mere torment of continued inaction became intolerable, but as to material danger, nothing definite came. The keen-eyed young soldiers on their beat night after night, day after day, caught no sight or sound of any lurking enemy, and began to feel resentment at the arduous hours asked of them. Once in a while one trooper would say to another that he saw no sense in people getting scared at nothing out in No Man's Land. The laborers of the camp were more or less incurious. They did their allotted hours of labor each day, passed at night to the bunk house, and fell into a snake-like torpor. Life seemed quiet and innocuous. Liquor was prohibited. The regime was military. Soon after the bugle had sounded Retreat each evening the raw little settlement became silent, save for the unending requiem to hope which the great waters chafing through the turbines continually moaned. It was apparently a place of peace.

Doctor Barnes felt reasonably sure that the attack, if any, would come through the valley at the lower dam, for that would be the only practical entry point of the marauders marooned somewhere back in the hills. The trail between these two dams lay almost wholly above the rocky river bed. It would have been difficult if not impossible to patrol the bed of the river itself, for close to the water's edge there were places where no foothold could have been obtained even now, low as the water was. Therefore it seemed most needful to watch the main wagon trail along the canyon shelf.

It was sun-fall of the third day after Doctor Barnes had left Mary Gage for her long wait in the dark. The men had finished their work about the great dam, and were on their way to their quarters. Sim Gage, scout, beginning his night's work and having ended his own attempt at sleep during the daytime, was passing, hatted and belted, rifle in hand, to the barracks, where he was to speak with the lieutenant in charge. The two men of the color guard stood at the foot of the great staff, dressed out of a tall mountain spruce, at whose top fluttered the flag of this republic. The shrilling of the bugle's beautiful salute to the flag was ringing far and near along the canyon walls. The flag began to drop, slowly, into the arms of the waiting man who had given oath of his life to protect it always, and to keep it still full high advanced. It must never touch the earth at all, but remain a creature of the air—that is the tradition of our Army and all the Army's proud color guards.

Sim Gage stopped now, as every man in that encampment, soldier or laborer, had been trained punctiliously to do, at the evening gun. He stood at attention, like these others; for Sim Gage was a soldier, or thought he was. His eyes were fixed on this strange thing, this creature called the Flag. A strange, fierce jealousy arose in his heart for it, a savage love, as though it were a thing that belonged to him. His chest heaved now in the feeling that he was identified with this guard, waiting for the colors to come to rest and shelter after the day of duty. It stirred him in a way which he did not understand. A simple, unintelligent man, of no great shrewdness, though free of any maudlin sentiment, he stood fast in the mid-street and saluted the flag, not because he was obliged to do so, but because he passionately craved to do so.

He turned to meet Annie Squires, who was hurrying away from her own quarters. She held in her hand a letter which she waved at him as she approach.

"Look-it here!" she exclaimed. "Look what I found. Where's the Doc? I want to see him right away."

"He's like enough down at the lower dam by now," said Sim.

"Well, he'd ought to see this."

"What is it?" asked Sim, looking at it questioningly. "Who's it to?"

"Who's it to?" said Annie Squires. "Why, it's to Charlie Dorenwald, that's who it's to!"

"What? That feller that was up there—one you said you knew before you come out here?"

"Yes. But how does this Waldhorn chump in there know anything about Charlie Dorenwald? That's what I want to know."

"What chump? Mr. Waldhorn?"

"I found this in his desk. Well, I wasn't rummaging in his desk, but I had to slick things up, and saw it. I only run on it by accident."

"What's in it?" said Sim Gage.

"Well, now," said Annie, naively, "I only just steamed it a little. It rolled open easy with a pen-holder."

"Huh. What you find in it?"

"Why, nothing but nonsense, that's what I found. Listen here. 'Price wheat next year two-nineteen sharp signal general satisfaction.' Now, what does that mean? That's foolishness. That man's a nut! I bet he gets alone up in here and smokes hop, that's what he does, all by himself. No one but a dope fiend would pull stuff like that.

"But still," she added, a finger at chin, "what bothers me is, how does Charlie know Waldhorn? Unless—"

"Unless what?" asked Sim Gage, his brows suddenly contracting.

"Unless they're both in on this deal! What do you suppose the Doc thinks? What makes him keep this Waldhorn close as he does? Is he a prisoner?"

"No, I reckon not. We all just got orders to shoot him if he tries to get away. I think Doc's holding him until he gets word in from outside. Things seems to me to move mighty slow."

"Well, this letter's addressed to Charlie Dorenwald, and anything that's got Charlie Dorenwald's name on it is crooked, and you can gamble on that. Can't you find the Doc?"

As it happened, Doctor Barnes had not yet left his quarters for his nightly trip to the lower canyon. He had been trying to sleep. He rose now, full-clad and all awake, when he caught sight of Sim Gage's face at his door.

"What's up?" he said.

"This here," said Sim, "is a letter that Annie brung me out of the house where them two is living. She says she found it in there. We can't make nothing out of it. Seems like this Waldhorn here had something to say to Charlie Dorenwald. Annie says it's the same Dorenwald that was up above, at the ranch, the one Wid didn't get. Well, how come him and Waldhorn to know each other, that's what I want to know. So does Annie."

"What I want to know, too!" said Doctor Barnes, reaching out his hand.

"Annie says it's plumb nutty, the stuff in it," commented Sim. The other looked at him quizzically.

"She read it then?"

He read it now, himself, and stood stiff and straight at reading. "This is a cypher—code stuff! They know what it means, and we don't. 'Two-nineteen sharp'—I wonder what that means! This is the nineteenth day of the month, isn't it? 'Signal general satisfaction'—Lord! I'd give anything for a good night's sleep. Gage, go on over and tell all the men to keep full dressed, and with equipment handy all night long. I don't have any clear guess what this is all about, but we can't take any chances."

"Wid, he thinks them fellers ain't coming down here a-tall," said Sim confidentially.

"He doesn't know anything more about it than I do or you do," said Doctor Barnes somewhat testily. "You go and tell Annie to shut that desk up, and see that she keeps it shut. I'm coming over to seal it up."

Annie Squires meantime had hastened back to discuss these matters with her patient in the hospital room. It only added more to the nervous strain that already tormented Mary Gage.

"Annie, I'm scared!" she whispered. "Oh! if I could only take care of myself. Tell me, Annie—I'll get well, won't I?"

"Sure thing, Kid—it's a cinch."

"Where is he?" Mary demanded after some hesitation.

"Who? Him?" Annie employed her usual fashion of indicating the identity of Sim Gage.

"No, I mean Doctor Barnes."

"He'll be going down below pretty soon. He don't know anything more than I do about what that fool stuff in the letter means."

"But say," she added after a time, "I been kind of looking around in desks and places, you know—I have to red things up—and I run across another thing, some more writing."

"You mustn't do these things, Annie! It may be private."

"Oh, no, it ain't. It's only some writing copied from a magazine, like enough. It was on one of the desks in this house—just in there."

"Copied?—What is it?"

"I don't know. Poetry stuff—sounds mushy. I didn't know men would do things like copying out poetry from magazines. Never heard of Mr. Symonds—did you?"

"How can I tell, Annie?"

"I'll read it for you if you'll let me. It's dark, in here—I'll just go outside the door and read it through the crack at you, so's the light won't hurt you anyways."

And so, faintly, as from a detached intelligence, there came into Mary Gage's darkened room, her darkened life, some words well-written, ill-read, which it seemed to her she might have dreamed:

"As a perfume doth remain
In the folds where it hath lain,
So the thought of you, remaining
Deeply folded in my brain,
Will not leave me; all things leave me:
You remain.

"Other thoughts may come and go,
Other moments I may know
That shall waft me, in their going,
As a breath blown to and fro.
Fragrant memories; fragrant memories
Come and go.

"Only thoughts of you remain
In my heart where they have lain,
Perfumed thoughts of you, remaining,
A hid sweetness, in my brain.
Others leave me; all things leave me:
You remain."

"Read them over again!" said Mary Gage, sitting upon her couch. "Read them again, Annie! I want to learn it all by heart."

And Annie, patient as ever, read the words over to her. The keen senses of Mary Gage recorded them.

"I can say them now!" said she, as much to herself as to her friend. And she did say them, over and over again.

"Annie," she cried, as she sat up suddenly. "I can't stand it any more! I can see! I can see!"

She was tearing at the bandages about her head when Annie entered and put down her hands, terrified at this disobedience of orders.

"Annie, I *know* I can see! It was light—at the door there! I can see. I can *see*!" She began to weep, trembling.

"Hush!" said Annie, frightened. "It ain't possible! It can't be true! *What* did you see?"

"Nothing!" said Mary Gage, half sobbing. "Just the light. Don't tell him. Put back the bandage. But, oh, Annie, Annie, I can *see*!"

"You're talking foolish, Sis," said Annie, pinning the bandages all the tighter about the piled brown hair of Mary Gage's head.

"But say now," she added after that was done, "if I was a girl and a fellow felt that way about me—couldn't remember nobody but me that way—why, me for him! Mushy—but times comes when a girl falls strong for the mushy, huh?

"Now you lay down again and cover up your eyes and rest, or you'll never be seeing things again, sure enough. I ain't going to read no more of that strong-arm writing at all."

Mary Gage heard the door close, heard the footsteps of her friend passing down the little hall. She was alone again. Her heart was throbbing high.

What she first had seen was the soul of a man; a man's confession; his recessional as well. Now she knew that he was indeed going away from her life forever. Which had been more cruel, blindness or vision?

CHAPTER XXXII

THE ENEMY

The night wore on slowly. Midnight struck, and the cold of the mountain night had reached its maximum chill. To the ears of the weary patrols there came no sound save the continuous complaint of the waters, a note rising and falling, increasing and decreasing in volume, after the strange fashion of waters carried by the chance vagaries of the air. At times the sound of the river rose to great volume, again it died down to a low murmur, the voice of a beaten giant protesting against his shackles. Came two o'clock in the morning, and the guards walked their beats with the weariness of men who have fought off sleep for hours. Sim Gage, sleepless so long, was very weary, but he kept about his work.

At intervals of half an hour he crunched down the gravel-faced slope of the bank which ran from the bench level to the foot of the dam. Here he walked along the level of the great eddy, along the rocky shore, examining the face of the vast concrete wall itself, gazing also as he always did, with no special purpose, at the face of the wide and long apron where the waters foamed over, a few inches deep, white as milk, day and night.

Any attempt at the use of dynamite by any enemy

naturally would be made on this lower side of the dam. There were different places which might naturally be used by a criminal who had opportunity. One of these, concealed from the chance glance of any officer, was back under the apron, behind the half-completed side columns of the spill gate, where a great buttress came out to flank the apron. A charge exploded here would get at the very heart of the dam, for it would open the turbine wells and the spillway passage which had been provided for the controlled outlet.

Ragged heaps of native rock lay along the foot of the dam, flanking the edge of the great eddy eastward of the apron. Here often the laborers stood and cast their lines for the leaping trout, which, wearied by their fruitless fight at the apron, that carried them only up to the insurmountable obstacle which reached a hundred feet above them, sometimes were swept back to seek relief in the gentler waters of the deep eddy, that swung inshore from the lower end of the apron.

Sim Gage saw all these scenes, so familiar by this time, as they lay half revealed under the blaze of the great search-light. It all seemed safe now, as it always had before.

But when at length he turned back to ascend to the upper level, he saw something which caused him to stop for just an instant, and then to spring into action.

The power plant proper of the dam was not yet wholly installed, only the dam and turbine-ways being comp-leted. In the power house itself, a sturdy building of rock which caught hold of the immemorial mountain foot beneath it, only a single unit of the dynamos had been installed. This unit had been hooked on, as the engineers phrased it, in order to furnish electric light to the camp itself, for the telephone service of the valley and for the minor machinery which was operated by this or that machine shop along the side of the mountain. A cable from the power house ran up to another house known as the lighting plant, which stood in the angle between the street level and the dam itself. Here was installed a giant searchlight which could be played at will along the face of the dam, to make its examination the more easy and exact by night. The steady stream of this light was a fixed factor, being held at such a position as would cover the greatest amount of the dam face.

Now, as Sim Gage topped the grade, gravel crunching under his feet, a trifle out of breath with his climb, since the incline itself was a thing of magnificent distances, he saw the searchlight of the power dam begin a performance altogether new in his own experience.

The great shaft of light rose up abruptly to a position vertical, a beam of light reaching up into the sky. An instant, and it began to swing from side to side. It swung sharply clear against the bald face of the mountain at the farther end of the dam. It swept down the canyon itself, or to its first great bend. It rose again and swept across the dark-fringed summit of the mountains on the hither side of the stream. Not once, but twice, this was done.

It was a splendid and magnificent thing itself, this giant eye, illuminating and revealing, fit factor in a wild and imposing panorama of the night. But why? No one ever had known the searchlight to be used in this way. What orders had been given? What did these zig-zag beams up and down the surface of the sky indicate? Was it a signal, or was some one playing with the property of the Company, there in the cupola of the light station?

Sim Gage reached the side of the plant just as the light came down to its original duty of watching the face of the dam. At first there was not any sound.

"Who's there?" he called out. No answer came. It seemed to him that he heard some sort of movement in the little rock house.

"Halt! Who goes there?" he called out in a formula he had learned.

He got no answer, but he heard a thud as of a body dropping out of the window of the further side of the house, against the slope of the dam which lay above it.

He ran around the corner of the little building, rifle at the ready, only to see a scrambling figure, bent over, endeavoring to reach the top of the dam, where the smooth roadway ran from side to side of the great gorge. That way lay no escape. The sentry was across yonder, and would soon return. This way, toward the east, a fugitive must go if he would seek any point of emergence from these surroundings.

"Halt! Halt there! Halt, or I'll fire!" cried Gage. "Halt!" He called it out again, once, twice, three times. But the figure, whoever or whatever it was, ran on. It now had reached the top of the dam, and could be seen with more or less distinctness, sky-lined against the starlight and the gray sky behind it.

Sim Gage, old-time hunter, used all his life to firearms, was used also to firing at running game. He drew down now deep into the rear sight of his Springfield, allowing for the faint light, and held at the front edge of the running figure as nearly as he could tell. He fired once, twice and three times—rap!—rap!—rap!—the echo came from the concrete—at the figure as it crouched and stumbled on. Then it stopped. There came a scrambling and a sliding of the object, which fell at the top of the dam. It slipped off the dam top and rolled and slid almost at his feet. He dragged it down into the edge of the beams of the searchlight itself.

Up to this time he had not known or suspected who the man might be. At first he now thought it was a woman. In reality it was a Chinaman, the cook and body-servant of Waldhorn, engineer at the power operations! He was dead.

Sim stood looking down at what he had done, trying in his slow fashion of mind to puzzle out what this man had been doing here, and why he had come. He heard the sound of running feet above him, heard challenges, shouts, every way. Others had heard the shot. "This way, fellers—Come along!" he heard Wid Gardner call out, high and clear; for that night Wid also was of the upper guard.

But they were not running in his direction. They seemed to be back on the street. All at once Sim Gage solved his little problem. This Chinaman had been sent to do this work—sent by the owner of that house yonder, the engineer, Waldhorn. That prisoner must not escape now. He knew! It was he who had given the searchlight signal! Waldhorn—and Dorenwald! He coupled both names now again.

Sim Gage himself, having a shorter distance to go than his comrades, left his dead Chinaman, and started after the man higher up. He reached the Waldhorn quarters slightly before the others.

He heard the screen door of the log house slam, saw a stout and burly man step out, satchel in hand. The man walked hurriedly toward a car which Sim Gage had not noticed, since there was so much unused machinery about, wheel scrapers, wagons, plows and the like. Now he saw that it was Waldhorn and Waldhorn's car. He was taking advantage of this confusion to make his own escape.

This hurrying figure halted for a half instant in the dim light, for he heard footsteps on each side of him. He knew the guard was coming.

Sim Gage's summons rang high and clear. Yonder was the man—he was going to escape. He must not escape. All these things came to Sim Gage's mind as he half raised his weapon to his shoulder, challenging again, "Halt! Who goes there? Halt!" The bolt of his Springfield clinked home once more.

The man turned away, toward the sound of the greater number of his enemies, weapon in hand. The patrol was closing in. But before he turned he both gave and received death in the last act he might offer in treachery to this country, which had been generous and kind to him.

Sim Gage fired with close, sure aim, and cut his man through with the blow of the Spitzer bullet of the Springfield piece. But even as he did so Waldhorn himself had fired with the heavy automatic pistol which he carried. The bullet caught Sim Gage high in the chest, and passed through, missing the spine by but little. He sprawled forward.

Waldhorn's body was no better than a sieve, for he received the fire of the entire squad of riflemen who had approached from the other side, and so many bullets struck him, again and again, that they actually held him up from falling for an instant.

Now the entire street filled. Foreign or half-foreign laboring folk came out, soldiers and sailor boys came, jabbering in a score of tongues. None knew the plot of the drama which had been finished now. All they knew was that the chief engineer had been killed by the guard. Very well, but who had shot Scout Gage?

Sim Gage, looking up at the sky, felt the great arm of Flaherty, the foreman, under his head.

"Easy now, lad," said the big man. "Easy. Lay down a bit, till I have a look. Where's the Docther, boys?—Get him quick."

"What's the matter?" said Sim Gage. "Lemme up. I fell down—Who hit me?"

He felt something at his chest, raised a hand, and in turn passed it before his face in wonderment.

"Well, look at that!" said he. "Did that feller shoot me? Say, did I get him?"

"Sure, boy!" said Flaherty. "You got him. And so did a dozen more of the fellies. He's deader'n hell this minute, so don't you worry none over that. Don't worry over nothing," he added gently, folding his coat to put under Sim's head. He had seen gun shot wounds before in his life on the rough jobs, and he knew.

"Get a board, or something, boys," he said. So presently they brought a plank, and eased Sim Gage gently to it, men at each end lifting him, others steadying him as he was carried. They took him into the house which Waldhorn had just now left.

It was the turn of dawn now. The soft light of day was

filtering through the air from somewhere up above, somewhere beyond the edge of the canyon.

"Better tell those women to stay away," said Flaherty to the young lieutenant. The latter met Annie Squires at the door of her house, ejaculating, demanding, questioning, weeping, all at once. It was with difficulty that she was induced to obey the general orders of getting inside and keeping quiet.

Other men came now, telling of the discovery of the dead Chinaman near the lighting station. The bits of information were pieced together hurriedly, this and that to the other.

Doctor Barnes had seen the light's play on the sky, had heard echoes in the mountains. He now reached the scene, coming at top speed up the canyon trail in his car. He met answers already formed for his questions.

"They got Sim," said Wid Gardner. "Waldhorn—"

He hurried into the room where they had carried the wounded man. "Why, of course," said Sim Gage dully, "I'll be all right. After breakfast I'll be out again all right. I've got to go over and see—I've got to go over to her house and see—" But he never told what he planned.

Doctor Barnes shook his head to Flaherty after a time, when the latter turned to him in the outer room. The big foreman compressed his lips.

"He's done good work, the lad!" said Flaherty; and Wid Gardner, still standing by, nodded his head.

"Mighty good. It was him got the Chink all right—hit him twict out of three, and creased him onct; and like enough this Dutchman first, too. Tell me, Doc, ain't he got a chanct to come through? Can't you make it out that way for pore old Sim?"

"I'm afraid not," said Doctor Barnes. "The shot's close to an artery, and like enough he's bleeding internally, because he's coughing. His pulse is jumpy. It's too bad— too damn bad. He was—a good man, Sim Gage!"

"What was it, Annie?" asked Mary Gage, over in their house. "There was shooting. Was anybody hurt?"

"Some of the hands got to mixing it, like enough," said Annie, herself pale and shaking. "I don't know."

"Was anybody hurt?"

"I haven't had time to find out. Oh, my God! Sis, I wish't we'd never come out here to this country at all. I want my mother, that's what I want! I'm sick with all this." She began to cry, sobbing openly. Mary Gage, now the stronger, drew the girl's head down into her own arms.

"You mustn't cry," said she. "Annie, we've got to pull together."

"I guess so," said Annie, sobbing, "both of us. But I'm so lonesome—I'm so awful scared."

The morning came slowly, at length fully, cool and softly luminous. The friends of Sim Gage, all men, stood near his bedside. His eyes opened sometimes, looking with curious languor around him, as though some problem were troubling him. At length he turned toward Wid, who stood close to him.

"Hit!" said he.—"I know, now."

No one said anything to this. After a time he reached out a hand and touched almost timidly the arm of his friend. His voice was laboring and not strong.

"Where's—where's my hat?" he whispered at length.

"Your hat?" said Wid. "Your hat?—Now, why—I reckon it's hanging around somewheres here. What makes you want it?"

But some one had heard the request and came through the little hallway with Sim Gage's hat, brave green cord and all.

The wounded man looked at it and smiled, as sweet a smile as may come to a man's face—the smile of a boy. Indeed, he had lived a life that had left him scarce more than a boy, all these years alone on outskirts of the world.

He motioned to them to put the hat on the bed side him. "I want it here," he said after a time, moving restlessly when they undertook to take it from him.

He touched it with his hand. At length he reached out and dropped it on the chair at the head of his bed, now and again turning and looking at it the best he might, laboring as he did with his torn lungs; looking at it with some strange sort of reverence in his gaze, some tremendous significance.

"Ain't she *fine*?" he asked of his friend, again with his astonishingly winsome smile; a smile they found hard to look upon.

A half hour later some man down the road said to another that the sagebrusher had croaked too.

That is to say, Sim Gage, gentleman, soldier and patriot, had passed on to the place where men find reward for doing the very best they know with what God has seen fit to give them as their own.

CHAPTER XXXIII

THE DAM

Doctor Allen Barnes turned slowly toward the house where the wife of Sim Gage still lay. His heart was heavy with the hardest duty he had ever known in all his life.

But as he reached a point half way between the two houses he suddenly stopped. At that moment every man on the little street stopped also.

The routine of the patrol had been relaxed in the excitement of these late events. Indeed, it seemed tacitly agreed that the climax had come, so that there was no need now for further guardianship of the property. It was not so.

The sound was a short, heavy moan, as nearly as it may be described, and not a sharp rending note; a vast, deep groan, somewhere deep in the earth, as though a volcano were about to erupt. It was not over in an instant, but went on, like the suppressed lamentations of some creature trying to break its chains. It might have been some prehistoric, tremendous creature, unknown to man, unknown to these times. But it was our creature. It was of our day. Else it could never have been.

Then the ground under the feet of every man on the little street lifted, gently, slowly, and sank down again. As it did so a tremendous reverberation gathered and broke out, ran up and down the canyon, up the opposite cliff face, echoing and rising as dense and thick as smoke does. The rack-rock charge, of no one may know how many hundreds of pounds, had done its work.

And then all earth went back to chaos. A new world was in the making. There arose in that narrow, iron-sided gorge a havoc such as belike surpassed that of the original breaking through of the waters. That first slow work of nature might have been done drop by drop, a little at a time. But now all the outraged river was venting itself in one epochal instant. Its accumulated power was rushing through the wall that held it back from the seas—the vast vengeance of the waters, which they had sought covertly all this time, now was theirs.

An uncontrollable and immeasurable force was set loose. No man may measure the actual horse power that lay above the great dam of the Two Forks—it never was a comprehensible thing. A hundred Johnstown reservoirs lay penned there. That there was so little actual loss of life was due to the fact that there were few settlements in the sixty miles below the mouth of the great canyon itself. A few scattered dry farms, edging up close to the river in the valley far below, were caught and buried. Hours later, under the advancing flood, all the live stock of the valley was swept away, all the houses and all the fences and roads and bridges were wiped out as though they had never been. But this was fifty, sixty, seventy miles away, and much later in the morning. Those below could only guess what had happened far up in the great Two Forks canyon. The big dam was broken!

The face of the giant dam, more solidly coherent than

granite itself, slowly, grandiose even in its ruin, passed out and down in a hundred foot crevasse where the spill gates were widened by the high explosive. A vast land slip, jarred from the cut-face mountain side above, thundered down and aided in the crumbling of the dam. A disintegrated mass of powdered concrete fell out, was blown apart. The face of the dam on that part slowly settled down into a vast U. Then the waters came through, leaping—a solid face of water such as no man may comprehend.

An instant, and the canyon below the dam was fifty feet deep with a substance which seemed not water, but a mass of shrieking and screaming demons set loose under the name of no known element. There came a vast roar, but with it a number of smaller sounds, as of voices deep down under the flood, glass splintering, rocks rumbling. The gorge seemed inhabited by furies. And back of this came the pressure of twenty miles of water, a hundred feet deep, which would come through. The river had its way again, raving and roaring in an anvil chorus of its own, knocking the great bowlders together, shrieking its glee. The Two Forks river came through the Two Forks canyon once more! Against it there stood only the fragmental ruin of the great, gray face, buttressed with concrete more coherent than granite itself, but all useless here.

The tide rose very rapidly. The canyon was too crooked to carry off the flood. The lower part of the town, where the street grade sank rapidly, went under water almost at once. Horses, cows, sheep, chickens, the odds and ends of such an encampment, gathered by vagrant laborers, were swept down before opportunity could be found to save them. Men and the few women in that part of town, employees of the cook camp, abandoned their possessions and ran straight up the mountain side, seeking only to get above the tide. Their houses were swept away like cheese boxes. Logs were crushed together like straws. The sound of it all made human speech inaudible anywhere close to the water's edge.

The east half of the dam, that closer to the camp, still held. The buildings here were still under the dam—a mass of water fifty feet in height rose above them, would come through if that portion of the dam broke. But at the time only the suction of the farther U, where the break was made, caused a gentle current to be visible at this side of the backwater. If the dam held, it would be quite a time before the level of the lake above would be appreciably altered. Slowly, inch by inch, each inch representing none might say how much in power of ruin, it would sink, and in time reveal the ancient bed of the river. If the remnant of the dam held, that would be true. Happy the human race aspiring to erect such a barrier, that so few suffered in this rebirth of the wilderness. Had the settlements been thick below, all must have perished. The telephone was out, there was no way for a messenger to get out ahead of the flood. Only the quick widening of the valley, below the canyon's lower end, eased down the volume of the flood so that it was less destructive. There was no settlement at all in the canyon proper.

After the first pause of horror men here at the broken dam began to bestir themselves. Discipline was a thing forgotten, and *sauve qui peut* was the law. It was some time before Doctor Barnes pulled himself together and began to try to get his men in hand. He ordered them to the lower end of the street, to drive the people out of their houses without an instant's delay; for none might say at what time the break in the dam would increase, in which case it soon would be too late for any hope. He himself hastened at last to the house where the two women were, Wid Gardner with him, after he had issued general orders for all the men to get up the trail above the dam as soon as possible.

"Come out!" he cried as he opened the door. Mary Gage and Annie came arm in arm, both of them hysterical now.

"It's all gone," said Doctor Barnes, not even bitterly, but calmly after all. "It's out. The dam's gone."

"Gone? What does it mean? Where shall we go? Is there danger?" These questions came all at once from the two women. The roar of the waters drowned their voices.

"Come quick! Get into my car. It's only a step up the grade—we'll be safe on the upper level."

They came, Mary Gage still with her bandages in place, stumbling, terrified, but leading the little dog, Tim, who cringed down in curious terror of his own. Doctor Barnes hurried them, guided them, and the little car quickly carried them up the incline above the top of the dam.

They paused here at the first sharp curve under the lee of the cut bank, where they might take breath and look down. There came up and grouped themselves near them and beyond them now several of the people of the camp, and practically all of the soldiers from the barracks, who fell into a stiff, silent line, looking down. It was a scene singular enough which lay before them, this wild remaking of the wilderness.

There came another cosmic cry from the chaos below them, more terrifying than anything yet had been. Two Forks was throwing in the reserves. The enemy was breaking! Doctor Barnes knew what this meant. The break was widening. He stood looking down. And then he heard a human voice cry out, a voice he knew.

He turned—and saw Mary Gage fall as though in a faint upon the ground. Her eye-bandages were off, her eyes wholly uncovered to the light.

"Well, it's over now," said he quietly to Annie Squires. "One way or the other, it's done."

He lifted her gently, attended her until at length she moved, stood—until at length he knew that she saw!

She turned her face back from the ruin which had been her first vision of her new world, and looked into the eyes of the man who had given back to her eyes with which to see. And he looked deep, deep into her own, grave and unsmiling.

She spoke to him at last. "I can see," said she simply.

"I'm very glad," said he, trying to be as simple. But he turned her away, giving her into Annie's arms.

"Look!" cried other voices.

A section of the side of the great U, running clear back to a seam which had formed in the dam face, slowly broke out and went down. The water rose like a tide now, very rapidly, because the canyon itself, so narrow and so full of abrupt curves, made no adequate outlet for this augmented flood. The entire lower part of the camp was covered, and the flood, eddying back from the mountain wall, came creeping up toward the top of the grade, covering now this and now that portion of the settlement. One house after another was swept away before their eyes.

Doctor Barnes stood looking out over it all moodily. He did not go back to Mary Gage. Back beyond a few of the soldiers were chattering idly, but no one paid attention to them, for not even they themselves knew that they were talking. But at length a voice, clear and distinct, did come to Doctor Barnes' ears.

"Where is my husband!" cried Mary Gage, breaking away from Annie. "Which is he?"

He turned to her silently. He shook his head.

"I want to see him! I've got to see him. Who's that man?" She pointed.

"That's Wid Gardner," said Doctor Barnes, slowly and gently as he could.

"Those men yonder—those soldiers—is one of them my husband? You said he was a soldier."

"Yes," said Doctor Barnes, "he was a soldier."

Then she guessed at last.

"He *was* a soldier? Where is he *now*?" She turned upon him, laying her hands upon his arms. "Where is he now?" she demanded.

But Doctor Barnes was looking at the foam-flecked surface of the water, eddying against the mountain side, crawling up and up. The little log house where Sim Gage's soul had passed was no more to be seen. It had gone. The house where the women had stopped was swept down but a short time later. Doctor Barnes could not speak the cruel truth.

"Annie!" called out Mary Gage, sobbing openly, imploringly. "Tell me, won't I *ever* see him? You said he was a good soldier."

"One of the best," said Doctor Barnes at last. "Listen to me, please. Your husband died believing he had saved the dam. And so he had, so far as his work was concerned. It was he who discovered their work last night. He took care of two of them—it makes three for him. It was he that killed Big Aleck, up on the reserve, and avenged you, and never told you. He was shot—you heard the firing. He died before we came up here. I couldn't bring his body till you were cared for. Now it's too late. He's gone. Well, it's as good a way for a good man to go."

"Blow 'Taps,'" he ordered of the bugler near by. It was done. And then, at his order, the rifles spoke in unison over a soldier's grave.

"But I've never *seen* him!" she said to him piteously, after the echoes of the salutes had passed. It was as though she was unable to comprehend.

"No," said Allen Barnes. "But keep this picture of him— think that he died like a gentleman and a soldier. A good man, Sim Gage."

He turned away and walked down the grade apart from them, hardly seeing what lay before him, hardly hearing the rush of the waters down the canyon.

When men began to question as to the cause of the disaster, it became plain that some man, whose name no one will ever know, must have crept along the side of the river bank below the road grade, and have fired the fuse of a heavy charge of rack-rock, which, none might know how long, had been hid between the buttresses and back of the apron of the dam.

Doctor Barnes reasoned now that that man in all likelihood had come from below. If so, in all likelihood he was one of the Dorenwald party. His face lighted grimly. There were but few places where they could have found a place in the canyon for an encampment. If they had found one of these places—where were they now? Their fate could now be read in this flood forcing its way down through the crooked gorge of the mountain range. The flag staff had not been swept down—the flag still fluttered now, triumphant over the attempted ruin—the answer of America to Anarchy! And the flag had been avenged. Dorenwald and his "free brothers," leaders of the "world's revolt," would revolt no more. The sponge of the slate had wiped off their little marks. No one would ever trace them. They would find no confessional and no shriving, for their way back to that underworld of devil-fed minds, out of which they had emerged to do ruin in a country which had never harmed them, but which on the contrary had welcomed them and fed them in their want.

CHAPTER XXXIV

AFTER THE DELUGE

In one elemental instant there was loosed in the soul of Mary Gage a pent flood of emotion. She let her heart go, let in the wilderness of primitive things again. She was alive! She could see! She could be as other women!

The flood of relief, of joy, of yearning, was a thing cosmic, so strong that regret and grief were for the time swept on and buried in the welter of emotions running free.

It was as though she had stepped absolutely from one world into another. Suddenly, the people of her old world were gone. There had been a shadow, a strange, magnified shadow of a soul, this man who had been called her husband. But now with astonishing swiftness and clarity of vision she knew that he never had been a husband to her. What another had told her was the truth. He never had allowed her to touch his hand, his face, he never had laid a hand on hers, never had called her by any name of love, never had kissed her or sought to do so. And he was gone now, so absolutely that not even the image of him could remain had she ever owned an image of him. She never had known him, and now never could.

Emerson Hough

Alas! Sim Gage, shall we say? By no means. Happy Sim Gage! For he passed at the climax of his life and took with him forever all he ever could have gained of delight and comfort. Happy Sim Gage! to have a woman like Mary, his wife, stand and weep for him now. He had lost her had she ever seen his face, and now, at least, he owned her tears. A vast and noble flood carried happy Sim Gage out to the ocean at the end of all, to the rest and the absorption and the peace.

Mary Gage pushed back the bandage from her eyes furtively, unable to obey longer any command which cut her off from this new world to which she had come. Before she dropped the bandage once more she had caught sight of a figure not looking toward her at the moment.

Allen Barnes was standing with his head up, his eyes looking out over the abysmal scene below. Behind his back he had gripped tight together his long and sinewy hands. He was a lean and broad man, so she thought. He stood in the uniform of his country, made for manly men, and beseeming only such. The neatness of good rearing even now was apparent in every line of him. Dust seemed not to have touched him. He was clean and trim and fine, a picture of an officer and a gentleman.

Light, and the new music of the spheres—to whom did she owe those things? It was to this man standing yonder.

"McQueston," she heard a sharp voice command, "take your men and go down to the lower dam—any way you can get across the mountains. Bring your report up by one of these cars when you get back here. I'll go up above to the upper station with these people. It's going to rain. That will end the fire."

He saluted sharply in return, and turned again to those under his personal charge.

"Get into the car," he said. Mary Gage felt his hand steadying her arm. He took his place at the steering wheel, Wid Gardner alongside, Annie and herself being left to the rear seat of the tonneau. It was reckless driving that Doctor Allen Barnes did once more. They out-ran the approaching valley storm, and so presently came into the gate of that place where once had lived Sim Gage. They dismounted from the car and stood, a forlorn group, looking at the scene before them as funeral mourners returning, not liking the thought of going into a deserted home from which a man is gone never to return.

CHAPTER XXXV

ANNIE ANSWERS

All at once Annie Squires, usually stolid, now over-strained, gave way to a wild sobbing. "I can't go in there," said she. "I'm scared. I want to go home! I want my mother, that's what I want."

"Where is your mother?" asked Wid Gardner. He had come over near to her when Doctor Barnes was helping Mary into the house.

"Dead—dead long ago," wept Annie. "When I was a little girl. Like her, Mary, there—we didn't neither of us ever have a mother. We done just the best we could, both of us. We've tried and tried to find some sort of place where we belonged, and we couldn't. We haven't got any place to go to. I haven't got a place on earth to call my home.

"And it's something a woman wants sometimes," she added after a while, dabbing her wet handkerchief against her eyes. "That's the Gawd's truth."

Wid approached more closely the weeping girl, touching her arm with a brown hand now gentle as a child's.

"Now look-a-here," said he. "I can't stand to hear you go

on that way. Do you reckon you was ever any lonesomer fer a home than what I am, living out here all my life?"

"And now I'm worse off than I ever was before," he went on frowningly. "I didn't know nothing before you come out here. But now I do. I can't think of your going back, Annie."

She did not answer him, but went on weeping.

"What's more, I ain't *a-going* to stand it," he added savagely. "I ain't *a-going* to let you go back a-tall. Talk about home!—there's a home right acrosst the fence. We can make it any way we like. It'll do to start with, anyhow. Here's where you belong—you don't belong back there in them dirty cities. You belong right out here—with me."

"I couldn't—I can't," said Annie. "I couldn't let her go back alone. I got to take care of that kid."

"She ain't blind no more," said Wid. "But she don't have to go back! This here place where we stand is hers, ain't it? What more does she want? And we'd be right here, too, all the time, to help her and watch her, wouldn't we, now?"

"You don't know her," said Annie Squires. "I do."

"But, Annie," he went on, "you'd ought to see this out here in the valley when the spring comes! It's green, all green! The sage has got five different colors of green in it—you wouldn't think that, would you? And some blue. And you ain't seen the mountains yet when they're white with snow on them—that's something you got to see fer to know what a mountain is. And look at that little creek— it's plumb gentle up here, ain't it? It's pretty, here. You ought to see the moonlight on the meadows when the moon is full,—I was telling you about that, Annie."

"I ain't never been married in my life," he went on, arguing now. "I ain't never seen a woman that I loved or looked at twicet but you. I was too damn lazy to care anyway about anything till I seen you. I just been drifting and fooling along. But now I ain't. I want to go to work. I want to be somebody. Why, Annie, I reckon all the time I was homesick, and didn't know it. But I tell you it wouldn't be no home unless you was in it with me. I ain't fit to ask you to run it fer me. But I do!"

It was the ancient story, even told direct in the open, unwhispered, even told now, at such an hour and place. She did not answer at all, but her sobbing had ceased. He stood still frowning, looking at her, his hat pushed back from his forehead.

"I can't say no more'n I have," he concluded. "Years and years, Annie. Wouldn't it settle a heap of things?"

"I got to have some sort of time to think things over, haven't I, then?" She spoke with apparent venom, as though this were an affront that had been offered her.

"All you want," said Wid Gardner gently. "I've done my own thinking. I know."

"I've got to go in and get them folks something to eat, haven't I?" said Annie, using her apron on her eyes. "It's going to be about the last time all of us'll ever eat together any more."

"Well, we can invite them over, sometimes, can't we, Annie?" said Wid Gardner calmly. And he kissed her brazenly and in the open.

CHAPTER XXXVI

MRS. DAVIDSON'S CONSCIENCE

It was fall, and the flame of the frost had fallen on the aspen and the cottonwoods, and shorn the willows of most of their leaves. A hundred thousand wild fowl honked their way across the meadows toward the black flats where once had been a lake, and where now was immeasurable food for them. Up in the mountains the elk were braying. The voice of the coyotes at the pink of dawn seemed shriller now, as speaking of the coming days of want. But the sun still was kind, the midday hour still was one of warmth. A strange, keen value, immeasurably exalting, was in the air. All nature was afoot, questioning of what was to come.

Mary Gage came in from the stream side that afternoon, the strap of her trout creel cutting deep into the shoulder of her sweater. She placed the basket down under the shadow of the willow trees, and hung up a certain rod on certain nails under the eaves of the cabin. Her little dog, Tim, soberly marched in front of her, still guiding her, as he supposed; but she no longer had a cord upon his neck, a staff in her hand. A hundred chickens, well grown now, followed her about, vocal of their desire for attention. She turned to them, taking down the little sack which contained the leavings of the wheat that had been threshed not so long ago here.

"Chick, chick, chick!" she called gently—"*chick*ee, *chick*ee!" So she stood, Lady Bountiful for them as they swarmed about her feet in the dooryard.

She heard the clang of the new gate, and turned, her hand shading her eyes to see who was coming.

As she stood she made a splendid picture of young womanhood, ruddy and brown, clear of skin and eye, very fair indeed to look upon. The droop of the corners of her mouth was gone. Her gaze was direct and free. She walked easily, strong and straight and deep of bosom, erect of head, flat of back, as fit for love as any woman of ancient Greece. Such had been the ministrations of the sagebrush land for Mary Gage, that once was the weakling, Mary Warren.

She saw two figures coming slowly along the well-worn track from the gate. She could not hear the comment the one made to the other as they both advanced slowly, leaning together as gossiping women will, like two tired oxen returning from the field.

"Is that her?" asked one of the newcomers, a ponderous sort of woman, whose feet turned out alarmingly as she walked.

"Sure it's her," said Karen Jensen. "Who's it going to be if it ain't her? Ain't she nice-looking, sort of, after all? And to think she can see now as good as anybody! Yes, that's her.

"How do you do, Mis' Gage?"

She spoke now aloud as Mary came toward them smiling.

The dimples in her cheek, resurrected of late, gave a girlishness and tenderness to her face that it once had lacked in her illness.

"I'm well, thank you, Mrs. Jensen. It's a glorious day, isn't it? I've got some fish for you. I was going to tell Minna to take them down to you when she went home. She's a dear, your Minna."

"Well, it's right fine you should catch fish for us now," said Mrs. Jensen. "I'll be obliged for some—my man don't seem to get time to go fishing."

"Make you acquainted with Mis' Davidson, Mis' Gage," she continued. "This is the school teacher. She comes every fall to teach up above, when she's done living on her Idaho homestead, summers."

"How do you do, Miss—Mrs. Davidson," began Mary, offering her hand. "If you know Mrs. Jensen I ought to know you—she's been very good to me. Come in, won't you? Sit down on the gallery."

"Yes, this new porch is about as good as anywheres right now," commented Mrs. Jensen. "It's a little hot, ain't it?" They found seats of boxes and ends of logs.

Mrs. Davidson cast a glance into the open door. It included the spectacle of a neat, white-covered bed, a table with a clean white oil-cloth cover, a series of covered and screened receptacles such as the place might best afford out of its resources. She saw a floor immaculately clean. She spoke after a time ending a silence which was unusual with her.

"The latter title that you gave me, Mrs. Gage, is correct," said she. "I am a widow, having never encountered the oppor-r-r-tunity but once." It was worth going miles out of one's way to hear her say "opportunity"—or to see her wide-mouthed smile.

"As a widow," she resumed with orotundity not lessened by her absence from her own accustomed dais, "as a widow yourself, you are arranged here with a fair degree of comfort, as I am disposed to believe, Mrs. Gage."

"I cannot complain," said Mary Gage simply.

"A great trait in life, my dear madam; resignation! I endeavor to inculcate in my pupils the virtue of stoicism. I tell them of the Spartan boy, Mrs. Gage. Perhaps you have heard of the Spartan boy?"

"Yes," said Mary. "I know something about stoicism, I hope. But now I'm going to get you some berries—I picked some, up beyond, on the meadows." She rose now and passed into that part of her cabin which constituted the kitchen.

"An extr-r-r-aordinary young woman!" said Mrs. Davidson to Karen Jensen. "An extra*ordi*nary person to be here. Why, she is a person of culture, like myself. And once married—married to that man!"

Mrs. Davidson's lips were tight pursed now.

"I don't reckon she ever was, real," said Karen Jensen, simply. "I don't hardly believe they *was*."

Mrs. Davidson showed herself disposed to regard all the proprieties, hence she but coughed ponderously and shook her head ponderously, turning from side to side two or three times in her chair ponderously also.

"For what has happened here," said she at last, "I thank God. If things had happened worse it would have been my fault. Never again shall I address myself to the task of writing advertisements for men in search of wives. Great Providence! An extraordinary woman like this! To-night I shall pray on my two knees for forgiveness for what I did, and what it might have meant. When I consider how near I came to—to—"

"To raising hell?" inquired Karen Jensen sympathetically, seeing that her companion lacked the proper word at the time.

The other woman nodded in emphatic though unconscious assent. Always there was present before her mind her own part in the little drama of this place. It was she who had helped to bring this woman here—who had helped to deceive her. She thanked Providence that perhaps fate itself sometimes saves us from the full fruit of our follies, after all.

"Just a little sugar, thank you, Mrs. Gage," said she as Mary offered her some of the fresh whortle berries. "And these little cakes—you made them?"

"Oh, yes—I do most of my cooking, when I can keep Annie away. You know about Annie, of course. And Minna, Mrs. Jensen's little, girl, who is my companion here most of the time—as I said, she's a dear. I've been teaching her to read all summer—spoiling your work, Mrs. Davidson!"

"I wish more and more that I might have aid in that undertaking in this valley," said Sarah Davidson, herself a great soul in her way, and Covenanter when it came to duty. "It is perhaps primitive here, more so than elsewhere, but the people—the people—they need so much, and they—they—"

"They *are* so much," said Mary Gage gently. "They *are* so much. I never knew before what real people were. I'm so glad."

Mrs. Davidson's face worked strangely, very strangely, Mary thought, so that she believed her to be afflicted with some nervous disease of the facial muscles. But in truth Sarah Davidson was only endeavoring to get under control her own emotions, which, like all else about her, were ponderous and slow.

"Then, my dear—you will let me say 'my dear,' won't you? It's becoming such a habit with me at my time of life—you will permit me to inquire if that is an actual expression of your attitude toward the people here? You say you are glad? Do you mean that, or is it a mere conventionality with you?"

Mary turned toward her with that gravity which quite commonly marked her face when all her features were at rest.

"I quite mean it all, Mrs. Davidson," said she. "I'm thankful with all my heart that I came out here. It's a great place to fight things out. I'd never have been happy in all my life if I had not come here. I'm really glad, and you may believe that, because I do—now."

"You would forgive—you would cherish no malice against any who acted as the ah—instigators—of your original journey here?"

A sudden question arose in Mrs. Davidson's mind as to whether or not any of Mary Gage's associates and neighbors ever had told her all the story of that original endeavor, whose object was matrimony. Whereupon she concluded now to let sleeping dogs lie, and not to urge the matter. Nor was Mary herself the more disposed at the moment to speak of the past. She only looked out across the valley, as was her custom.

They passed on to some talk of the peace news, and demobilization plans for the men still abroad, for the visitors had brought the latest paper with them.

"Our men!" exclaimed Mary Gage as she read the headlines. "They're fine. They are always fine, everywhere, all of them. I'd have liked to see them in the great parades, in the cities."

"'Twould be a gr-r-r-and sight," said Mrs. Davidson, "for women who have had no oppor-r-r-tunity!"

"Ah? Women who haven't had what women wish?" said Mary Gage, a strange confidence in her own tones. "Don't you suppose God knows the way? Why be trying to change—" The word did not come at first.

"The plan?" suggested Mrs. Davidson.

"The plan!" said Mary.

"I must be going before long," said Karen Jensen, having finished her saucer of berries, and caring little for philosophizing. "I've got to milk seven cows yet."

"I will come often, if I may, Mrs. Gage, now that I am again located in this valley," said her companion, rising also.

"Oh, won't you, please!" said Mary Gage. "And—won't you do me a little favor now? I have a letter—I was just going up to the corner to put it in the box. If you're going that way, will you drop it in for me?"

Karen Jensen hesitated, looking across at the shortcut across the fields, but Mrs. Davidson, not being well organized for barbed wire entanglements, offered for the errand, which would take her around by the road.

"Surely, I shall be most happy," said she. "I will walk around by the box and drop your letter very gladly. No, no, don't mind coming. It's nothing—I always go home that way."

But Sarah Davidson after all was the school teacher when she had passed beyond the gate in the willow lane. She felt that in her were represented all the privileges of what priesthood might be claimed in this valley. She felt that her judgment was large enough to be infallible, since she so long had been arbiter here in all mooted matters. It was, therefore, surely her right to have intelligence as to the plans, the emotions, the mental process of all these people, including all newcomers. Were they not indeed in her charge?

Her right? Indeed, was it not her duty to know what there was in this letter from the woman whom she herself had brought out here not so long ago? It caused her vast perturbation, for she had a conscience which dated back to ages of Scottish blood, but she was not one to deviate from her duty once she had established it! This letter—to Major Allen Barnes, in yonder city—what was in it?

It was a letter going to that outer world, from the very person whom she, Sarah Davidson, had brought into this sagebrush world and had set down among these neighbors. Just now she had confessed herself to be happy here. Why? Could it be a violation of confidence—an eavesdropping—opening this letter? Not in the least! It was only oppor-r-r-tunity! As to that, who did not know that for years every letter to a soldier was opened and censored? Obviously it was her duty as social censor of Two Forks also to open and read this letter.

Therefore, looking behind her cautiously to see she was not observed, she stepped behind the cover of the willows and ran the point of her pencil along the edge of the sealed envelope—it had been sealed thoroughly. Still, she tore it but very little in the process.

There came out into her hand a single sheet of paper. It bore no address and no signature. It showed a handwriting evidently that of a lady of culture, of education. There was nothing to show that it was an answer—an answer long deferred but not now to be changed, a woman's answer to the great question.

Mrs. Davidson was standing in a sort of consternation, the two parts of the letter in her two hands, when she nearly sprang into the wire fence at the sudden voice she heard, the voice of a man speaking close at hand.

"Good Lord, Mr. Gardner!" said she, "you gave me a turn. I wasn't thinking of you."

"What was you thinking of, Mis' Davidson?" asked Wid, smiling. "You was all in a trance. Something on your mind, huh? I bet I know. You're sending out a ad on your own account—'object, matrimony!'"

"Sir-r-r!" said Sarah Davidson, flushing red for the first time Wid Gardner had ever seen it occur, "such conver-r-r-sation is not welcome on your part, not in the least! I prefer-r-r that you shall not again mention that act which I have so long regretted. The past is past. A woman's real

Emerson Hough

love is for to-day and to-morrow, when with her own eyes and her own hear-r-rt she has chosen honorably, sir-r—honor-r-ably! I bid you good evening, Mr. Gar-r-r-dner. I request you never to speak of that incident again!"

Nor did he, so far as known.

But when Wid himself, chuckling innocently, had passed on down toward the gate with the loaf of bread which Annie was sending over to Mary Gage for her evening meal, Sarah Davidson was passing up the road toward the school house—entirely forgetting to turn to the left toward Nels Jensen's, where she boarded.

She was wiping away large, ponderous tears—tears of joy that the world had in it love of men and women—that God, after all, did know—that the world still was as it was in the beginning, incapable of destruction even by war, incapable of diversion from the plan of peace and hope. She guessed so much—and guessed the future of Mary Gage's life—from data meager enough, but which may have served.

What she saw on the single, unsigned page, and what opened all the fountains of emotion in her own really gentle soul, was a part of what Mary once had heard come to her in a world of darkness. The words now were written by herself in a world of light.

She had promised him when he went away that, if ever everything was clear in her own mind regarding what was past, she might write to him one day. So now she had written:

"Only thoughts of you remain
In my heart where they have lain;
Perfumed thoughts of you, remaining,

A hid sweetness, in my brain.
Others leave me; all things leave me:
You remain."

ABOUT THE AUTHOR

Emerson Hough (1857-1923) was an American author, best known for writing western stories.

Hough was born in Newton, Iowa, and graduated from the University of Iowa with a law degree. He moved to White Oaks, New Mexico, and practiced law there but eventually turned to literary work by taking camping trips and writing about them for publication.

He is best known as a novelist, writing The Mississippi Bubble as well as The Covered Wagon, about Oregon Trail pioneers, which later became successful as a movie, running 59 weeks at the Criterion Theater in New York City, passing the record set by Birth of a Nation. Other notable works included Story of the Cowboy, Way of the West, Singing Mouse Stories, and Passing of the Frontier, and writing the "Out-of-Doors" column for the Saturday Evening Post.

Hough was also a conservationist, and was the catalyst behind a law passed by the U.S. Congress to protect the buffalo in Yellowstone National Park. He married Charlotte Chesebro of Chicago in 1897 and made that city his home.

Choose from Thousands of 1stWorldLibrary Classics By

A. M. Barnard	Booth Tarkington	Edward Everett Hale
Ada Leverson	Boyd Cable	Edward J. O'Biren
Adolphus William Ward	Bram Stoker	Edward S. Ellis
Aesop	C. Collodi	Edwin L. Arnold
Agatha Christie	C. E. Orr	Eleanor Atkins
Alexander Aaronsohn	C. M. Ingleby	Eleanor Hallowell Abbott
Alexander Kielland	Carolyn Wells	Eliot Gregory
Alexandre Dumas	Catherine Parr Traill	Elizabeth Gaskell
Alfred Gatty	Charles A. Eastman	Elizabeth McCracken
Alfred Ollivant	Charles Amory Beach	Elizabeth Von Arnim
Alice Duer Miller	Charles Dickens	Ellem Key
Alice Turner Curtis	Charles Dudley Warner	Emerson Hough
Alice Dunbar	Charles Farrar Browne	Emilie F. Carlen
Allen Chapman	Charles Ives	Emily Bronte
Alleyne Ireland	Charles Kingsley	Emily Dickinson
Ambrose Bierce	Charles Klein	Enid Bagnold
Amelia E. Barr	Charles Hanson Towne	Enilor Macartney Lane
Amory H. Bradford	Charles Lathrop Pack	Erasmus W. Jones
Andrew Lang	Charles Romyn Dake	Ernie Howard Pie
Andrew McFarland Davis	Charles Whibley	Ethel May Dell
Andy Adams	Charles Willing Beale	Ethel Turner
Angela Brazil	Charlotte M. Braeme	Ethel Watts Mumford
Anna Alice Chapin	Charlotte M. Yonge	Eugene Sue
Anna Sewell	Charlotte Perkins Stetson	Eugenie Foa
Annie Besant	Clair W. Hayes	Eugene Wood
Annie Hamilton Donnell	Clarence Day Jr.	Eustace Hale Ball
Annie Payson Call	Clarence E. Mulford	Evelyn Everett-green
Annie Roe Carr	Clemence Housman	Everard Cotes
Annonaymous	Confucius	F. H. Cheley
Anton Chekhov	Coningsby Dawson	F. J. Cross
Archibald Lee Fletcher	Cornelis DeWitt Wilcox	F. Marion Crawford
Arnold Bennett	Cyril Burleigh	Fannie E. Newberry
Arthur C. Benson	D. H. Lawrence	Federick Austin Ogg
Arthur Conan Doyle	Daniel Defoe	Ferdinand Ossendowski
Arthur M. Winfield	David Garnett	Fergus Hume
Arthur Ransome	Dinah Craik	Florence A. Kilpatrick
Arthur Schnitzler	Don Carlos Janes	Fremont B. Deering
Arthur Train	Donald Keyhoe	Francis Bacon
Atticus	Dorothy Kilner	Francis Darwin
B.H. Baden-Powell	Dougan Clark	Frances Hodgson Burnett
B. M. Bower	Douglas Fairbanks	Frances Parkinson Keyes
B. C. Chatterjee	E. Nesbit	Frank Gee Patchin
Baroness Emmuska Orczy	E. P. Roe	Frank Harris
Baroness Orczy	E. Phillips Oppenheim	Frank Jewett Mather
Basil King	E. S. Brooks	Frank L. Packard
Bayard Taylor	Earl Barnes	Frank V. Webster
Ben Macomber	Edgar Rice Burroughs	Frederic Stewart Isham
Bertha Muzzy Bower	Edith Van Dyne	Frederick Trevor Hill
Bjornstjerne Bjornson	Edith Wharton	Frederick Winslow Taylor

Friedrich Kerst
Friedrich Nietzsche
Fyodor Dostoyevsky
G.A. Henty
G.K. Chesterton
Gabrielle E. Jackson
Garrett P. Serviss
Gaston Leroux
George A. Warren
George Ade
Geroge Bernard Shaw
George Cary Eggleston
George Durston
George Ebers
George Eliot
George Gissing
George MacDonald
George Meredith
George Orwell
George Sylvester Viereck
George Tucker
George W. Cable
George Wharton James
Gertrude Atherton
Gordon Casserly
Grace E. King
Grace Gallatin
Grace Greenwood
Grant Allen
Guillermo A. Sherwell
Gulielma Zollinger
Gustav Flaubert
H. A. Cody
H. B. Irving
H.C. Bailey
H. G. Wells
H. H. Munro
H. Irving Hancock
H. R. Naylor
H. Rider Haggard
H. W. C. Davis
Haldeman Julius
Hall Caine
Hamilton Wright Mabie
Hans Christian Andersen
Harold Avery
Harold McGrath
Harriet Beecher Stowe
Harry Castlemon
Harry Coghill
Harry Houidini

Hayden Carruth
Helent Hunt Jackson
Helen Nicolay
Hendrik Conscience
Hendy David Thoreau
Henri Barbusse
Henrik Ibsen
Henry Adams
Henry Ford
Henry Frost
Henry James
Henry Jones Ford
Henry Seton Merriman
Henry W Longfellow
Herbert A. Giles
Herbert Carter
Herbert N. Casson
Herman Hesse
Hildegard G. Frey
Homer
Honore De Balzac
Horace B. Day
Horace Walpole
Horatio Alger Jr.
Howard Pyle
Howard R. Garis
Hugh Lofting
Hugh Walpole
Humphry Ward
Ian Maclaren
Inez Haynes Gillmore
Irving Bacheller
Isabel Cecilia Williams
Isabel Hornibrook
Israel Abrahams
Ivan Turgenev
J.G.Austin
J. Henri Fabre
J. M. Barrie
J. M. Walsh
J. Macdonald Oxley
J. R. Miller
J. S. Fletcher
J. S. Knowles
J. Storer Clouston
J. W. Duffield
Jack London
Jacob Abbott
James Allen
James Andrews
James Baldwin

James Branch Cabell
James DeMille
James Joyce
James Lane Allen
James Lane Allen
James Oliver Curwood
James Oppenheim
James Otis
James R. Driscoll
Jane Abbott
Jane Austen
Jane L. Stewart
Janet Aldridge
Jens Peter Jacobsen
Jerome K. Jerome
Jessie Graham Flower
John Buchan
John Burroughs
John Cournos
John F. Kennedy
John Gay
John Glasworthy
John Habberton
John Joy Bell
John Kendrick Bangs
John Milton
John Philip Sousa
John Taintor Foote
Jonas Lauritz Idemil Lie
Jonathan Swift
Joseph A. Altsheler
Joseph Carey
Joseph Conrad
Joseph E. Badger Jr
Joseph Hergesheimer
Joseph Jacobs
Jules Vernes
Julian Hawthrone
Julie A Lippmann
Justin Huntly McCarthy
Kakuzo Okakura
Karle Wilson Baker
Kate Chopin
Kenneth Grahame
Kenneth McGaffey
Kate Langley Bosher
Kate Langley Bosher
Katherine Cecil Thurston
Katherine Stokes
L. A. Abbot
L. T. Meade

L. Frank Baum
Latta Griswold
Laura Dent Crane
Laura Lee Hope
Laurence Housman
Lawrence Beasley
Leo Tolstoy
Leonid Andreyev
Lewis Carroll
Lewis Sperry Chafer
Lilian Bell
Lloyd Osbourne
Louis Hughes
Louis Joseph Vance
Louis Tracy
Louisa May Alcott
Lucy Fitch Perkins
Lucy Maud Montgomery
Luther Benson
Lydia Miller Middleton
Lyndon Orr
M. Corvus
M. H. Adams
Margaret E. Sangster
Margret Howth
Margaret Vandercook
Margaret W. Hungerford
Margret Penrose
Maria Edgeworth
Maria Thompson Daviess
Mariano Azuela
Marion Polk Angellotti
Mark Overton
Mark Twain
Mary Austin
Mary Catherine Crowley
Mary Cole
Mary Hastings Bradley
Mary Roberts Rinehart
Mary Rowlandson
M. Wollstonecraft Shelley
Maud Lindsay
Max Beerbohm
Myra Kelly
Nathaniel Hawthrone
Nicolo Machiavelli
O. F. Walton
Oscar Wilde

Owen Johnson
P.G. Wodehouse
Paul and Mabel Thorne
Paul G. Tomlinson
Paul Severing
Percy Brebner
Percy Keese Fitzhugh
Peter B. Kyne
Plato
Quincy Allen
R. Derby Holmes
R. L. Stevenson
R. S. Ball
Rabindranath Tagore
Rahul Alvares
Ralph Bonehill
Ralph Henry Barbour
Ralph Victor
Ralph Waldo Emmerson
Rene Descartes
Rex Beach
Rex E. Beach
Richard Harding Davis
Richard Jefferies
Richard Le Gallienne
Robert Barr
Robert Frost
Robert Gordon Anderson
Robert L. Drake
Robert Lansing
Robert Lynd
Robert Michael Ballantyne
Robert W. Chambers
Rosa Nouchette Carey
Rudyard Kipling
Saint Augustine
Samuel B. Allison
Samuel Hopkins Adams
Sarah Bernhardt
Sarah C. Hallowell
Selma Lagerlof
Sherwood Anderson
Sigmund Freud
Standish O'Grady
Stanley Weyman
Stella Benson
Stella M. Francis

Stephen Crane
Stewart Edward White
Stijn Streuvels
Swami Abhedananda
Swami Parmananda
T. S. Ackland
T. S. Arthur
The Princess Der Ling
Thomas A. Janvier
Thomas A Kempis
Thomas Anderton
Thomas Bailey Aldrich
Thomas Bulfinch
Thomas De Quincey
Thomas Dixon
Thomas H. Huxley
Thomas Hardy
Thomas More
Thornton W. Burgess
U. S. Grant
Upton Sinclair
Valentine Williams
Various Authors
Vaughan Kester
Victor Appleton
Victor G. Durham
Victoria Cross
Virginia Woolf
Wadsworth Camp
Walter Camp
Walter Scott
Washington Irving
Wilbur Lawton
Wilkie Collins
Willa Cather
Willard F. Baker
William Dean Howells
William le Queux
W. Makepeace Thackeray
William W. Walter
William Shakespeare
Winston Churchill
Yei Theodora Ozaki
Yogi Ramacharaka
Young E. Allison
Zane Grey

www.ingramcontent.com/pod-product-compliance
Lightning Source LLC
Chambersburg PA
CBHW021311250626
47155CB00002B/475